THE *Lady* IN THE COPPERGATE TOWER

OTHER PROPER ROMANCES
BY NANCY CAMPBELL ALLEN

My Fair Gentleman
Beauty and the Clockwork Beast
The Secret of the India Orchid
Kiss of the Spindle

PROPER ROMANCE

THE *Lady* IN THE COPPERGATE TOWER

NANCY CAMPBELL ALLEN

SHADOW
MOUNTAIN

Library of Congress Cataloging-in-Publication Data
Names: Allen, Nancy Campbell, 1969– author.
Title: The lady in the Coppergate Tower / Nancy Campbell Allen.
Other titles: Proper romance.
Description: Salt Lake City, Utah : Shadow Mountain, [2019] | "A steampunk Rapunzel"—Publisher's website. | "Proper romance"—Publisher's website.
Identifiers: LCCN 2019002128 | ISBN 9781629725543 (paperbound)
Subjects: LCSH: Mental illness—Fiction. | Twin sisters—Fiction. | Rapunzel (Tale)—Fiction. | Romania, setting. | LCGFT: Steampunk fiction. | Romance fiction. | Action and adventure fiction. | Novels.
Classification: LCC PS3551.L39644 L33 2019 | DDC 813/.54—dc23
LC record available at https://lccn.loc.gov/2019002128

Printed in Canada
Marquis, Montreal, Quebec, Canada

10   9   8   7   6   5   4   3   2   1

For Karin and Julie.
Your resilience is a source of strength for me.
How I love you both.

The mysterious Tower had no door to enter. Within were grand and beautiful apartments brightly lit with garnets that shone like sunlight. Every curiosity was collected in this place . . . She was alone in this beautiful abode where she had nothing to desire but companionship . . .

—*PERSINETTE,* BY MLLE DE LA FORCE, 1698

Prologue

Dr. Samuel MacInnes lay on his back in his bed at Blackwell Manor, arms behind his head, and looked at the night sky. Rather than a traditional guest room, his accommodations were in the third-floor observatory, complete with a domed glass ceiling. He preferred this room to other guest suites at the manor when he visited his good friend, Miles Blake, Earl of Blackwell. While other rooms boasted luxury and comfortable amenities, the observatory offered an enormous view of the night sky, and since his time spent on a battlefield in India, when the night closed in, he wanted to see the stars.

There were no stars out tonight because a storm raged. Even that was comforting, though, because it mirrored how he felt inside of late. Since his return from India, he had achieved enormous professional success as a surgeon at the forefront of his field, and as an inventor of transplant organs for the wounded or terminally ill, but his social life still remained on the back burner, where he'd tossed it upon coming home. He'd lost all desire for meaningless pursuits, and attending balls and soirces only when his mother insisted.

His current worries consisted of perfecting the heartclock he was crafting for Miles, and caring for his patients. Miles was living on borrowed time, and Sam felt a sense of urgency about completing the device. Strange things were afoot at Blackwell Manor, most notably the continued sightings of Marie Blake, the ghost of Miles's sister. Her angry spirit, combined with an odd illness afflicting Miles's sister-in-law that had Sam baffled, created an unsafe environment for Miles.

Sam closed his eyes, tired, but determined to enjoy the comfort of the observatory with its crackling fire that provided the only light. As he felt himself sliding into the mesmerizing fog of sleep, he thought he heard a crash. His eyes flicked open, and after a long moment, he heard a roar.

He sat up on the narrow bed, frowning. His telescriber dinged, then, and his heart thudded. He grabbed his scriber and saw a new message from Miles.

Library. Med bag. Accident!

He quickly dressed and seized his medical bag before running down the three flights of stairs to the main level. As he entered the library, he found Miles crouched on the floor next to an unconscious woman. With Miles was Lucy Pickett, a houseguest and sister to their good friend, Daniel Pickett.

" . . . vampire in black mist form," she was saying to Miles.

Sam noted, with alarm, Lucy's upper back, where her

dress was torn to shreds and bloodied. Angry claw marks slashed down her spine and shoulders. The wounds were beginning to show a faint green tinge, confirming her statement about a vampire.

He looked at the woman on the floor, and his heart jumped into his throat.

"Miss Hughes?" he asked.

He'd not seen Hazel Hughes in years, but he would know that head of honey-gold hair anywhere. At his mother's suggestion, he had recommended her as a Medium to Miles. He quickly squatted down next to her and began his examination. She was unconscious, her clothing was singed, and blood seeped onto Lucy's dress where she cradled Hazel's head.

"A vamp?" he addressed Lucy. "Then we must treat your back immediately. We will need a mix of Abelfirth and Chromaxium. We shall have to rush you to the airfield and head straight for London—I don't have any with me."

Lucy shifted, sliding her hand from beneath Hazel's head, and Sam braced the wounded woman's neck. "I have some upstairs," Lucy said, wincing.

Sam's jaw dropped, as did Miles's, and he stared at her. "How on earth do you have a supply of anti-vamp? It's all I can do to secure some, and even then I must jump through a series of hoops that make it nigh impossible."

"I am part of the botany research team. I told you this." Lucy looked down at her hands, which were red and would soon blister, and cradled them to her chest. Sam considered Hazel's singed clothing and realized Lucy must have batted out the flames with her hands.

Sam looked down at Hazel. He monitored her breathing and felt her pulse, while flipping open his bag with one hand and grabbing a cloth. He gently turned Hazel's head and assessed the damage, while Miles and Lucy began a familiar argument about whether Lucy's brother was entitled to limit her dangerous activities.

Sam had thought the entire house had turned in for the evening. What on earth had the two women been doing?

Lucy sat back on her heels, and winced.

Sam turned Hazel slightly to inspect her back where her clothing had burned away. His jaw tightened. He was glad for her sake that she was unconscious; the pain when she awoke would be unbearable. He would need to take her to London immediately for proper treatment.

He glanced up at the other two, and said, "We must apply the anti-vamp immediately. Have a 'ton bring it down, Miles."

"No," Lucy said and struggled to her feet. Miles stood with her and caught her elbow when she stumbled. "I can't have just anyone rummaging through my things. I'll do it myself." She paused, looking down at Hazel. "Will she be well?"

"I hope so," Sam said, trying to slow the bleeding. "Where is Oliver?" he asked Miles and reached back into his bag for a bandage he could secure around Hazel's head.

Miles told him their friend, Oliver Reed, an Inspector with the Yard, had been called to London, and Sam cursed inwardly. Something was happening at Blackwell, and Oliver's calm head and resources would have been hugely beneficial.

"Help Lucy." Sam thumbed back one of Hazel's eyelids and shone a light across her pupil.

Lucy's face was pale, and a light sheen of sweat had appeared across her forehead. She wobbled on her feet, and Miles, for the first time since Sam had known him, seemed frozen in place.

"Hurry," Sam barked.

Miles picked up Lucy and carried her quickly from the library, and Sam hoped they wouldn't be forced to tell Daniel his sister had been killed in a vampire attack.

"Miss Hughes . . . Hazel," Sam said as he secured the bandage around Hazel's head, pleased that the bleeding was gradually slowing. "Awaken for me, won't you?" The blood was a garish contrast to her golden-blonde hair, and he winced.

He cleared his throat. "I do hope we shall avoid cutting some of your hair away," he said, speaking nearly as much to break the silence as to bring her around. "The wound will require stitching, but fortunately for you, I am quite proficient with a needle."

Hazel moaned and turned her head.

"There we are! That's a good girl. Can you open your eyes?"

She winced and squeezed her eyelids, then fluttered them open. She squinted against the muted light. "I hurts," she whispered.

He nodded. "I should think so. Where do you hurt?"

"Everywhere." Her eyes were gold, like her hair, and had flecks of green in the irises that magnified as tears gathered. "My head . . . my back—"

"I am taking you to a hospital in London. We'll contact your mother, and we will get you well." He paused, realizing she may not recognize him. "I am Dr. MacInnes—Sam. We met several years ago, our mothers are friends—"

She nodded and sucked in a breath of pain at the movement. "I know who you are."

He fished his telescriber from his pocket to contact the airstrip. He'd need a Traveler brought around from the garage first. Movement at the doorway caught his eye, and he glanced up to see Mrs. Farrell, the housekeeper, blinking in confusion and wearing a housecoat.

"Oh, good," he said. "Please have Martha Watts deliver a Traveler to the front door."

Her eyes widened, but she nodded and hurried away.

Hazel groaned and tried to move. Tears flowed, and he helped her roll to her side to ease some of the burden from her back.

"Can you tell me what happened?" he asked her gently.

"I am the world's worst Medium," she mumbled and closed her eyes. Tears dripped across the bridge of her nose. "I did not conjure a ghost. Somehow, I drew the attention of a vampire."

A door slammed down the hall, and the sound of running footsteps grew louder until Martha Watts, Blackwell's vehicle and stable mistress, entered. She was of middle age, striking in her appearance with long, curling black hair. She wore breeches, always, and was one of the most efficient people Sam had ever met.

He quickly explained everything to her, all the while gently holding Hazel's head. He needed to clean Hazel's back before applying a burn salve, but her head wound worried him. When her eyes fluttered closed, his worry increased.

"You'll remain here for a moment?" he asked Martha. "I must leave quick instructions for Miles."

"Of course. And I've brought the fastest Traveler to the front yard."

He nodded his thanks, made sure Hazel was comfortable, then grabbed paper and pen from his medical bag, before running upstairs to the South Wing. He stopped at Miles's suite and knocked a pattern they'd used in India, and then began scribbling on the paper. Miles opened the door, and Sam glanced up after a moment, handing him the paper.

"I need to take Miss Hughes to London immediately," he said. "I've scribed ahead to the airstrip. They have an emergency airship at the ready. Miss Watts will take us."

"How badly is Miss Hughes hurt?"

Sam shook his head. "I'll know better when I get her to the hospital. I've written instructions for Lucy's care." He pointed to the paper he'd handed Miles. "Scribe me immediately if her fever spikes above the red line. She should have a thermometer with her other medicines."

Miles nodded. "Travel safely."

"I will scribe as soon as Miss Hughes's condition is stabilized." Sam clasped Miles's hand and then jogged quickly down the hallway. He made his way back to the library, where Mrs. Farrell and Martha Watts hovered over Hazel.

"I'll drive, so you can sit with her inside," Martha Watts told him firmly.

"Thank you." He scooped up Hazel, who had lapsed again into oblivion, and shifted her as high against his chest as he could to keep from exacerbating the wounds on her back. "Mrs. Farrell, will you have my belongings in the observatory shipped to my London address?"

The woman nodded, her eyes still huge. Martha Watts picked up his medical bag and carried it to the front door, which she opened wide for Sam.

The gleaming, black vehicle with the Blackwell crest emblazoned on the door waited for them. The Traveler looked like an elaborate carriage without horses to draw it. The engine was running, steam releasing from a large pipe on top. The driver's seat was situated out front, slightly lower than a horse-drawn perch to facilitate efficient maneuvering.

Sam carefully lifted Hazel into the conveyance and climbed in after, pulling her partially across his lap and switching on an interior Tesla torch while Martha Watts secured the door and settled herself in the driver's seat. As the Traveler moved forward through the rain and the wind, Sam heard the mechanism engage that controlled the external canopy, covering the driver from the elements.

"Hazel," Sam murmured. "I will care for you. You are going to be fine." As blood continued to seep through the heavy bandage, he held another to the back of her head, which rested on his leg, and wrapped a long curl of her hair around his fingers. It was thick, and as soft as spun silk. Light from the interior torch glinted off the locks; they gleamed gold with hints of bronze. He rubbed the strands between his fingers and tipped his head against the seat, tired.

"You will be well," he whispered as the carriage sped and

bumped along the road to the airstrip, under a tunnel of trees with thick branches that met overhead. He thought of the procedures he would need to perform to close the gash in her head and treat the burns on her back, and he hoped he was right.

Chapter 1

The dream had always been the same. Hazel looked in a mirror and saw her reflection, yet it was not exactly her. Hazel's hair was golden, like honey. The reflection's hair was so blonde it was nearly silver. And the eyes—Hazel's were gold and green, while the Hazel in the mirror had eyes so blue they seemed purple. The curls were the same; the smile was the same. And when she tilted her head, the reflection tilted her head as well, but something was off. The reflection wasn't quite right.

The dream had begun in childhood, and as Hazel aged, the reflection kept pace. Dream Hazel was always in a beautiful room, with a lovely forest scene painted on the walls and a canopy of stars on the ceiling. There were toys and books, and clothing rich in color and design—much fancier than anything Hazel ever wore in her real life.

She'd once mentioned the dream to her mother, but Rowena Hughes was an easily excitable woman who reacted to Hazel with a dismissive wave of her hand. Dreams were nonsense, so why on earth would someone dream about having different hair and eyes, and more to the point, why would someone be foolish enough to dwell on it?

Hazel never mentioned the dreams again, but they continued. The sense that something was missing—some vital part of her—grew alongside the strange images until Hazel, as an adult, accepted that there must be a piece of herself missing and she would know it when she saw it.

But something else disturbing had developed over time. The dream was changing. Dream Hazel was slowly going mad.

Hazel Hughes lay on her back and stared up at the early morning sky, waiting for the world to stop spinning. She hoped it would stop, and soon, before a crowd gathered. Landing flat on her back in Hyde Park because she fell off a horse while racing with a pair of dandies would not endear her to her social betters. *I must be mad,* she thought.

"Hazel!" Mr. Landon Price's face came into view, eyes large and freckles pronounced. Her childhood friend hadn't changed in appearance through the years, except to grow bigger. "Oh, Hazel! Are you— Can you move? Blast it all, Trent, you said that mount was harmless!"

Lord Trent was Landon's old school chum and the third son of an obscure baron who held onto high society's coattails with clenched hands. He hurried over, leading his and Landon's horses by the reins. "Is she dead?" he asked, breathless. He sounded nearly as breathless as Hazel felt; her quick, violent contact with the cold, hard earth had forced all air from her lungs, and sharp pain radiated through her abdomen and chest.

"She is not . . . dead," Hazel finally managed and sucked in a desperate breath of air. "She may never walk again, however."

"Oh dear, dear, dear . . ." Landon touched her arm with a fingertip but quickly drew it back.

"You'll not be afflicted, Landon." She groaned and turned onto her side. "I've not contracted an infectious disease."

"Miss Hughes, I cannot imagine what happened. Lucifer is usually the most docile of creatures. His gentle nature prompted his ironic name, in fact."

She shoved herself into a sitting position, wincing at the sharp pain radiating through her shoulder. "Where is the rotten devil?" She squinted down the path after her horse. The last she had seen of him was the moment when he'd reared up on hind legs, thrown her spectacularly to the ground, and then raced off.

"Do not worry about him for an instant, Miss Hughes," Trent hastily told her. "I shall track the beast down."

She hadn't been worried about finding the horse. "I am"—she shifted painfully—"much relieved to hear it." She glanced at Landon, who hovered close, his brow pinched in a worried frown. "Do you suppose you might lend me an arm?"

"Oh. Oh!" He stuck out his elbow, and when she swiped at it twice without success, he finally cupped her arm and helped her, awkwardly, to stand. "You know, this rather brings to mind yesteryear, does it not? Constantly falling out of trees, you were."

Hazel swayed on her feet and clutched Landon's hand when he released her. "I was never the tree climber, Landon. Emme was the tree climber."

"Ah, yes. Quite right. That Emme." He chuckled. "Trent, you remember Emme? Saw her last week at the shifter symposium."

Lord Trent edged closer with the horses, one of which roughly nudged Hazel's shoulder. "Nattie!" He tugged on the reins. "What is the matter with these horses? Miss Hughes, you have my word this will not happen again. Next time—"

"Trent, I cannot thank you enough for agreeing to this mad scheme and meeting me here. Now that I have done it, I shall move forward." She tested her balance before releasing her grip on Landon's arm.

"But, Hazel, you ride beautifully! Only your third time on horseback and you looked every inch the natural!" Landon's protest soothed her ego, if not her bruised and battered body.

"Thank you, but I do not need to further improve my skills. I only wanted to race through the park in the early morning hours." She frowned, regretting it as pain stabbed through her head.

There was the rub, truly. Why had she been so determined to race through the park? Likely it had been the same prompting that had placed her on a bridge, high above a river, from which she'd jumped with a rope attached to her feet. Or the same inducement that had insisted she and Emme search for adventure at the dockside late one night. The bridge leap had resulted in a sprained wrist when she hit the water, and the dockside had seen her imbibing cheap ale, vomiting on Emme's shoes, and getting mugged while attempting to hail a hack.

The strangest part of all was that Hazel was not adventuresome by nature—to the contrary. Over the course of the last several months, she had felt compelled to attempt things she had no desire to even think about, let alone try. When such compulsions overtook her, they brought with them a sense of desperation, along with a heavy dose of despair. She was consumed by the idea that life in all its fullness was passing her by as she sat trapped in her staid existence.

She quite enjoyed her existence, normally, and her odd sense of dissatisfaction struck randomly and without warning. The only way to dispel the despair was to surrender to the compulsion. It made little sense to her as she made plans and tried new things, and even less after completion of the task. The only relief she felt was that the insanity had passed, even if only momentarily.

"Shall we see you home, Miss Hughes?" Trent looked genuinely concerned.

She took a deep breath, caught herself with a wince, and took a shallow breath instead. "My lord," she said, with a hand on her heart and slight nod, knowing he enjoyed the flattery, "I am grateful for your indulgence with this excursion, but I must go or I'll be late for the clinic. I shall hire a hack."

"Yes, of course." He nodded.

She massaged the back of her neck with a dirt-smudged

hand that shook. "I do hope Lucifer makes an appearance, soon."

As if she'd called him, the horse trotted up the path and came to an innocent stop at Landon's shoulder.

"Oh, good," she said flatly. "You've returned."

By the time Hazel had gathered her gloves and reticule, and climbed into the rented carriage pulled by an aging mechanical horse, the sky was fully light. She looked out the smudged carriage window and managed a wave at the two worried young men who stood in the road, watching her departure.

The carriage was cold, and now that the excitement of the accident had passed, she shivered. Small rocks were embedded in one palm, and her other hand bore a long abrasion that began at the side and traveled the length of her arm to her elbow. Her white blouse was a torn, dirtied mess. She was glad she kept a fresh ensemble of clothing at the clinic for changing into after messy surgeries.

She winced as the carriage bumped and bounced over the cobblestones. The driver must have considered reins an optional feature; he seemed to give the horse its head and didn't object when the conveyance swayed dangerously around corners.

The hack pulled to a sudden stop, throwing her forward. She gasped and planted her foot on the seat opposite to keep from falling on the floor. The carriage tilted, the door opened, and the automaton driver smiled, motioning for her to exit.

She managed to extricate herself from the vehicle without groaning aloud; a paltry success, but she would claim it. She paid the driver and straightened her coat and corset before entering the tidy building that housed Dr. Samuel MacInnes's medical clinic.

She closed the door with relief, glad to shut out the gusting autumn wind, and unwound her scarf. She made her way through the waiting area to her small office in the back, noting the light coming from Sam's office, one room down.

"Good morning!" He was irritatingly cheerful in the early hours of the day, and she grunted a response, which elicited a chuckle from him. "Your tea awaits."

"An entire pot, I hope." She switched on the Tesla lamp attached to the wall near her desk. Her scarf and coat were dark, and the dirt she'd acquired on her mad dash with Lucifer wasn't noticeable. Her hat, which was a new affair— green velvet, goggles, and ostrich plumes—had amazingly emerged from the fiasco unscathed.

She smoothed her matching forest-green corset and black skirt, noting again the dirt and snags on her sleeve, then retrieved a fresh blouse from the small wardrobe in the corner of her office. She took great pride in her appearance, piecing her clothing and accessories together with care, and always dressed in the height of fashion through careful budgeting, smart shopping, and exceptional skills with a needle and thread.

Sam appeared in her doorway with a cup and saucer, and his mouth dropped open. "What on *earth*? Hazel, what happened to you? Were you accosted? Are you hurt?"

She grimaced and took the cup of tea from him. "I fell."

His features tightened, and she braced herself for a lecture. "What were you doing when you fell?"

She sighed. "Riding a horse."

He paused for a long moment. "You fell from a horse."

She nodded. The movement made her neck hurt. Her head hurt. Everything hurt. "I am well and whole, as you can see." She sipped the tea and closed her eyes in appreciation.

"Hand over the tea, if you please."

She opened her eyes. "Never."

He held out his hand, and she reluctantly placed the cup and saucer in it. He set them aside and then turned her head gently with his fingertip, first left, then right. She hoped he would mistake her swift intake of breath as discomfort from her fall. Would she never be able to control the thrill she felt at his nearness, at his touch?

He carefully ran his fingers over her head, and when he found the bump where she'd made contact with the ground, she winced and involuntarily pulled back.

He shook his head, his lips thinning, and looked into her eyes, one at a time. She knew he was checking her pupils.

"It is not unusual to be riding a horse," she told him. "Plenty of people begin their days enjoying a leisurely ride."

"Something tells me you were not enjoying a leisurely ride. Come." He put his hand on her elbow and led her from the office, down one door to one of the clinic's examination rooms. He motioned for her to sit on the padded table and proceeded to treat her as she'd seen him treat his patients hundreds of times. The same way he'd treated her more than once in recent months.

"Tell me honestly," he said as he cleaned the cut on her arm, "what were you doing?"

She sighed. "My childhood friend, Landon, and his friend, Lord Trent, accompanied me on an early morning ride through Hyde Park. I wanted to race." She held up her hand before he could interrupt with questions. "I do not know what prompted it, other than I've been wanting to add horse racing to my list of accomplishments."

He drew in a measured breath and slowly released it. He finished treating her cuts and scrapes, listened to her heart and lungs, probed for broken bones, and seemed satisfied she was well enough. He washed his hands and dried them with a clean towel as he continued to eye her with clear suspicion.

He leaned a hip against the counter and frowned. "Hazel, are you mad? You've nothing to prove to yourself, to anyone. You are the smartest woman I know."

He was so handsome, and so incredibly talented. She resisted sighing dramatically. She was extraordinarily proud of the restraint she'd honed after nearly a year's worth of practice. He was her social superior, her employer, and entirely out of her reach. She'd met him once in passing as a young teen when her mother had been a seamstress for his mother, and then again a year ago when he'd saved her life.

Though her feelings had begun as hero worship, working with him daily had deepened her emotions. As colleagues, her natural gifts as a Healer dovetailed nicely with his brilliance as a surgeon, and the clinic had quickly gained an impressive reputation. On the non-surgical front, his talents, combined with her ability to read and retain every word as if she had taken a mental photograph, made for a good combination.

She was always aware of him, knew the moment he entered a room. Their working relationship had become a warm friendship, but she did not fool herself into believing it would, indeed *could*, ever be more. He was charming with her, but he was charming with everyone. He often bestowed a breath-stealing smile on her, but he was generous and shared such smiles with all and sundry.

He wore shirtsleeves, vest, and dark trousers, and while she relished the casual nature of their relationship, his informal dress in her presence was a reminder that they were mere colleagues. If she were a contender for the role of Mrs. Doctor MacInnes, his behavior and bearing would be properly formal.

She quite adored him, and he was quite clearly *not* meant to be hers.

"I do not know that I can explain it with any degree of sensibility," she said. "I've a hard time understanding it, myself. If I ever make sense of the state of my brain, you shall be the first with whom I share the information."

He smiled, and throwing aside her natural reserve, she said, "I've had a recurring dream since childhood, and it grows increasingly more bizarre."

He lifted a brow. "Odd."

She nodded and explained the childhood elements of her dreams, and added, "But now, she's—I call her Dream Hazel—she is most certainly mad." She paused, thinking. "In last night's dream, I was in the room with her. The only view to the outside world were large windows that overlooked a vast forest, and the ground, which was impossibly far away. I felt this overwhelming desire to just . . . run."

"Hmm. New psychological science suggests there may be meaning behind recurring dreams."

"The reason is likely that I am daft."

He chuckled. "I would never have hired you as my assistant if you were daft."

"There is that, I suppose. Now, I've wasted enough time, and we've a day to attack."

"You feel well enough to work? I understand if you would rather go home and rest."

"I am perfectly well, just sore. Please, I would much rather stay here and be busy." She paused. "Where is Eugene?"

Sam scowled. "Bane of my existence, that one. He is charging, nearly done. He's taken it into his head—well, his processors—that since he now acts as my valet as well as my medical assistant, he requires a change of uniform to differentiate his duties."

Hazel laughed. Eugene was a high-functioning automaton, or "'ton," with exceptional programming. He had been a gift from Sam's friend, Daniel Pickett, who had a similarly designed 'ton he utilized as his first mate aboard his airship.

Eugene was so humanlike that Hazel often had to remind herself he was an automaton. One of the personality traits Sam had requested was that Eugene possess a dry sense of humor, which manifested in Eugene more as dry sarcasm. Hazel found it hilarious. Sam found it tedious.

"What would it hurt to allow him a change of uniform?"

Sam rolled his eyes. "If I give him an inch, he'll take a blasted mile. Next he will request a top hat and cane."

Hazel smiled as he helped her down from the table. She led him from the room and back to her office, where she again retrieved the fresh blouse and a long, starched white apron. "With a top hat and cane, people would see you as two chaps about town. Perhaps he might draw in the future Mrs. MacInnes." She tossed the comment out casually, though once it left her lips she regretted it. She didn't want to discuss anything even approaching his social life.

Sam laughed. "Eugene would frighten away any prospects with his interminable chatter and litany of useless facts. I don't know that I could be attracted to a woman who found him charming."

She had set the trap and then walked straight into it. She didn't find Eugene charming, but she did find him highly amusing. Was that the same thing? She blew a curl out of her eyes and tucked it back into place with the rest of her hair, trying to muscle her tangled mane of braids and curls back into submission.

She straightened, smiling. "So, our duties for the day?"

"Nora filled the schedule. Mostly minor injuries, no surgeries until next week. The first appointment is in an hour. I'd like to review yesterday's notes when you're ready. The typewriting machine is still in my office; I'm adding some options to the Atkins boy's file. I believe the new prosthetic foot design will serve him better than the old one. I'll need to tweak a few bits, of course." He gave her another smile before disappearing into his office.

Hazel closed her door and leaned against it. "'Tweak a few bits,'" she murmured fondly. For anyone else, medical invention was a daunting task. For Sam, it was inconsequential.

She changed her clothes, doing her best to ignore the bruises and scrapes. Her head ached abominably. She would need copious amounts of tea over the next several hours in order to keep her wits about her.

After all, the only thing madder than horse racing in Hyde Park would be to allow herself to fall in love with Dr. Samuel MacInnes.

Chapter 2

S am had finished with the day's final patient and listened to Hazel offer instructions to the woman for the medicines she'd prescribed. Hazel's brain was like a steel trap—whatever went in did not come back out—and her knowledge of herbs and medicinal remedies was varied and thorough. She often expressed gratitude to Sam for hiring her as an assistant despite her lack of formal training, but he knew full well he was the more fortunate. Someone else would have snapped her up eventually.

Her friendship with Lucy Pickett Blake had introduced her to social and professional circles to which she might not otherwise have gained access, and the medical world—and his office, certainly—would have been lesser for it. She had a comforting yet practical approach to patients, and he had yet to find fault with any of her recommendations for post-visit care. She read the medical journals to which he subscribed, and she was medically conversant with him and improving daily. She was a natural Healer, and he had noticed that her presence when he operated was an extra boost. If she chose to pursue it, she would make a fine physician.

He washed his hands at the newly plumbed sink in the examination room and dried them as he joined Hazel, who was tidying the waiting area. She was, quite possibly, the most beautiful woman he'd ever met, and if she knew it, she never acknowledged it. She was a complex combination of humility and confidence, wit and refinement, and as her employer, he spent entirely too much of his free time lately thinking of her.

A small scratch on her cheek and a rather large one hidden under her sleeve were reminders of her early-morning escapade. The more he grew to know her, the more her sometimes unpredictable behavior baffled him. She was steady and intelligent with the wisdom of an old soul. Why she pursued activities that placed her in danger made no sense to him, which was made worse by the fact that she claimed they made no sense to her, either.

Perhaps Hazel's friendship with Lucy and Isla, both of whom were unconventional, bold women, had prompted an unconscious desire to prove herself their equal in some way. But she was already their equal. She had strengths they did not. She had strengths Sam, himself, did not.

He looked at her now, at the knot—invisible beneath her hair—that had formed when she'd been thrown from a horse that morning. He'd watched her throughout the day, and other than a headache she nursed with tea and some herbs, she'd not seemed much worse for the wear.

"Do you suppose she'll heed your advice this time?" He

nodded toward the door that had just closed behind the patient.

She smiled and untied her apron. "I do believe she might. Consistent nighttime pain when she needs to sleep seems to have worn her down. The tea makes all the difference in the world if she would only drink it."

"Are there further instructions for me, Miss Hughes?" Nora, the office 'ton, asked from the reception desk.

"If you've finished labeling the new files, I have nothing further. Dr. MacInnes?"

"No, the cleaning service will arrive in a few hours, and if everything is ready for morning, you may dock in your charger, Nora."

The 'ton tipped her head and left the room, efficient but not nearly as advanced as Eugene. Hazel also left the reception area, saying over her shoulder, "Eugene is in my office perusing a tailor's catalog."

"I beg your pardon?" Sam shook his head. "Is he still looking for a new uniform?" He followed Hazel to her office, where he found Eugene standing next to her desk and making notes in a book that bore pictures of trousers, shirts, vests, and coats. "Eugene," he said firmly. "You have four full sets of clothing and are never at a loss for a clean ensemble."

As a 'ton, Eugene was of average height and weight, with dark hair and eyes, and his pleasant features could truly be called "handsome." Now, he frowned. "If you are content with your valet resembling a working-class assistant, then I suppose my current wardrobe will suffice."

"You *are* a working-class assistant." Sam gestured to

Eugene's nondescript black trousers, durable jacket, and white shirt. "Your appearance is perfectly respectable."

Eugene looked at Hazel with a flat expression and set the catalog on her desk. He capped his fountain pen and tucked it into his interior jacket pocket, then straightened his lapels. "One could hardly ask for anything more than *respectable*. Shall I bring the carriage 'round, then?"

Hazel snorted but covered it by clearing her throat and moving out of Eugene's path.

"Yes, Eugene, and make haste, please." Sam looked at Hazel once Eugene left the room. "He is trying my patience."

Her lips twitched, and she scratched the side of her nose. "He is dreadfully entertaining. You cannot deny his brilliance as an assistant."

It was true. In surgical procedures especially, Eugene was worth his weight in gold. His processors allowed for him to gain additional knowledge through experience, and the 'ton had learned to anticipate Sam's needs before they arose. "No, I cannot deny it. It is a steep price to pay, however."

She smiled. "Isla says the same thing, or rather, Daniel does. Samson is a brilliant first mate, but subtly insolent."

"When will they return from Port Lucy?"

Hazel folded her apron and set it in the bin to be laundered, and smiled. "Next month. With Lucy and Lord Blackwell also on holiday, I find myself quite friendless."

Sam leaned against the doorframe, reluctant to leave. "You are the sort of person who will never be friendless, Hazel Hughes. In a related vein, I have it on good authority that Lady Hadley's final ball of the season is this evening, and that you have received a coveted invitation."

Hazel scrunched her brow. "You did hear me say that my friends are out of town, did you not? I would be entirely out of my element without them. Besides, those in your circles invite me only to court the favor of the famed Dr. Isla Cooper Pickett and Lady Lucy Pickett Blake. The invitation for tonight's event was sent before the esteemed hostess realized my friends would be unable to attend."

Sam frowned. "You're uncomfortable at such social events?"

She leaned against her desk and folded her arms. "Do not dare to suggest you are unaware of the chasm between your status and mine."

He looked at her carefully, but her expression gave nothing away. "I do not ever think of it. I suppose I view us as . . . colleagues. Employer and employee."

She nodded.

"Friends, I should think." He certainly hoped she felt the warmth of friendship with him. "As it happens, I also have an invitation to Lady Hadley's ball, and my mother insists I attend. If I must go, so must you." He paused. "Unless you are fatigued, which, given your injuries this morning—"

She sighed and dropped her arms, bracing her hands on the desk by her hips. "I am not fatigued, and the head pain is nearly gone. The Gladwells, however, are hosting a book discussion this evening."

Of course. He'd seen her at intellectual and academic gatherings, soirees and events that embraced a variety of people and stations. Professionals, mostly, who worked for a living. Sam had a foot in both worlds. His father was a Scottish textile merchant with more money than nearly anyone but the queen—and thus held society's reluctant respect though he had made, not inherited, his money—and his mother was the British daughter of a viscount. After spending a year of military service in India, he'd returned home with a simplified mind-set. Securing society's good graces had fallen to the bottom of his priority list. His parents' friends and associates thought him daft, but his resolve to continue his career as a surgeon only solidified.

He had the advantage of being a man who could take high society or leave it. Hazel had no such advantage. In fact, because of her association with Isla and Lucy, she'd been elevated to a strange place somewhere on the fringes. She never showed discomfort at society events, certainly hadn't voiced it, and he'd not considered she might be uncomfortable. Rather obtuse of him, really. He had grown fond of her in the year since that fateful evening at Blackwell, and he admired her greatly. Anything beyond that friendship, however, was inappropriate because she was his employee. Still, he'd thought he knew her relatively well. Apparently he'd missed some cues.

He tried again. "The Gladwells will have their book group again next month, but this is the last major event of the Season. I am dreading it, and misery loves company, so you must attend. We will have a drink and some refreshments, bow and curtsy to those we must, and then wash our hands of it. I know for a fact that your mother would rather you make a showing at Lady Hadley's than the Gladwells'."

She rolled her eyes. "My mother is easily impressed with shiny objects."

"Your mother was my mother's favorite confidante, still is."

"Because she is highly strung enough to be entertaining, but not so much as to lock away in Bedlam." She sighed. "She means well, and I love her, but she doesn't understand certain events are quite . . . awkward." Hazel looked at the toe of her boot and tapped her foot for a moment before stilling and looking back at him. She rarely fidgeted. "You belong there. I do not."

He felt an ache in his chest, and he absently rubbed it with his fingertips. "The last thing I would do is see you uncomfortable, Hazel. Forgive my insensitivity."

She waved a hand and laughed, but it lacked true mirth. She crossed the room to the coat-tree, where she retrieved her outerwear. "I shall make a showing this evening at Lady Hadley's, as a gesture of gratitude for her gracious invitation—and for the fact she did not rescind the invitation when she realized my friends of consequence were away. Then, I'll go to the Gladwells'. That way I shall conclude the evening on a pleasant note and still be home early enough to be rested for tomorrow morning. We all need good sleep, after all, and mornings are unpleasant enough for me as it is."

He looked at her carefully. She was rambling, something else she rarely did. Hazel was well and truly uncomfortable, and he was torn between sympathy and a tender sort of humor. His lips lifted, but he kept any comments to himself, instead holding her cloak for her as she slipped her arms into it. A few of her golden curls had fought their way free of her hair pins and caught on her collar. He lifted the strands, rubbing them between thumb and forefinger and marveling at their softness.

The last time he'd had that mass of hair in his hands, he'd been afraid for her life. He released the curls, which fell in a spiral down her back. Hoping she hadn't noticed his presumption or the inappropriate intimacy such a gesture implied, he shoved his hands in his pockets and backed against the doorframe while she secured her hat atop the silky mass—barely wincing as she bumped the knot on her head—and pulled on her gloves.

"May I drive you home?"

She smiled and shook her head. "My thanks, but no. I've some shopping to do first; I'll catch a hack."

"You'll take care, of course?"

"Of course. Isla taught me to shoot, and I carry my ray gun in my reticule."

He choked on a laugh. "You do?"

"I have a permit." She frowned at him. "I am a rather excellent shot, as well."

"I would never doubt it."

The front door opened, and Hazel stepped into the hall to peer around the corner. She looked back at him with a grin. "Your 'ton and his *respectable* clothing are ready to take you home."

He chuckled in spite of himself. "At least let us drop you at your shopping destination. The evenings grow dark earlier, now."

"Dr. MacInnes, I manage quite well on my own every day. I have for a year."

"Your employer has not done well by you." He meant

it sincerely. He'd been so consumed with work, keeping his mind busy so he wouldn't dwell on gruesome memories of battlefield surgery and the soldiers he'd tried—but failed—to save, that he'd not paid much attention to those around him. He had gone through the motions, maintained his charm, put on a bright face, but now it felt as though he'd been drifting along in a fog.

"My employer has allowed me to be a woman of independent means." She tipped her head to him with a smile, and he returned it, regretting the loss of her company before she even left. "You are generous with both salary and opportunity, and I am grateful." She opened the door and added on her way out, "I shall see you tonight at Lady Hadley's. I am already holding you accountable for my miserable time."

He stopped himself from calling after her to save a dance for him, and instead lifted a hand in farewell.

He walked through each room to be certain the lights were switched off, gathered his work satchel, and his hat, coat, and gloves. He locked the front door and stepped to the curb, turning back as he always did to admire the nameplate next to the entrance. Doctor Samuel MacInnes, Surgeon. He had worked long hours and sacrificed sleep and entertainment to achieve his goals. Now that he was finally, truly settled, he might turn his attention to other facets of life, even consider the benefits of sharing hearth and home.

He climbed into the carriage, and Eugene closed the door behind him and then guided the automated carriage into traffic.

The trouble with entertaining such domestic notions, however, was he couldn't think of a single woman in his social sphere who piqued his interest. Unbidden, his thoughts turned to Hazel's comments about the differences in their stations.

She was right, of course. She was trapped in her odd circumstances as effectively as was he. His only advantage was that he'd already bucked convention by pursuing a career when he could have easily lived on the family money, taking up a few charitable causes to justify a gentleman's lifestyle. Nobody expected him to fall in step like the rest of his acquaintances and marry a woman of good breeding and acceptable status for convenience or title or for the sake of checking off the next item on the list. He'd always chafed at the notion that he was not fully in control of his life. No, his choices were his own to make.

He wouldn't go looking for a wife; he would allow events to progress naturally. Perhaps he might attend social functions with a broadened perspective, be open to the possibility that he was ready to consider sharing himself with someone who would interest him.

Friendship, he decided, was an element he wanted in a potential companion. Someone with common interests and a sense of humor. A subtle sense of humor, an intelligent wit. Someone who could grasp nuances and see that people were often quite ridiculous. Someone who worked diligently toward her own goals, who found satisfaction in helping others, who looked beyond herself and saw the world for the amazingly complex feast it was. Someone who cared that there was a world beyond London worth exploring, who kept an open mind to possibilities. Golden hair, perhaps, and a good head for fashion might also be pleasant.

He looked out the window at the rapidly darkening city and hoped Hazel concluded her shopping quickly. He should have insisted that she allow him and Eugene to see her safely home after work. The home she shared with her mother was in a smaller section of town on the outskirts, quiet and respectable, but a world away from his townhome on Charrington Square. He wouldn't mind the extra time it would require if it meant keeping her safe. The city was full of miscreants who would find her easy prey, ray gun or no.

Rowena Hughes had raised Hazel by herself since Hazel's infancy when Mr. Hughes contracted an illness and passed away. Rowena was an exceptional seamstress and had taken in projects, quickly making a name for herself among some of society's more exclusive households. Sam's mother had been captivated by Rowena's odd charm and what she referred to as her "quirky" personality, and the two had been friendly acquaintances for years.

In some manner, Sam felt he was responsible for Hazel's accident last year at Blackwell. Rowena had told Lady MacInnes that Hazel was most certainly a Medium, claiming something vague about her blood or birthright. So, when Miles had told Sam he needed someone to communicate with the lingering ghost of his sister, Sam had suggested Hazel. Miles had sent for her, and the rest had unfolded disastrously. The only bright spots, he supposed, were that now he and Hazel worked together, and Hazel had formed a warm friendship with Lucy Pickett Blake.

He rubbed his eyes and stifled a yawn. The thought of freshening up for a formal social event was the last thing he wanted to do. He'd promised his mother, though, and figured it was the least he could do since he'd not yet come close to providing her with a daughter-in-law and grandchildren. His elder brother, Scott, had done his duty, adding to the family pedigree chart with a wife and, subsequently, three precocious little girls. His mother dropped subtle hints at Sam, however, and he dreaded the day when they became less than subtle.

Eugene pulled alongside the curb in front of Sam's house, but remained in the driver's seat. They'd argued about it all week. Sam insisted he could climb out of the carriage on his own, so Eugene should remain in place to park the vehicle in the carriage house around back. Eugene had told him he was happy to act as driver, but a man of status should never perform menial tasks, and the neighbors would surely find him substandard if Sam didn't allow him to conduct his duties properly. Now, as Sam stepped down and approached his front door, he glanced back at Eugene, who pointedly did not look at him as he drove the carriage away with his nose in the air.

Sam's 'ton butler opened the door, took his hat, coat, and gloves, and said, "You have a visitor in the parlor, sir."

"Oh?" Sam entered the parlor to find Oliver Reed, a detective-inspector with Scotland Yard, who had also served as Sam's captain during their India service. Sam smiled, surprised, and crossed the room to the sidebar. "Wasn't expecting you today, Oliver. Would you care for a drink?"

"Yes."

Sam looked over his shoulder as he poured two glasses. "Must be something serious for you to actually accept, Detective-Inspector."

Oliver shook his head and rubbed his eyes, taking a seat near the hearth. Sam grew concerned. Oliver was professional, steady, and had nerves of steel. He rarely allowed anyone a glimpse of weakness, emotional or otherwise.

Sam handed his friend the glass and raised both brows high when Oliver tossed back the drink in one swallow. "Well, now I am concerned."

Oliver looked at the glass for a moment and then at Sam. "I am going to kill Emmeline O'Shea."

Sam took a seat opposite Oliver. "What has she done now?"

Oliver sighed. "She intercepted a message meant for my office concerning activities across the northern border."

Sam blinked. "Activities?"

"I am not at liberty to share details. But she has evaded me for three days, and the powers that be are growing angrier by the hour."

"One would assume the matter relates to the Predatory Shifter Regulations Committee."

Oliver lifted his empty glass in acknowledgment.

"You're certain she has it?"

Oliver pinched the bridge of his nose. "A reliable source believes she does. The chief inspector now questions my ability to objectively investigate this issue, as it may have ties to my brother. The case may be reassigned."

That surprised Sam. Oliver was the best in the business, an undisputed expert at investigation. He worked day and night to uphold his reputation, and he had an uncanny ability to intellectually insert himself into a criminal's mind to reason through their motivation and intention.

Sam studied his friend, realizing that in all the years of their acquaintance, he'd never seen Oliver so outwardly frustrated or affected. One year ago at Blackwell Manor, Sam, Oliver, and Daniel had helped Miles defeat an enemy, but in the process, they'd learned that Oliver's estranged brother was a vampire who was climbing through the ranks of the criminal underworld. Oliver had grown quiet, introspective, and had never discussed the matter with his friends. Now, Sam realized Oliver must be pursuing elements of a crime that somehow involved his brother, and Emme O'Shea stood between Oliver and pursuit of his goal.

"I don't imagine you've ever had a case reassigned," Sam observed, hoping Oliver would divulge more information.

Oliver shot him a dark look. "Of course not." He took a breath and blew it out slowly through his nose. "The O'Sheas have been at their country estate, but their staff here in Town have been frantically readying the house for an early return."

"Mr. O'Shea's daughters would be aghast at the prospect of missing the Season's last event." Sam paused, brow wrinkled. "Except for Emme. Her only interest in social events is to cultivate contacts for her cause."

"Exactly. My superior has secured an invitation for me to attend Lady Hadley's gathering, and I wonder if I might tag along on your coattails. I would appear much less conspicuous as your guest."

"Of course, Oliver. I hope you know the invitation to appear anywhere as my guest is always extended." He tipped his head at Oliver's clothing. "That would account for your formal attire. I shall change and return straightaway. As the event itself will be some time before becoming a decent crush, I had planned to visit the club first. You'll join me?"

"Yes, many thanks."

Oliver seemed no more thrilled at the coming prospects than Hazel had, and Sam chuckled as he climbed the stairs to his rooms. If nothing else, the evening should prove entertaining.

Chapter 3

Hazel slowly made her way around the ballroom's perimeter, inwardly cursing Sam and wondering if she'd been in attendance long enough to justify slipping away. Chatter swirled around her as she edged through clusters of matrons and their charges. The room was abuzz with news of a Romanian count who had recently purchased property in London and was in the process of furnishing it with items gathered in extensive travels. Some pieces had even been made by London artisans. He was rumored to be quite handsome, of indeterminate age, and best of all—single.

"Surely he's here seeking a bride," Lady Weston said to Lady Miller. "Why else would a single man of his consequence set up house in London? I told my Cynthia that even if he wishes to reside mostly in Romania, his home there is a castle surrounded by an ancient medieval fortress. Can you imagine the wealth?"

Lady Miller nodded. "Surely once he has secured an heir,

he will not quibble about where his wife wishes to spend her time. She might find herself back in London indefinitely."

Hazel managed to look away before rolling her eyes. For the count's sake, she hoped he was aware that the matrimonial horde was primed and ready to attack from the front, sides, and rear. Perhaps that was his aim, however, and if so, she wished him luck. He'd find himself inundated with attention from an entire population suddenly enamored of Romania.

" . . . so exotic," one woman said to her friends as Hazel squeezed past them. "He funds archaeological excursions and has amassed more treasure than the finest museums. Only last week, the Smalleys hosted a sarcophagus opening, and Mother said the refreshments were divine and the company exclusive. Invitations to the event were highly coveted. Imagine if Count Petrescu has decorated his home with items from Egypt or the Orient! The parties will be the talk of the town . . ."

Hazel spied the doors leading to Lady Hadley's extensive back gardens and decided if she couldn't go home, she could at least escape the crowded room, which was becoming oppressively warm. She was exhausted from the early morning ride and the aches and pains that were the result.

She skirted a trio of young women, one of whom caught Hazel's eye before turning to her friends.

"I have it on good authority that Dr. MacInnes will be in the market for a bride before long. Of course, he has always preferred women of status and consequence. When he begins courting in earnest, one assumes his preferences will remain consistent."

Hazel felt her face flush, but hurried past with her eyes averted. She'd not give the girl the pleasure of seeing her flustered. Many people knew Hazel worked in Sam's clinic, but the gossipy girl could have saved her breath and her pointed barbs. Hazel was well aware that Sam's interest in her lay within the sturdy bounds of professionalism.

The balcony doors were nearly in reach when a group of rowdies beat her there. They were a crowd of young men of marriageable age, who found her pretty enough to tease but not important enough to court. She did not care for the lot of them and had nearly decided to make her escape for the evening when Emmeline O'Shea appeared at her side with a smile. She kissed the air next to Hazel's cheek.

"Emme!" Hazel smiled at her friend, who was also Isla's cousin, genuinely pleased for the first time since entering Lady Hadley's vaunted halls. "You've returned early."

Emme smirked. "The princesses hate the countryside, and Lysette was positively expiring at the thought of missing the Season's last ball."

Hazel regarded her with sympathy. Emme's younger stepsisters had decided quite young that the universe revolved around them, and age had not disabused them of the notion. She glanced around the room, then leaned closer. "Have you any protests planned?"

Emme's moss-green eyes sparkled, and she tucked a strand of glossy black hair behind her ear. "This week," she whispered, "Mr. Randolph is planning a retreat in the country for PSRC officials. I've a friend who works in the carriage houses—he suspects an axle or two might be loose. The lot of them tend to travel at a snail's pace, so no lasting harm done."

Hazel gasped and then laughed. "Emme," she whispered and pulled her friend by the elbow into the shadows, "you'll find yourself arrested again!"

Emme's eyes hardened, but a ghost of a smile remained. "All publicity is good. The sooner we convince the Prime Minister to dissolve the Predatory Shifter Regulations Committee, the better. I do not mind being a sacrificial pawn for the cause."

Hazel eyed her sideways. "You're more queen than pawn. What will the movement do if you are eventually charged with a crime that sticks? Your mother's money will buy only so much tolerance."

Emme straightened her shoulders. Hazel was of average height, and Emme was a head shorter. What her physical size lacked, however, her spirit compensated. "The cause is just and will continue with or without me." She gave Hazel a definitive nod and then laughed. "I shall be absolutely fine. I fear no one."

"And I am envious."

Emme's attention snagged on someone beyond Hazel's shoulder, and her eyes widened. "Drat," she muttered.

"What is it?" Hazel looked behind her. She spied Sam, who conversed most handsomely with his equally handsome friend, Oliver Reed, and her heart tripped.

"That blasted detective. He has called at the house twice in the past month. I managed to escape out the back both times, but my luck will not hold forever." Emme ducked behind Hazel.

"Why is he calling at the house? Does he intend to court you?"

Emme snorted. "Hardly. He wants to question me about a theft."

Hazel choked on a laugh. "Is he justified?"

Emme scowled and moved further into the shadows. "Of course not. But someone has made me look like the guilty party." Her eyes flicked to the right. "And the night grows worse! Not only is Lysette here, but my blasted stepfather has joined her. Should anyone ask, I have left the country." Emme kissed her fingertips and waved them at Hazel. She darted behind three matrons and their charges, losing herself in the crowd.

Hazel didn't know whether to laugh or be concerned. There was ill will between Emme and her stepfamily, but she never elaborated. Hazel glanced back at Sam and Mr. Reed, dismayed at their steady approach. "Thank you, Emme," she muttered to the shadows. She was comfortable with Sam, of course, but Mr. Reed made her nervous. It was as if he suspected her of committing a crime though she knew full well she hadn't.

"Miss Hughes," Sam said when they reached her. "You're looking splendid, as usual."

She bared her teeth, knowing it was a sad approxima tion of a smile. She was overheated, attending a ball she had no wish to be at, her friends were out of town, and Emme had teased her with company only to make a quick escape. Sam was handsome and wonderful, Hazel's social betters eyed him from across the room like cats on cream, and she was frustrated in the extreme. The sight of him in formal clothing was a torture to which she was not yet immune.

And Emme had had the right of it—Oliver Reed was not pleased.

"Miss Hughes," the detective said, inclining his head. "Did I see Miss O'Shea here a moment ago?"

Hazel smiled. "Yes, Detective-Inspector. She was obliged to make a short appearance and then was called away."

His lips twitched at one side, but Hazel wasn't certain it indicated mirth. "Called away?"

Sam raised a fist to his mouth and cleared his throat, but there was no mistaking his amusement.

Hazel nodded. "Her mother requires assistance at the shop. Inventory accounting, I believe."

Now Mr. Reed smiled, but it was at odds with his narrowed eyes. "Odd, that, seeing as I spoke with Mrs. O'Shea not ten minutes ago. She also arrived late, said she was here with her husband and children."

Drat that Emme! "I clearly misunderstood. It was my impression that—"

Lady Hadley's laugh tittered across the ballroom, drawing their attention. Through the swirling mass of couples on the floor, Hazel saw the hostess standing next to an imposing gentleman dressed in formal black. She'd never seen him before, but an intense energy slid subtly through the room and reached her on the other side. He locked dark eyes with Hazel, and then couples swirled in the middle of the room, blocking her view. Through glimpses of moving people, however, she realized his focus remained on her. She took an involuntary step back and touched a delicate gold chain she wore always on her left wrist. For a reason she'd yet to divine, she always found comfort in gold.

"Dravor Petrescu." Oliver Reed nodded in the man's direction. "A Romanian count, recently acquired vacation residence in London."

Hazel studied the foreigner. "Vacation? A pity—the bulk of attendees here tonight had hoped his move was permanent."

"Count Petrescu arrived one week ago, has purchased property, but rumors have already grown around him. His purposes are unknown." Mr. Reed's brows drew together. "I do not care for mysteries."

Hazel lost sight of the nobleman for a moment, and when she saw him again, he was smiling genially at Lady Hadley. At that moment, Count Petrescu again turned his attention through the crowd and caught Hazel's eye. His mouth lifted at the corner, and he gave a slight nod.

"Do you know him?" Sam edged closer to Hazel.

"I've never seen him in my life." She flicked open the small fan hanging from her wrist. The heat was becoming intolerable. "Perhaps we should prop open a door," she muttered.

Sam looked down at her, his expression speculative. "Suddenly warm? In need of some fresh air, are we?" he murmured.

"It is positively stifling in here." She tipped her head, unable to read his undertone.

"Never met him, you say?" Mr. Reed interjected.

Hazel shook her head and looked across the room, feeling an odd sense of relief when the crowd continued to swirl between her and the stranger who seemed to find her of interest.

"I believe he seeks to remedy that." Sam's tone was sharp, clipped. "I want whatever information you can find on the man," he said to Oliver.

Hazel looked at Sam, whose eyes narrowed as he searched the crowd. "Dr. MacInnes, you needn't research a stranger on my account. I sincerely doubt he has an inkling of who I am, nor does he want to."

Sam looked as though he might respond, but instead held his tongue.

Mr. Reed glanced from the gentleman to Hazel, one brow raised. He clapped Sam on the shoulder, leaned close, and said, "I shall dig deeper."

He moved as though to leave but paused as Count Petrescu approached them with Lady Hadley leading the way and talking animatedly. Mr. Reed murmured something to Sam, who nodded once, tersely.

Sam shifted closer to Hazel, their arms brushing. She would have loved to believe he stood protectively near her because he fancied her, not because he felt a sense of professional obligation. He probably wanted to guard his employee from some perceived harm, protect his business investment. She refrained from grinding her teeth together, but only just.

"Dr. MacInnes, Detective-Inspector Reed, Miss Hughes—allow me to introduce my guest," Lady Hadley said, breathless. "This is Count Petrescu. He is Romanian nobility, here in London, if you can imagine!" Lady Hadley fanned herself.

Hazel curtsied, and when Count Petrescu bowed lightly and held out his hand, she placed hers in it only because convention required it. She felt self-conscious by the attention, and there was something about him that unnerved her. He kissed her gloved fingers, and then straightened with a smile. "I have traveled a long distance indeed to meet you, Miss Hughes. I am most grateful to our lovely hostess for providing the introduction. I wonder, would you grace me with a dance?"

Hazel searched for an intelligent response. Though she wanted to decline, she knew it would be poor manners. "I would be delighted," she finally managed.

He'd timed the introduction perfectly, as the orchestra ended one set before playing the opening strains of a waltz. She registered Sam's fingertips on the back of her arm and then Mr. Reed's subtle head shake. Sam dropped his hand, and Hazel placed hers in Petrescu's. He led her to the floor and settled into the dance, his movements sure and measured to match hers.

Petrescu stared at her in silence for a moment before smiling. He had dark hair and eyes, was handsome in a classically aristocratic fashion, his expression pleasant. "You must forgive my abrupt behavior, but my entire purpose here in London revolves around you, Miss Hughes."

He guided her in a comfortable rhythm, and as they turned, she spied several shocked faces. Had his statement not been so baffling, she might have enjoyed the moment.

"I cannot imagine why, my lord. Surely we've not met, as I would have remembered you." Her social triumph would be fodder for gossip by morning, but she didn't want the attention or scrutiny that would be heaped upon her. The count might as well have placed a target on her chest.

"We have not met, that is true, but I knew your mother. I am certain you will understand my shock when I say that you are the very image of her."

She tilted her head, confused. "You are the first to ever say it, and I confess, I cannot see a resemblance."

"My dear, I do not speak of Rowena Hughes." He paused. "I bear news that will shock you, I fear. Clearly, you have not ever been told of the true circumstances of your birth."

Hazel's heart beat faster as they continued to move in concert, heat suffusing her face and adding to the room's stuffiness. She licked her lips and, despite the warmth, felt a chill run down her spine. Her shoulder ached from her early-morning fall at the park, and her head began to throb. "Perhaps anything shocking might be best discussed . . . anywhere but here." She looked again at the people who whispered behind their fans, and the openly curious glances from even the other couples on the floor.

Before she could protest, the count had guided her effortlessly to the balcony doors. "Then let us continue away from prying eyes. Will you join me outside for a moment? You are flushed."

She nodded and took his arm. They were nearly to the exit when Hazel felt the warmth of Sam's hand on her elbow. She paused, and beyond Sam's shoulder noted Detective-Inspector Reed's careful scrutiny, and Lady Hadley's unabashed, possibly dismayed, curiosity. The hostess had only invited Hazel as a matter of concession to Isla and Lucy; now, her prime guest paid exclusive attention to the young woman she openly disliked.

"Count Petrescu, in the absence of family to speak for Miss Hughes, I must ascertain your intentions." Sam's grip on Hazel's elbow tightened.

Petrescu's brows climbed high. "A request for conversation is cause for concern, Dr. MacInnes? I can assure you, I mean Miss Hughes no ill will."

Hazel grew irritated with the conversation that flowed around her as though she were a child. "I would certainly share a moment of my time." She smiled and pulled her elbow from Sam's grasp. "It is insufferably warm in here," she added, pointedly not looking at their hostess, "and I would welcome a respite on the balcony."

Lady Hadley bristled, but Hazel ignored her. She looked back at Sam and Mr. Reed, adding, "I'll be perfectly visible through the glass. Thank you for your concern for my welfare, gentlemen."

She put on a brave face, but a sense of unease began at the base of her spine and inched upward. The cool air she'd been so anxious to feel moments earlier now seemed much less comfortable, and she shivered slightly. The balcony doors closed behind them, and Hazel noted that many guests had moved down the wide staircase and onto the lawns and gardens.

Count Petrescu walked with her to the balcony railing and turned, resting lightly against it. "Miss Hughes, as I said, this will come as a shock to you, but I know of no other way to present it. When I said I knew your mother, I was not speaking of Rowena Hughes."

"I wonder if you've mistaken me for another," Hazel finally said. "Rowena Hughes is my mother."

49

Count Petrescu shook his head. "I speak of the woman who gave birth to you, twenty-three years ago in a small Transylvanian village. She died in childbirth, leaving you orphaned. Along with your twin sister."

Chapter 4

Hazel sat across from Count Dravor Petrescu in a lavish carriage, numb with shock. Seated next to her was a young woman named Sally Tucker, whom he had brought along to act as a maid and chaperone for Hazel. The situation was ridiculous, really. She didn't require a chaperone; she was an independently working woman who went about each day entirely on her own. He was a foreign nobleman, and likely did not understand.

The things he had told her, although sparse on detail, clicked into place in her brain with the sensation of truth. She had a twin sister. Of course she did. She'd been dreaming of her since childhood.

"Is her hair the color of platinum? Nearly silver?" Hazel's question was the first she'd asked since leaving the ball.

The count nodded, studying her carefully. "Indeed. Has been since birth." He smiled faintly. "Her nursemaid told me it would darken with time, but it did not."

"She bears my features in every other way, yes? Except for her eyes, which are a deep blue."

"What you say is true, but may I ask how you know such details?"

"I've seen her in dreams all my life."

There was a stillness to him while he studied her. His direct gaze both drew her in and made her uneasy. The silence stretched to the point of discomfort.

"I find this incredible, Miss Hughes, and I am filled with a sense of hope for the first time in . . . such a very long time."

On Lady Hadley's balcony, the count had told Hazel that her twin, Marit, was ill, and had asked if Hazel would receive him in the morning to discuss the matter in detail. Hazel had known she wouldn't sleep a wink, so had invited him home that very moment.

"What is your relationship to my sister?" A thought struck her, and she added, "To me?"

He took a breath, and a smile twitched at the corner of his mouth. His expression was paternal, and he hesitated.

"Please. Do not keep me in suspense. I would rather know all, and immediately."

He tilted his head in acquiescence. "Of course. Miss Hughes, your mother was my sister. I am your uncle, and I have raised Marit from birth."

Hazel frowned. It made no sense. How on earth had she come into Rowena Hughes's care, and as her daughter?

The question was logical, and he anticipated it. "There was an issue with the midwife."

She arched a brow, and she was struck by the thought that her expression mirrored his. "What sort of 'issue'?"

"Your birth mother struggled in the delivery. We were

unaware she carried twins—indeed, I did not know of it until recently—and after the midwife delivered both of you, your mother passed. Your father was beside himself with grief. With the help of her daughter, the midwife spirited you away. I do not know her original intent, but in the end, you were sold to a traveling English merchant and his wife who had always wanted a child."

Hazel's mouth was dry, and she tried to swallow. "My mother—Rowena."

He nodded. A muscle worked in his jaw. "You can imagine my dismay when I realized my own flesh and blood had been sold, and to a foreign merchant."

Hazel hadn't realized she'd clenched her fists tightly in her lap until her fingers protested the grip. "What happened to my father?" She straightened her fingers slowly. They were chilled despite the warmth of her gloves and the heated carriage interior. She was cold everywhere.

"He passed shortly after your mother. They were soul mates from youth, and he was bereaved beyond consolation at her death."

His expression was sympathetic, but there was a thread of cynicism running beneath his statement that had Hazel questioning his sincerity.

"That was when you took in my sister?"

"Yes. Raised her as my own." He frowned. "I have done everything in my power, but she is not . . . well."

"You mentioned that earlier. What ails her?"

"Nothing modern medicine can cure. I have brought in experts from every field. Her problems stem from her mind, and I am at a loss."

Hazel's heart thumped, and she looked out the window. Dream Hazel—Marit—had been slowly growing mad. Hazel's own dreams of late had become increasingly dark, full of fear, hopelessness, and a desperate sense of loneliness.

"You know something," Count Petrescu said. It sounded almost like an accusation.

Hazel looked back at him and hoped her fear didn't show on her face. "I wish I did. I wish I knew how to help her, but frankly, you must understand my skepticism about this entire situation."

He smiled. "You doubt my claims?"

"I do not doubt my sister's existence; I feel as if I have always known it. I do not, however, know anything about you."

"Let us speak with Rowena. I've no doubt she'll verify my story."

They fell into silence, and Hazel looked at Miss Tucker, who sat as far in the corner of the seat as she could manage. The girl seemed desperate to remain invisible.

Hazel felt a stab of sympathy. "You're newly employed by the count?" She gestured toward the nobleman as she addressed Sally.

"Yes, miss. Only just."

"Have you family here in Town?"

"Yes, miss. A mother and five younger siblings."

Hazel smiled. "A full house, then."

"Indeed."

Hazel took in the young woman's tidy but worn clothing, and her pale features. Work was often hard to come by, and employment with a Romanian nobleman would be a boon to a family consisting of so many hungry little mouths.

The conveyance carried them through the streets to Hazel's home. Her head swirled with thoughts; she imagined her brain had been replaced with feathers that blew topsy-turvy around her skull.

She peered outside the window at the inky world beyond. A light rain had begun, and now gathered strength, pattering on the carriage roof. Her heart beat in time with the drops, and she absently shook her fingers against the chill that had shot through her extremities when Count Petrescu had turned her reality on its head.

She was afraid, horribly afraid, that Rowena would confirm what he'd said. If she was a twin, one mystery would be solved. But it would also open several more. Why had she been abducted? Why had Rowena never told her the truth? And ultimately, what was wrong with Marit?

When they reached the cottage, the 'ton driver flipped the steps down and helped her alight. She turned back to Sally and bid her good night, and then made her way to the door, aware of Count Petrescu murmuring instructions for the driver to wait and to keep the heater on so Sally could wait in warmth and comfort. Hazel hesitated, her hand poised over the door handle. As soon as they entered and confronted her mother, everything would change.

Count Petrescu stood a respectful distance behind her, but his presence crowded Hazel against the small home. She took a shuddering breath and opened the door, calling for her mother and motioning her guest inside. "Please, come in. To the left is the parlor," she said. "Take a seat near the fire, and I will locate my . . . my mother."

Rowena Hughes descended the stairs, then froze. "Hazel?"

Hazel clasped the stair railing and looked up at her. "We have a visitor from Romania, Mother."

Rowena sat slowly, heavily, on the step, and her face had leeched of all color. Hazel wondered if her mother would faint.

So it was true. It was all true.

On shaking legs, she climbed the few steps to Rowena and clasped her limp fingers. "We should offer our guest some tea," Hazel said quietly. "And then perhaps we have some things to discuss." She was amazed her voice remained steady. Everything felt wobbly, from her head to her feet.

Rowena's mouth worked, but no words formed. She swallowed and looked rapidly from the count to Hazel and back again. "Hazel," she finally whispered. "I . . . I . . . you must go . . . you cannot . . ."

"Come." Hazel tugged on Rowena's hand and pulled her up. "Is Celina already charging for the evening?"

Rowena licked her lips and shook her head, following Hazel slowly down the stairs. "I was just about to shut her down." Her voice was a thread of sound.

"You instruct her to prepare tea," Hazel told her, "and I shall hang the count's wrap."

Their guest had remained silent since entering, and he watched Rowena with a flat expression. Hazel grew defensive for her mother. As much as Rowena exasperated her, she loved her and had always been secure in Rowena's love for her.

Rowena made her way down the short hallway to where their automaton servant, Celina, worked in the kitchen. Hazel took a deep breath and wordlessly hung Petrescu's coat on the stand by the door.

She gestured for the count to enter the parlor again, hearing Rowena's hushed instructions to Celina for tea. It was odd, really. Rowena wasn't usually the quiet sort. Shorter and rounder than Hazel, she'd always had the verbal volume of a giant, and friends had often laughed at the difference between mother and daughter.

Rowena joined Hazel and the count in the parlor, and they sat in furniture that was comfortable but faded. The home was cozy and tidy, and spoke of Rowena's penchant for herbal remedies and minor Light Magick concoctions. Hazel viewed it through Petrescu's eyes, now, and again felt a surge of defensiveness.

Petrescu crossed one leg over the other and placed his hands together on his lap. He regarded Hazel with one brow raised, waiting as if in deference to her, allowing her to assume the role of host. It felt strangely farcical, almost a mockery, yet his expression was pleasant, his features a mask of patience and compassion. Even sitting near the fire, Hazel felt cold.

Hazel cleared her throat. "Mother, this is Count Dravor Petrescu. Have you, perhaps, met him before?"

Rowena swallowed, looking at him with wide eyes. "I do not know him, but perhaps I might have met a fellow country-woman, years ago."

Petrescu inclined his head. "Indeed, Mrs. Hughes. You were acquainted with Mrs. Romanescu, a midwife, were you not?"

Rowena blanched further, something Hazel wouldn't have thought possible.

Hazel reached over and took her mother's hand. "My lord, perhaps you will tell my mother what you've shared with me."

"Of course. Years ago, Mrs. Hughes, your husband traded in wools and textiles, and you traveled with him to Romania on a business venture. The final evening of your journey, at a village called Vania, in the Carpathian Mountains, you were approached by Mrs. Romanescu, a midwife."

Hazel looked at Rowena, who nodded. All Hazel knew of her father was that he'd died before she was born. Rowena never spoke of him.

"Mrs. Romanescu approached you with a strange proposition. The midwife had just aided a young villager who had given birth to a daughter and then died. She knew the infant would face scorn as the bastard child of a fallen woman, and she said the baby was yours if you wanted her."

Rowena cleared her throat. "We had always wanted a child. Of course, we said yes." Her fingers tightened on Hazel's. "Mrs. Romanescu told us the mother had been a practitioner of Light Magick and a Medium, and I knew it was a sign, as I am also from a witch family."

Petrescu nodded sympathetically at Rowena, wincing slightly. "I regret to inform you, dear lady, that you were told a lie." He gestured elegantly to Hazel. "Your daughter's mother was a respected woman who died giving birth to twin

58

girls. Mrs. Romanescu spirited away one infant, telling their grieving father nothing and, instead, selling her to you." He raised a brow, his manner grave. "You paid handsomely, did you not?"

"She . . . she seemed desperate and terrified . . ." Rowena straightened, color returning to her face. "We paid her all the gold we had, keeping only enough to return home." Her voice rose in pitch, and she spoke quickly. "She told us to go, that we must run and never return to the village because the poor dead mother's family wanted to kill the child!" Rowena's breath came faster. "She said we might even be followed, that we should hide. We sold our farm, our business, everything we had and moved here. Then Mr. Hughes fell ill that winter and died, leaving me alone with the baby."

Hazel's emotions veered from sorrow to frustration. "Why did you never tell me this?"

Rowena looked at Hazel, eyes wide. "To keep you safe, of course. I couldn't tell you!"

"Mother, I am not a child anymore. You ought to have told me."

Rowena looked back at the count, who seemed content to watch the drama unfold. "When you entered my front door tonight, I thought you meant to kill my child." Her eyes filmed over, and Hazel felt sick for her.

"On the contrary," Petrescu soothed. "And I did send a letter some weeks ago, but never received a response from you."

Rowena swallowed.

Hazel murmured, "Mother, did you receive a letter?"

"I did." Rowena lifted her chin. "And I burned it. I was

not about to allow my child to travel to a place where her life would be at risk, to be with strangers we had never met."

"I certainly understand your concern, Mrs. Hughes, but I believe your daughter has a mission to fulfill."

Hazel looked at Petrescu. "Helping my sister," she said quietly.

"Yes. I fear the time is already upon us." The count looked to Rowena. "Mrs. Hughes, Hazel's sister, Marit, is ill. She is from a Light Magick family—in that much, Mrs. Romanescu did not lie—and I believe Hazel's tie to Marit as her twin will be beneficial. I am hoping Hazel will help me find a cure."

"You'll not involve Hazel in this madness." Rowena's eyes flashed. "I have kept her safe all these years!"

"And an admirable feat it has been," Petrescu said, his voice soft.

Rowena's grip on Hazel's fingers relaxed, and Hazel looked sharply at the man. His attention was focused entirely on Rowena, and Hazel felt the subtle but unmistakable surge of energy emanating from him.

She felt seeds of anger take root, and she welcomed the emotion. Who did he think he was, coming into their home and using some sort of mind control on her mother?

"Mr. Petrescu," she said, deliberately omitting his title and pulling his attention to her. "As I said, I do not doubt the existence of my sister. I still do not, however, have any proof of your tie to her or to us."

He reached into his jacket and pulled out a pouch. He opened it and slid into his palm a delicate platinum chain fastened with a clasp. "You wear a gold chain around your wrist, like this one." He looked at Hazel for confirmation.

She nodded, swallowing.

"That chain was a talisman your mother placed around your neck when you were born." He glanced at Rowena. "Hazel was still wearing it when Romanescu gave her to you?"

Rowena nodded wordlessly.

"This one belongs to Marit." He extended his hand to Hazel. "Here."

She took the platinum chain and sucked in a breath, stunned. The bracelet seemed to stretch toward her wrist and her own chain, like metal filings to a magnet, but where her gold bracelet always gave her a tangible sense of calm and comfort, a mellow glow, the platinum was uncomfortably warm and unsettling.

Petrescu watched her closely, one corner of his mouth lifting in a triumphant smile. He extended the open pouch, and she dropped the platinum chain into it. She rubbed her palm with her fingers, her heart thudding.

"Why do you have that?" she asked hoarsely.

"She gave it to me, temporarily."

Hazel's lips tightened. She was never without her bracelet. It was a familiar comfort, and on the rare occasion she removed it, she noted its absence. She couldn't imagine Marit was content without her bracelet.

"Perhaps this will provide the best proof." Petrescu replaced the pouch in his breast pocket. "You have a tiny birthmark shaped like a star on the inside of your left wrist."

Hazel stared, and she placed her finger on the birthmark she'd had her whole life.

Petrescu nodded and pulled his cuff back to reveal an identical star. "It is a family trait that lands on some and avoids others," he told Hazel. "Miss Hughes, I am truly your blood relative."

Chapter 5

S am sat in his carriage, watching the Hughes' home from a distance as though he expected something to happen. He wondered if he was losing his mind. Hazel had left the ball nearly an hour before, after emerging from the balcony with the count, whom he did not trust as far as he could throw.

Hazel had been white as a ghost, and Sam was sick with worry. He'd followed them as they left the ball, Eugene driving the automated carriage, a canopy cover protecting him from the rain. The carriage's Talk function activated, sounding with a ding in the carriage interior before Eugene spoke.

"Still raining, Doctor. Quite impressively. Perhaps you were wondering."

Sam counted to ten. "I am aware, Eugene. And you are in no danger from it."

"You sound as though you would benefit from some intelligent conversation."

"Which I am unlikely to get from you."

"My, my." Eugene said, and Sam could practically see the

'ton arching one eyebrow. "Perhaps your contact with Miss Hughes outside a professional setting ought to be limited. You're ever so surly."

Sam closed his eyes. "Silence, Eugene."

A sniff. "Very well." There was a pause, and Sam braced for the parting shot. "You'll see that I am correct, though, and my earlier observation stands. Miss Hughes has no need of your protective nature and may well be enamored of the Romanian nobleman. In fact—"

Sam flipped a switch, terminating the conversation on his end. He wasn't about to admit Eugene may have the right of it. But Hazel had no male relatives to watch out for her, and her mother was flighty, at best. He wiped the window clear of the fog from his breath and stared again at the cottage. That man was still in the house, and the sense that all was not right sat heavily in Sam's gut.

His telescriber dinged with a message from Oliver. The words scrolled across the device, the text similar to that used in typewriting machines.

Dravor Petrescu is an antiques collector. No criminal record. Old Romanian family, has business interests with British museums. Will advise if anything nefarious surfaces.

Sam frowned. Oliver's report should have put him at ease, but there was something indefinable about Petrescu. He looked again at the cottage, raindrops on the carriage window distorting the gaslight and shadows on the small front garden. The house was quiet, there was no screaming to be heard, lights glowed in the parlor—Sam had no legitimate reason for lingering.

More to the point, he had no legitimate reason to suspect

a visiting nobleman of anything untoward. He had just decided to approach the cottage when the door opened and the nobleman stepped outside. Sam quietly slid his carriage window open an inch to better view Hazel, who stood in the doorway and conversed with her guest. Petrescu was speaking, Hazel nodding. She wasn't smiling, though.

Petrescu took his leave, climbing into an opulent carriage and disappearing into the night.

Hazel closed her door without glancing in Sam's direction, but why would she? She would hardly be expecting him to lurk outside her home. Feeling uncomfortably like a voyeur, he put on his hat, climbed out of the carriage, and turned to give Eugene instructions.

"Oh, excellent, Doctor. You've decided to join me out here instead of inviting me into the carriage where it is warm and dry," Eugene said before Sam could utter a word.

Sam squinted up at him. "You require neither warmth nor dryness, Eugene. Regardless, you have that lovely canopy to keep you from getting wet."

"Except for when the wind blows." As if summoned, a gust blew up the street and spattered the 'ton with rain. Eugene shot him a look.

"Wait here. And while you're waiting, use your processors to gather any information you can find on Dravor Petrescu."

"Perhaps I could wait inside the carriage."

"I'll not be long." Sam turned to the cottage, anxious about Hazel and irritated with his 'ton. "As though he needs to escape the elements . . ." Sam muttered when he reached the door and knocked. The house was hushed, and he felt churlish thinking the women may already be retiring for the evening.

As he debated whether to leave, and growing wetter and colder by the moment, the door cracked open, and Hazel regarded him in surprise.

"Sam?" She blinked, and the light from the small lamppost reflected in the golden hue of her irises. Golden eyes with flecks of green, golden hair with thick curls that felt like spun silk.

"Sam." She was frowning, now.

He shook his head. "Apologies. I wanted to see personally that you are well." Rain dripped from the brim of his hat into his eyes.

She pulled the door open. "Come in from the weather, then."

He stepped over the threshold and removed the hat, raking a hand through his hair. He fought the urge to shake like a dog all over the small entry.

"I am well," Hazel said. "Thank you for looking after me. I have . . ." She glanced at the parlor, then lowered her voice. "I've received odd news.

He edged forward and peered into the parlor, where Rowena stared into the hearth. She didn't seem aware of anything beyond the dancing flames.

Hazel cleared her throat and stood by the front door, placing her hand on the handle. "We've had a strange evening, and my mother needs me."

"Is she ill? What is it, Hazel? Let me help."

She sighed, and her eyes closed briefly. She looked infinitely weary, as though she carried the weight of the world's troubles. "The Romanian count we met at the party? He is my uncle. Rowena adopted me—" She interrupted herself with a short laugh. "Purchased, really. And I have a sister, apparently, who is ill."

Sam stared at her. "Are you . . . are you certain the man speaks the truth?"

Hazel nodded. "He does have odd proof, and my mother confirms his story. The parts of it she knew, at least. And now I have a sister in distress and a family I knew nothing about before tonight." Her brows knit, and she lowered her voice. "And yet I did know. I knew about her."

"What? How?" Sam asked, his thoughts whirling in confusion.

"I've been dreaming about her my whole life."

Sam shook his head. "What was his purpose in coming here?" Unease began to spread throughout his gut. He sensed she hadn't told him everything yet.

"He wants my help finding a solution to her illness. My sister. In Romania."

Sam exhaled. "Hazel, you cannot go anywhere with that man."

She looked at him sharply, her shoulders stiffening, and he inwardly groaned.

"I most certainly am going," she said. "If I can help Marit somehow, I would be selfish indeed not to make the attempt."

He felt sick, panic settling in his chest. "You cannot go alone." He grasped her shoulders. "Hazel, you mustn't go alone."

"And who shall I take with me?" she demanded. "My

mother? Impossible. Isla and Lucy are out of town. Emme . . ."
She paused. "Emme would go with me."

Her announcement brought on a greater sense of alarm.
He gave her shoulders a little shake. "You cannot take Emme
O'Shea! Not only will she be unable to protect you, she will
find trouble!"

Her shoulders slumped, and she stepped away. "I do not
know what else to do, Sam. I cannot remain here, not now
that I'm aware of my sister and that she needs help. I have
talents, you know I do, and perhaps I may be effective in
finding a cure."

He took a deep breath and tried to still the inexplicable
panic that filled him at the thought of her facing possible
danger alone. The notion that she was leaving *him* fought
for equal footing, but surely that was no reason for him to be
frantic.

"Let me go with you, then."

She stared at him, slack-jawed. He was nearly as stunned
by the suggestion, himself.

"I cannot, in good conscience, see you do this thing
alone."

Her expression softened into a sad smile. "Sam, you
have too much here that requires your attention. Surgeries
are scheduled; you have meetings with the patent board. You
cannot leave."

He leaned toward her, his fingers itching to pull her into
his arms. Bewildered by the sudden urge, he shoved his hands
into his pockets but remained close, gratified that she didn't
move away.

"The surgeries can be referred to colleagues, and the

patents have been filed. I've needed some time away, and this is the perfect opportunity."

"Sam, I—"

"Hazel."

Her eyes flew to his, bright with unshed tears.

He lifted the corner of his mouth. "If you refuse, I shall be forced to petition my good friend Count Petrescu for an invitation. I'd much rather be your guest than his."

She laughed and sniffed. "We would both be his guests; I do not see the difference ultimately."

"The difference is night and day to me." He smiled and reached for a handkerchief. He handed the square of linen to her, and she dabbed at her eyes and nose.

"Truly, I am grateful for the offer, but I would feel incredibly selfish." She smiled, but he wasn't fooled by it. "I shall be completely fine. The count is a . . . wonderful person."

He chuckled. "You and I both know that to be a generous assessment. You're an astute judge of character, one of the finest I know, and you'll never convince me you feel at ease with him."

She lifted a shoulder, but didn't disagree.

"Let me go with you," he said softly.

"I cannot keep you from it."

"You certainly can. I'll not bully my way into your affairs, so I am hoping you think well enough of me to allow it."

"You are not fighting fairly. As though this is a privilege I would deny you." She frowned, but he sensed a crack in her resolve.

"It is indeed a privilege. I'd not rest easy knowing you are far away and at the mercy of a complete stranger. One I do not trust."

"Why? Why would you do this?"

Why, indeed? He had money enough to hire an army of security to accompany her. He didn't need to go along. He looked down at her, at the gown that fit to perfection and the curls on her head that gleamed gold in the lamplight. He saw her as she'd been earlier at Lady Hadley's. She'd been uncomfortable there, but he had been amazed it hadn't shown in her face or demeanor. She possessed more substance than anyone in that ballroom.

"You are my esteemed colleague," he said, "and more to the point, a dear friend. It would be an honor to help you."

She bit her lip and looked away, her eyes again suspiciously bright. "I—" She cleared her throat. "Thank you, Sam. I welcome the help and am grateful to you, more than I can express."

He smiled, relieved. He exhaled softly, realizing he'd been holding his breath. "When shall I be ready to depart?"

She raised her brows and again caught her lip between her teeth. "Tomorrow evening."

He blinked. "Well. Not wasting any time, is he?"

She shook her head. "This is madness. It's too sudden, and you could never make arrangements in time—"

He held up his hand. "Not a word. I have people at my disposal to make any and all arrangements necessary. You'll not put me off so easily."

She flushed, which he found adorable. "I meant nothing of the sort, I—"

"Hazel, do not fret." He ducked to catch her eye. "All right, then?"

She nodded. "All right."

They lingered. She swayed slightly, and he wondered if she was aware of it. Her eyes flickered from his own, to his mouth, and back again. Awareness flared in his chest, something dormant that woke with a familiar need.

"Hazel?" Rowena's voice sounded from the parlor.

Sam breathed deeply, close enough to Hazel to note the soft lavender scent he'd come to associate with her. Kissing her suddenly seemed the most natural thing in the world to do, so he straightened, putting a respectable distance between them.

He exhaled quietly again, noting her flushed cheeks and beautifully large, golden-green eyes that held a hint of wariness and something else he wasn't sure he could define.

"Please give my apologies to your mother for the lateness of my visit," he said, still watching Hazel. "I'll take my leave."

"This excursion will be unseemly," she murmured. "People will talk."

"I shall bring Eugene. Properly chaperoned—all problems solved."

She laughed softly. "Eugene is the answer to any dilemma."

He donned his hat and rolled his eyes. "Never let him hear you say such a thing. He will become unspeakably smug."

"He already is unspeakably smug."

Sam turned the door handle, but paused. "Tomorrow, then. I'll contact the count and then call again here."

The door closed quietly behind him, and he jogged across the wet cobblestones to his carriage. He looked up through the rain, which had grown to a steady downpour, to see the driver seat empty. A quick glance inside the carriage showed Eugene, who touched two fingers to his brow in a salute.

Sam opened the door with unnecessary force and jerked his thumb to the side. "Out. We have a week's worth of details to arrange before morning."

Chapter 6

The next morning, Hazel finished dressing and sat at her vanity, trying to muscle her curls into submission.

"You mustn't go," Rowena said for the fifth time. "I knew when we took you as an infant that returning to that wretched place would mean your peril. I do not know this man, and I do not know if he is trustworthy in the least." She took a hairpin from Hazel, who was trying in vain to anchor it into her coiffure. "We have nobody to look after your interests, no one to keep you safe." She bit her lip and met Hazel's eyes in the vanity mirror. "I cannot even afford to hire someone." Rowena's eyes shone with tears, and Hazel shook her head. "I used all of our savings to send you to school, and—"

"Mother, no, I am fine." Hazel spoke quickly. Once Rowena wandered into crying wilderness, the recovery mission would take hours. "Please do not fret. Isla taught me to handle my ray gun, and that which I cannot accomplish with brawn I shall manage with my brain." She smiled, but it felt and looked strained.

"What sort of mother would I be if I allowed such madness?" Rowena sniffled, and the tears continued gathering.

Hazel turned in her seat to grasp her mother's hands. "Please, please no theatrics this morning. I shall be fine."

"I shall accompany you." Rowena's jaw set, and Hazel inwardly groaned. If she didn't say something, her mother would anchor herself to the proverbial spot and refuse to move.

Hazel sighed. "Dr. MacInnes has offered to accompany me."

Rowena's face brightened. "Oh, yes! Yes, that's very good." She wiped her eyes and nodded. "I tell his mother constantly she has no need to hide her head in shame that her second son chose the life of a simple doctor rather than the military. I mean, he did spend time at war and all, but he didn't remain in service to Queen and Country and rise through the ranks as do most respectable second sons."

Hazel blinked. "And you tell his mother that her brilliant son is no cause for shame—her son who is a surgeon and a pioneering medical inventor who is literally performing miraculous feats with limb and organ replacement?"

"I am aware it is hardly traditional, Hazel, but you must learn to broaden your horizons. The man has given you gainful employment, after all, and I am surprised you would be a harsh judge. Prejudice does not become you."

Hazel closed her eyes.

"I sincerely hope you'll not embarrass me to Lady MacInnes by slighting him. Just because you now keep company with Countess Blackwell does not mean you ought to forget your own humble roots—"

Hazel stood and put an arm around her mother and propelled her to the door. "I believe I hear Celina at the front door. We must have guests."

Rowena's eyes widened, and she nearly took Hazel's bedroom door from its hinges in her haste downstairs. Her voice echoed back up as she gave Celina instructions for tea.

Hazel released a breath and quietly closed her door, leaning against it. Her mother had raised her, though she would probably never truly understand her.

Hazel's life was predictable, rather staid, and for all that she'd unwittingly tried to face her fears over the last year, nothing had changed, not really. Nothing except that a dashing, devastatingly handsome and charming man had once saved her life and then insinuated himself into it so neatly that her heart would be torn when he married another.

While Sam's solicitous concern was kindness on his part, a sort of patient benevolence, she knew her heart was in line behind dozens of others whose private dreams included capturing the affections of the paragon with blond hair, deep blue eyes, and an impressive physique.

He was so much more than merely handsome to Hazel. He was funny and kind and intelligent. He brightened the energy in the room, drew others to him as moths to a flame. Hazel understood she was one of many moths, and she flew dangerously close to that flame. Her wings were already singed, and every ounce of self-preservation screamed at her to fly away, and quickly.

It was one thing to see him during work hours and the occasional social event. It was another entirely to spend hours on end in his company, traveling to strange places—with strangers—and growing ever closer to him because he was the only familiar thing there.

She pushed herself off the door and sat at her vanity. She scanned her packing list and picked up her fountain pen, scratching off the items she'd already stowed in her trunk. Cupping her chin in her hand, she absently flipped through her notebook, which was thick with letters from friends, quotations from her favorite books, lists of tasks, dreams, disappointments, and the mundane. She'd clipped in playbills from the theater and receipts from café visits with notations about the company and the conversation.

She traced her finger along one page, absently registering voices downstairs in the parlor but shutting it out. She didn't want anything more complicated in her life than the list before her, though her current situation might be the very definition of the word. Her eyes drifted across the letters, her head jumbled with thoughts of a newly discovered uncle, a sister she'd never met, and a man she loved with her whole heart.

A soft knock at her door startled her, and she opened it, surprised to see Emme on the other side. "The count and your mother are exchanging words in the parlor, and you would not believe the rumors I have heard this morning. I ought to have braved Detective-Inspector Reed's interrogation and remained at the Hadleys'. What on earth is happening? Are you Romanian royalty?"

Hazel smiled and opened the door wider, glancing around her room, viewing it through another's eyes. Various items of clothing—different colored corsets and blouses, trousers, skirts, netting overlays, bustles, belts and accessories—were strewn across her bed and hanging from wardrobe doors. "Pardon the mess. I will explain as much as I know."

Emme sat on a stuffed ottoman next to Hazel's vanity. "Tell me everything."

Hazel sat at the vanity and recounted what had transpired from the time Emme had left the ball.

Her eyes grew wider as Hazel spoke, her expressive face giving away her every thought, and she finally smiled, smug. "Well, well. Lady Hazel. What I wouldn't give to see Lady Hadley and her ilk this morning."

Hazel shrugged. "Nothing will change, except that I'll be labeled an 'upstart' now."

"Apparently you've not read the society pages yet today. Your uncle, the count, has legitimized your birth and status. He also exonerated Rowena and implied she saved your life in a time of peril."

Hazel's mouth slackened. "What . . . what does this mean for me?"

Emme smiled. "It means whatever you would like it to mean. You're free to move about in loftier circles with every claim to that right. Nobody can argue that you aren't 'old money,' even. I've felt those barbs, although I couldn't care less."

The significance of Emme's words penetrated some of the fog around Hazel's brain, but she wondered if her life truly would change. She was already on the fringes of high society, and she wasn't certain her uncle's legitimizing efforts would alter people's perceptions much. "Is it odd that, beyond the friends I already have, I do not crave association with my social 'betters'?"

Emme's expression softened. "You have a rich life already, with wonderful people in it. Truth be told, I would much rather attend an academic symposium than a high society soirée. And you, Hazel, have always carried yourself with an air of refinement that class cannot bestow or remove." She paused and chuckled. "Do you know that when we were children, I looked for your reaction to choices we made even before I looked to Isla? And she was my wise elder cousin."

Hazel couldn't hide her surprise. "Isla was the undisputed leader—she cared for all of us."

Emme nodded. "She did, but yours was the voice of reason. I did not always follow it, but I always heard it. To this day, I admire your sense of self, the control you maintain over emotion, even in times of duress. You're steady."

Hazel's shoulders slumped. "I am boring. I am also a coward. Here I am on the brink of something momentous, and all I can think about is how afraid I am to leave this room with a packed trunk."

"Of course you are. Anybody with half of a good brain would be apprehensive. But you are the farthest thing from *coward* that I have ever known."

"You would not be afraid."

"Most certainly I would be! I am just reckless enough to throw caution to the wind and leap before looking. You do not make those kinds of mistakes. You're methodical and organized, and you learn all you can about a topic before wrestling it to the ground with your big brain."

Emme leaned forward, grasping Hazel's hands. "You've mentioned feeling as though something has been missing from your life, and now you've learned of a twin. I've heard tales about twins, about a connection that defies logic. And now, you're going to find her, save her from peril. I cannot wait to hear the tales when you return." She gave Hazel's hands a squeeze. "And you will have Dr. MacInnes for support."

Hazel sighed. "There is another issue."

"But you said he visited last night and insists on joining you."

"Yes, and I accepted, but it will be awful. I'll be in his company without the benefit of work as a buffer."

Emme paused and scrutinized her closely. "Hazel, are you in love with him?"

"Of course not." Hazel snatched her hands away and sat up straight.

Emme slowly straightened, and a smile touched her lips. "Of course. I do not know why I did not reason it through before. You work together every day—you spend more time with each other than individually with your families."

"I am not in love with him," Hazel insisted, and heat suffused her cheeks. "Even if it were so, we are from two different stations in life."

Emme's smile broadened. "Not anymore."

Hazel put a hand to her forehead. "Emmeline O'Shea, he has no idea! He is blissfully unaware of my presence as anything but an employee, or a . . . a . . . family acquaintance. I am trusting that he will remain ignorant of it."

Emme raised her hand, palm out. "I'll not breathe a word to anyone. Your secrets are your own. You should know, however, that it is a splendid match, and I approve wholeheartedly." She tapped a fingertip against her lip. "And he *insists* on accompanying you. There is significance in that, I wager."

Hazel rolled her eyes. She brushed her hands against her skirt and stood. "Help me finish packing. I could use another set of eyes. What am I missing?"

Emme's answering smile was wry. "A great deal, apparently. Very well, show me what you've selected thus far. And when you return, I will enjoy hearing every detail of your romantic adventure."

Chapter 7

S am studied Dravor Petrescu's rigid posture as they stood silently in the small parlor of the Hughes' home. They'd not spoken two words since their early morning meeting at the count's hotel when Sam had explained his wish to accompany Hazel to Romania. Sam's pronouncement was met with stony silence, but in the end, Petrescu had agreed with a tight smile. He must have realized any refusal on his part would seem suspect, at the very least. What possible objection could a caring relative have to allowing his niece the comfort of a friend when embarking on something new and potentially frightening?

Petrescu met Sam's eyes as the silence stretched taut between them. "I wonder what has you so concerned for Miss Hughes's welfare. I am family and have her best interests at heart."

Sam smiled. "I am certain you do. Surely you understand my position, however."

Petrescu tipped his head to the side. "What is that position? You are not her suitor, or so I've been told, and there is no obvious family connection beyond an acquaintance between your mother and hers. Perhaps as her nearest male relative, *I* ought to be concerned for her reputation."

Sam's temper rose a notch, but he tamped it down. "No need for concern, I assure you. As the Hughes family has been notably without support all this time, it is my honor to fill the role."

He was taller than Petrescu by an inch, and grateful for any small advantage. The man had a large presence in the room, an energy Sam couldn't define. He possessed classically aristocratic good looks and bearing, with dark hair and eyes, but there was a coldness about him that showed itself in snippets, whether due to natural reserve or something else entirely, Sam didn't know.

He had hoped to reach the Hughes' home before the count. He wanted a word with Hazel in private. A shouting match greeted him upon his arrival as Rowena Hughes was soundly berating Petrescu, and when Sam entered the parlor, she'd burst into tears of gratitude. For his part, the Romanian had seemed mildly amused. Sam had wondered if the amusement would give way to irritation, though, so when Sam suggested Rowena see to refreshments, he'd been relieved when she'd agreed. Petrescu appeared mild enough for the moment—mild as a snake coiled to strike when provoked enough.

Sam slowly paced the length of the small parlor, restless. Petrescu remained by the hearth, still and aloof, only his eyes tracking Sam's movement. Footsteps sounded outside the room, and Hazel entered a moment later with Emme O'Shea.

He felt a moment's panic, wondering if Hazel had made good on her suggestion to invite the other woman.

Hazel was pale. Her eyes flicked from her uncle to Sam and widened fractionally; she clearly hadn't expected to see both of them. Sam pasted a smile on his face and moved forward to greet the women. He bowed first over Emme's hand and then Hazel's, keeping hold of her fingers when she attempted to withdraw.

"Hazel, you will be pleased to know arrangements have been made, and your long-lost uncle has graciously invited me to join the two of you as you travel to Romania."

She looked at Petrescu, as did Sam; the man raised one aristocratic brow but then finally nodded.

"A physician will be most welcome on our trip," the count said. "One never knows when unexpected illness or the presence of wild animals—natural or mechanical—might cause trouble." Petrescu smiled. "Besides, I am pleased to share our beautiful homeland with all."

Hazel nodded and withdrew her fingers from Sam's. "Emme has been assisting me on clothing choice. I understand with winter approaching I ought to include many layers. Please," she added, gesturing toward the sofa and chairs, "I believe tea will soon be served."

As if summoned, Rowena Hughes and Celina entered, the latter carrying a tea tray, and began to serve.

Sam noted Hazel's deliberate choice of a solitary chair, and he took one next to it while Petrescu sat on one end of the couch, and Emme, the other.

He sat back in his chair and studied Hazel. Her posture was stiff, hands clasped firmly in her lap. He wondered what that brain of hers was sorting. She had the quickest comprehension and best information recall of anyone he'd ever met. She was brilliant, but also had an innocent naivete about her. His protective instincts increased tenfold, and a glance at Petrescu reaffirmed his determination to remain close by her side. Petrescu was charming and very smooth. Too smooth.

Petrescu gave Hazel an affable smile, responding to something she'd said, and chuckled. Her hands remained firmly clenched, but Sam noted her shoulders relax the slightest degree. He wasn't certain if that was a good sign or bad.

"I daresay the climate will agree with you," the count was saying as Sam made an effort to focus on the conversation. "You've certainly lived in cold environs here, and after all, Romania is in your blood." Petrescu paused as though considering his words. "I wonder if your mother's mind will be put at ease if I share something I've not yet mentioned. Our family line, you see, is directly descended from a distinguished Turkish prince. You and Marit, by blood rights, are princesses."

Rowena's hand flew to her chest, and her mouth dropped open as she sat slowly into the final empty chair. "A prin . . . a princess? Hazel! Do you know what this means for you? For us?"

Petrescu sat forward and accepted a cup of tea from Celina. He leaned back with a smile and crossed his legs. "It means, dear Mrs. Hughes, that all of your dreams for Hazel are about to become reality. But do bear in mind that the title is not an official one, of course, as our bloodline is not currently in power and has been rather diluted throughout the years. Still, I find it a great source of amusement and entertainment." He turned to Hazel. "Once the good people of London read the papers today, you'll find yourself at the center of social events rather than on the fringes."

"Ah, but the fringes suit me well. I am much more contented to observe than be observed."

Petrescu inclined his head. "That is fair, and humility is admirable in its own right. But unofficial princess or no, you'll find yourself elevated simply by your connection to me. I am a count, and as my niece, you are 'Lady Hazel Hughes.'" He shrugged. "You might enjoy it, my dear. You'll find yourself in circles that would be to your benefit."

Hazel glanced at Sam, and a light blush stained her cheeks. One finger tapped restlessly against her other hand, and Sam frowned. She was clearly uncomfortable with the conversation; one needn't have known her for long to realize that attention from high society would be her last desire. He didn't blame her in the least.

The count kept his attention on Hazel. "Are there any other details I might facilitate before our departure this evening?"

Hazel shook her head. "I will retrieve my travel papers from the notary in an hour, and have a few small items to purchase. Otherwise, I am ready." She inhaled a shaky breath and smiled.

Sam fought the urge to reach over and take her hand. "I'd like to join you on your errands, Hazel. As it happens, I also have papers to retrieve. I brought my Traveler today, and we could accomplish your tasks in no time."

"Thank you for the offer, Dr. MacInnes. If you'll wait a moment, I'll get my reticule and wrap." Hazel nodded at him but quickly broke eye contact. She stood and gave Petrescu her hands when he reached for them.

"My dear," he said, "you've no idea how happy I am you've agreed to do this thing. I am certain I speak for Marit as well, when I express my gratitude. Unless I hear otherwise from you, we shall see you at the docks at six o'clock. I believe you'll find the *Magellan* a most entertaining craft."

Chapter 8

S am fastened the buckles on his traveling trunk and clicked the lock into place. "I believe I have everything we'll need," he said to Eugene, who stood in the dressing room with Sam.

"You seem to be bringing an inordinate amount of surgical supplies." Eugene hefted the trunk up by the leather handles on the sides. As an automaton, he possessed the strength of several men, a decided convenience when traveling.

"Cannot be too prepared," Sam said as they made their way down the front stairs and out to the waiting rented carriage. Where Hazel was concerned, he was leaving nothing to chance.

Eugene returned inside to retrieve Sam's portmanteau, which held practical toiletries and some common medical supplies. Sam frowned, reviewing a mental checklist and hoping he wasn't leaving behind something vital. A carriage pulled alongside the curb behind his conveyance, and Oliver stepped out. "May I join you to the docks?" he called.

"Of course." Sam nodded.

Oliver paid the driver and joined Sam. "I thought I might have missed you."

"You are just in time," Sam said. "Have you learned anything new about our Romanian friend?"

"Not much beyond information on some property. I will scribe if something turns up. Once you've reached land, of course, you'll need to telegraph. I doubt the scribers will be up to the distance."

Sam frowned. "New coils and rods have been installed everywhere."

"Not where you're headed. I checked. Bulgaria, Romania, and Hungary are behind the technological wave." He paused. "You're certain you want to do this?"

"Not a question of whether I want to," Sam told him, feeling a touch nervous in spite of himself. "I cannot let Hazel go off with these people alone."

Oliver studied him for a moment. "You're a conscientious man, but this course of action seems more intense than concern for an employee."

Sam brushed the comment aside as Eugene returned with a smaller trunk under one arm and Sam's portmanteau in the other. "What is that?" he asked his 'ton, pointing to the small trunk.

Eugene secured the portmanteau atop Sam's large trunk. "I have need of travel items." His gaze flicked to Oliver and then back to Sam. "Sir."

Sam would have been delighted if the "sir" had been a genuine utterance of respect. The 'ton clearly sought to appear the faithful servant for propriety's sake, but his tone was unconvincing and bordered on insolent.

"What items could you possibly need?" Sam asked. "Your uniform never varies beyond the black jacket and trousers with a white shirt; we've discussed that. I packed your necessities in the larger trunk, and you stood there with me. Offered suggestions and criticized the placement of nearly every item, in fact."

"When you connected me to the charging station in the Tesla room this morning, I acquired additional information about our destination. I also have news about the *Magellan* you may find interesting."

Sam shook his head. "Tell me when we arrive. We must be off, or we'll miss departure altogether. Inform Stanley that we are leaving, and then ride up top with the driver."

Eugene's expression, had he been human, would have best been described as a smirk. Therein lay the problem, though. Eugene was so very much like a human that Sam was often hard-pressed to remember he wasn't. The 'ton returned to the house as Oliver and Sam climbed into the carriage.

Oliver shook his head and looked out the small window as Eugene returned a moment later. "I cannot imagine why you allowed Daniel to sell you on the benefits of such advanced programming," Oliver said. The carriage dipped with Eugene's weight as the 'ton climbed onto the driver's perch.

Sam often wondered the same thing himself. "There are advantages. His knowledge base is unparalleled, and his ability to apply new information to different circumstances is extremely useful in medical situations, especially."

"But he is exhausting to deal with."

"Yes. Well, technology comes at a price."

Oliver shook his head. "Daniel nearly has Miles convinced of the benefits."

Sam smiled. "I'm sure Lucy would be in favor of having a highly evolved 'ton at their disposal."

The four men—Miles, Daniel, Sam, and Oliver—were close friends, bonded together by the fury of war and boredom of military life between battles. That Miles had married Daniel's sister, Lucy, had provided an additional cog that slipped in nicely with the others.

Oliver's mouth turned up in a half-smile. "I'm certain she would."

Sam hadn't seen any joy in his friend for some time, not since they'd learned Oliver's brother had become a vampire of some notoriety. Oliver was duty bound and an extremely focused person who took his responsibilities seriously. He became absorbed in the criminal cases he investigated and deeply internalized any failures. Sam worried for his friend's health, and wished, sometimes aloud, that Oliver would make time for a pleasant social life. He attended functions as Sam's guest on occasion, but only if there was an investigative tie to explore. The only woman Oliver had mentioned more than once lately was Emme O'Shea, and it was hardly with affection.

"You need more sleep," Sam observed as the carriage rocked gently along the streets.

"I get plenty of sleep." Oliver scowled. "Does your doctor brain never rest?"

"Does your detective brain never rest?"

Oliver inclined his head. "Touché." He reached inside his coat pocket for the small, black notebook he always carried and flipped it open. "Petrescu owns property in Romania, of course, but this morning I received records of additional property in Istanbul, Cairo, New Orleans, and Port Lucy."

Sam's gaze sharpened. "Why would he want property in such far-flung places? I suppose it's too much to hope he merely enjoys travel."

Oliver lifted a shoulder. "Perhaps. The man has money, and he travels extensively and often."

"You do not believe such a simple explanation, though."

"No, I do not."

Sam inhaled and let the breath out slowly. He looked out the carriage window. Dry leaves scuttled along the cobblestones. Ladies wore hats sporting goggles, flowers, ribbons, and colorful ostrich plumes that danced in the breeze. The wind plucked a handkerchief from a child's hand and sent it flying. A young woman, a sister, perhaps, scolded the boy, who knocked into pedestrians as he chased after the square of fabric. Sam envied the lightheartedness the scene evoked, suddenly imagining the scene with him standing beside Hazel, laughingly calling out after a child.

His concern for Hazel's safety on this journey climbed another notch. "What on earth does he want with her?" he muttered.

"Whatever his motives, I doubt they involve harm to Miss Hughes, at least initially. You, however, are expendable. He is allowing your involvement as a means of securing her passage from England with as little fuss as possible. I worry for your safety when he has Miss Hughes where he wants her."

Sam looked at Oliver, who sat comfortably in the opposite

seat—one foot resting on the other knee—but his casual posture was at odds with the razor-sharp directness of his focus. "I advise you to be vigilant on your own behalf as well, Sam. Keep a weapon on your person at all times."

Sam nodded. "I wish . . ." He shrugged. "It's neither here nor there. She is determined to go."

They rode in silence the rest of the way to the docks. When Eugene opened the door, crying seagulls and the unmistakable scents of the wharf greeted them. Evening neared, and the sun would soon sink below the horizon. Another carriage pulled alongside Sam's, and he spied Hazel's face through the window. He'd offered to give her a ride, but she'd insisted she could do that much on her own. He opened the door and flipped down the steps for her, and she took his hand and offered a tight smile.

"Where is the ship?" Oliver asked, scanning the docks.

Sam frowned. "Eugene, is this the correct location?"

Eugene set the luggage on the ground. "Just to the left, I believe."

Hazel shielded her eyes against the waning light. "There's nothing there."

Eugene nodded. "Yet."

Hazel's hired driver set down her steamer trunk and a large portmanteau next to Sam's, and she clutched a smaller valise in her gloved hands. She, Sam, and Oliver looked out over the water at the ships dotting the harbor.

Hazel frowned. "One of those, perhaps?"

Oliver wandered closer to the water's edge. His eyes widened slightly, and he put a hand to his mouth and ran his thumb along his lip. He glanced back at Sam and cleared his throat. "I believe I see the *Magellan*."

Sam's head suddenly throbbed, and his mouth went dry. His suspicions grew as he moved to Oliver's side and saw, down in the water, an eerie green-yellow glow that grew in intensity and size as it drew near.

Hazel rushed over, and then with a gasp, grasped Sam's arm. "What on earth . . ."

Eugene finished paying Hazel's hired driver and joined the three, who stared mutely into the water. "That is what I tried to tell you earlier, sir. The *Magellan* is a submersible."

Sam's heart pounded painfully in his chest. No, no, *no* . . . He'd never been one for tight spaces, and since the war, he'd made a habit of sleeping near windows, preferably open ones. He didn't rest easily unless he had a clear view of the sky, and he doubted very much he was likely to find such accommodations aboard a craft that propelled its passengers through the murky depths of the ocean.

Like a specter rising from the underworld, the submersible emerged from the water, growing until it stood as tall as some of the ocean liners that were becoming all the rage. The machine was massive, sleek, and adorned in silver and black with a huge raven crest along the side. The front boasted large panes of thick glass, revealing a brightly lit room that housed a large wheel and periscope with cushioned window seats along the periphery.

A uniformed 'ton maneuvered the behemoth into position alongside the dock. Sam sucked in a deep breath and hoped he'd not disgrace himself by fainting. He heard Eugene's gears quietly clicking and whirring—likely the 'ton was performing a bio-read on Sam, noting his elevated heart rate and rapid breathing.

True to his programming, Eugene stood behind Sam and murmured, "You are unwell?"

"I shall be fine," he managed, and when Hazel looked at him in concern, he turned his attention to the submersible with a roll of his shoulders. "I am fine."

Oliver whistled low under his breath as he examined the impressive bulk of the submarine and the rivulets of water that streamed down from the top of it. "I . . . well." He scratched the back of his neck. "Certainly looks seaworthy."

Sam glanced at him and hoped panic wasn't evident on his face.

Oliver looked at him for a moment and then turned to Eugene. "You're programmed to monitor his vitals, I would assume?"

"Yes," Eugene began, "and—"

"I am absolutely fine," Sam ground out.

"This is a horrible idea," Hazel murmured. "Sam, I do not think—"

A hatch atop the monster opened to reveal a stately Dravor Petrescu, lord of the castle and, apparently, the sea. He smiled broadly and extended a hand. "Gentlemen, my dear niece, I welcome you to the *Magellan*."

Chapter 9

A long gangplank extended from the submersible and led to the top hatch where Petrescu stood. Hazel climbed the length and took her uncle's hand as she stepped down into the massive craft. She stood in a small entryway with four steps leading down to a brightly lit hallway, painted white and adorned with evenly spaced Tesla sconces. She descended the stairs, followed by Sam and Eugene.

Sam was still pale as a ghost. A muscle worked in his jaw, and he nodded absently at something Eugene said. Petrescu delivered instructions to three 'tons, who carried the luggage down the hall and disappeared down another set of stairs.

With a light bump, the craft shifted and vibrated as engines far beneath their feet sounded. They were moving slowly through the water, and Petrescu smiled broadly. "I shall never tire of the thrill, the movement of this majestic creature of the sea."

Hazel cleared her throat. "It is most impressive, my lord.

I've certainly never had the pleasure of traveling in such style."

He placed a hand on his chest and inclined his head. "Please, you must call me 'Uncle,' or at the very least, 'Dravor.'"

"Very well. Uncle Dravor."

He beamed and gestured ahead. "The Grand Staircase. I shall show you to your quarters, and then I hope you'll join me for supper."

"That sounds lovely," Hazel said, but she doubted she'd be able to eat a bite of anything. Although she'd never suffered from motion sickness, her stomach churned with anxiety.

The Grand Staircase was wide and adorned with white-washed oak. They descended one deck to where an ancient suit of armor stood guard. The craft teemed with 'tons in matching uniforms: black shirt and trousers, with a single stripe down the arms that varied in color, likely dependent on their task or station.

"Are all of the servants automatons?" she asked Dravor.

"Mostly, however, I do employ a small human staff in case of emergency or mishap with the 'tons. I have a man of affairs you'll meet shortly—Renton—and I've taken the liberty of employing Sally Tucker as your personal maid. You've no objection, I hope?"

"None, thank you."

Directly facing the broad staircase was a set of open double doors, through which Hazel spied a large table. A man exited the room dressed in a plain suit of clothing. He was tall and broad, the sort of man Hazel imagined would find success as a prizefighter. His face even bore traces of just such activity. His nose had been broken at least once, and a jagged scar above his right eyebrow was evidence of a healed cut.

Dravor smiled and extended a hand outward. "Here is the man I just mentioned. Allow me to introduce Renton. He is my personal assistant and, on occasion, bodyguard. Renton, this is my niece, Lady Hazel Hughes, and her friend, Dr. Samuel MacInnes."

Renton placed a hand on his chest and inclined his head. "A pleasure."

The introduction marked the first time in her life Hazel had been formally presented as "lady," and she was uncertain if the flutter in her chest indicated excitement or discomfort. She and Sam murmured their greetings, and Petrescu added, "Meet me upstairs in the office, Renton. I'll be there shortly."

Renton bowed again and walked around them to ascend the stairs. He took them two at a time, his movements sure, and disappeared around the corner.

"The Main Room," Dravor told them, motioning to the double doors in front of them, "is where we dine as well as gather for conversation, company, and games." He smiled, and for a moment Hazel forgot he'd ever made her uncomfortable. "This craft is often my home for long stretches of time, and I like to enjoy the comforts I would on land. There is a library, my personal study for correspondence and business matters, a conservatory, and a well-equipped kitchen and pantry, even a billiard room, among other things."

Dravor gestured as they walked. "This level contains the

Main Room, of course, which is at the center like an island between two corridors. There are eight guest suites, although not all are in use at the moment."

Hazel's head swam. "It is enormous."

Dravor laughed. "It is indeed. There are four levels, simply numbered one through four from top to bottom, and the servants—human and 'ton—are located on Deck Three. We are presently on Deck Two. In addition to the *Magellan's* impressive size is her speed. We shall travel in a less than a week a distance that would take much longer overland."

Sam, who had been quiet since boarding, cleared his throat. "Which route are we taking?"

Hazel glanced at him. He was still pale, and a sheen of sweat dotted his brow.

If their host noticed Sam's discomfort, he refrained from comment. "We travel south along the Continent to Spain, through the Strait of Gibraltar, traverse the Mediterranean around Greece, up the Aegean, through the Bosporus, and northward along the Black Sea coast to Romania. I wish we could afford the luxury of stopping for an extended stay in Italy and Greece, but I fear time is of the essence."

Hazel nodded. "I hope we will reach my sister quickly."

Dravor nodded gravely. "Yes, as do I. I am gratified to note that your level of compassion is exactly as I'd hoped. I've no doubt our efforts will be not only fruitful, but expedient. We will find a cure for Marit, and all will be well."

Walking next to Dravor, Hazel wished she felt a sense of kinship to him. She studied books and people and was usually an astute judge of character, but Dravor Petrescu was an enigma, and she couldn't help but wonder if her partial sense of ease about him since boarding the *Magellan* was something fabricated. She imagined being aboard the huge vessel without Sam, and her heart lurched.

The entirety of the submersible's interior was whitewashed and lit with sconces that cast a warm glow. Portions of the ship's design sported walls of riveted metal, and though the large rivets and curved metal pieces that formed the gentle curve of the enormous hull were disconcertingly large, they were somehow comforting in their substance. What had Mr. Reed called it—*seaworthy*? She inhaled deeply. One would certainly hope.

Servants moved about quietly, nodding deferentially to the count as they passed. A thick Persian carpet lined the hall, muffling their footsteps, and doorways sported arched designs reminiscent of India. Subtle touches provided additional nods to Persian architecture and décor, evidence of the count's affinity for the exotic.

They passed several doors as they continued along the passageway. Dravor stopped at two adjacent doors near the stern of the craft and produced two keys with a flourish. "Your rooms, dear guests." He handed one to Hazel but paused as he placed Sam's key in his hand. "Are you unwell, Doctor? You seem peaked."

Sam shook his head. "Merely weary. I shall be fully restored after a good night's sleep."

Dravor frowned and pursed his lips. "Should you need it, there is a small infirmary on Deck Three. I'll show you after supper."

Sam nodded, but refrained from further comment. Hazel eyed him askance and then smiled at Dravor, who inclined his head in an informal bow, and walked away. She watched her uncle's progress down the hallway—his tall bearing, forbidding aura, impeccable clothing, and confident stride created a picture of a man who knew his place in the world and commanded his own destiny.

Sam was unlocking his door and hadn't spared her a glance, which was odd. Since the beginning of his involvement in the whole affair, his focus had been on her entirely, and now he seemed well and truly ill. She'd noted his panic upon first seeing the submersible, and while she didn't know the cause, she could see that it affected him profoundly. Her sense of guilt was crushing. This wasn't his concern, and what was worse, he was now adversely affected by it.

Eugene was quiet, save the subtle whir of gears.

Sam opened the door and entered the cabin. He still hadn't looked in her direction or uttered a word to her, and to her surprise, she realized he meant to enter the room and quickly close the door.

Her lips tightened, and she shoved her body against the door. "Sam," she hissed, "let me in."

She heard him huff in irritation, but he stopped pushing on the door. She entered the room and opened her mouth to say something, but stopped before uttering a word. The suite captured her attention. It was large and lavish, complete with a four-poster bed with gauzy white bed hangings, a table and two chairs, a seating area to the right, a small wardrobe, and an open door leading to a personal lavatory. His trunks had already been placed near the wardrobe, and the room was filled with softly glowing Tesla lamps and sconces, the same that adorned the hallways.

French doors at the side opened to a smaller room with a tidy bed and dresser, ostensibly for a maid or valet.

"Well," she said, taking in the whole of it. "This is . . . impressive."

Sam grunted noncommittally, pocketing his key. He sank onto one of the two chairs in the seating area.

Hazel glanced at Eugene, and then joined Sam. She sat slowly in the matching chair and watched him, her disquiet growing, as he leaned forward, elbows braced on his knees, and held his head in his hands. She tried to scoot her chair closer, but it was bolted to the floor.

She leaned forward, her elbows on her knees, and tried to see his face. "Sam," she murmured. "What is it?"

He drew in a deep breath and released it slowly. His fingers tightened in his blond hair, and Hazel realized she'd never seen him so vulnerable before. It was disconcerting, and she wanted to fix it. Sam MacInnes was charming and intelligent with a contagious sense of humor. Sam MacInnes, unwell, was an injustice the world should never have to know, and she resolved to help him or insist he disembark at the soonest possible moment and return home.

The silence stretched, and she wondered how to proceed. Lucy was competent and efficient; she took matters into her own hands and somehow made everything work. Isla was strong and brave and could help people as a natural empath. Emme was fueled by her passion for the downtrodden and pushed and shoved until people paid attention.

Hazel was none of those things, and she felt her limitations keenly. The only thing she knew for certain was that she adored the man who sat next to her, and she wished more than anything that he was hers, that she had the right to place her arms around his broad shoulders and hold him tight.

She felt her eyes burn as she watched him struggle. His breathing remained uneven, and his hands curled into fists on his head. She glanced at Eugene and realized she didn't know how much of Sam's personal history he had been programmed with. She widened her eyes at him in an unspoken plea for help. The 'ton, however, looked at her for a moment and then, as if having made a decision, nodded once and began unpacking Sam's belongings.

She gaped. What on earth was she supposed to do with that? Realizing that she was well and truly Sam's only companion, she shrugged aside her natural reserve and sank onto the floor next to his chair. She placed her hand on his knee, closing her eyes and genuinely feeling that her deepest wish was for him to be well.

"Sam?" she murmured again. "Please tell me what's wrong. There's a library here. Perhaps I can research a solution for you, or I might have read something already that will help. You must talk to me, though. The one thing I cannot read is your mind."

She paused, giving him time to speak if he chose to. His one concern over the last few days had been to help her, keep her safe. She wanted to help him, if she could.

"I am afraid," she told him, hoping to prompt a reaction. Perhaps if he felt the need to rescue her, it would pull him from this strange panic pouring off him in waves. "This ship is strange, and my new uncle is strange, and I have no idea what we are walking into."

He stirred, and she felt a mixture of triumph and guilt at having played on his vulnerability. He shuddered, rubbed his eyes, and finally lifted his head to look at her. His blue eyes were filled with discomfort and concern, and he placed his hand over hers, which still rested on his knee. "I am sorry, Hazel," he said.

She felt wretched for manipulating him. "What is it?" she whispered. "Tell me what's wrong. You've not been well since we saw this thing come out of the water." She paused. "Are you uncomfortable in tight spaces? This craft is massive, perhaps thinking of that will help?"

He nodded and winced. "I've never done well in any sort of confinement, and especially since the war . . . I need to see the sky, the stars." He flushed and rubbed his face with his free hand. "I sound like a child. I promise, I will manage it."

She smiled softly. "Have you read Milton?"

He lifted the corner of his mouth. "'The mind is its own place'?"

She nodded. "If only it were so simple, but there is something to it. I met a man not long ago at a dinner party who studies issues of the mind and behavior, observes patients in asylums and such. I was curious about his work, and he taught me an exercise. Close your eyes."

He kept looking at her.

"You must humor me. Close your eyes."

He obeyed.

"Now think of a happy memory, something in your life that happened, or perhaps a person who brought you great joy. Something that thrills you or prompts happiness or a sense of peace."

To her relief, he seemed to follow her instructions. He inhaled and exhaled quietly through his nose, his eyes still closed, and after a moment gave a small nod.

"I have it."

"Keep thinking of it, and gently pinch your thumb and forefinger together."

He obeyed. "Now what?"

"Continue for a few more moments. Repeat the same thing. Think of the memory and pinch your fingers gently together."

He inhaled and exhaled again, this time more deeply than before.

She thought of her own sense of comfort she felt when she touched the delicate gold chain on her wrist. Warmth suffused her skin where the bracelet lay beneath his hand and filled her with a familiar peace, and she imagined with her whole heart that the tiny bit of precious metal could help him, too.

He inhaled and exhaled a third time, then opened his eyes and looked down at their clasped hands. He opened his mouth as though to say something, but then closed it and lifted his eyes to her face.

Her heart beat faster. "Now," she said quietly, "whenever you feel that sense of panic, pinch your thumb and forefinger together and think of the good memory. The concept is that, after a time, the mere physical action of that small pinch will help alleviate stress." She smiled and lifted a shoulder. "I've used it myself with a fair degree of success. It certainly doesn't take away all the discomfort, but I do notice a difference."

His face relaxed by degrees, and he curled his fingers around hers. "Is it the method that works so well, or the one teaching it?" He paused. "It is an incredible sensation to be on the receiving end of your healing art."

She flushed. "Parlor tricks."

He gave her hand a small squeeze. "It is not parlor tricks, and you are fully aware of that. Do not diminish your talent, or bury it in insecurities."

"I . . ." She frowned. "I do not fully understand it. There are times I wonder if I even have control over it."

"You harness it during surgery without a second thought."

She lifted a shoulder. "Perhaps. I know the gift is there, but I feel I have so much to learn and nobody to teach me."

He watched her for a moment longer and then lifted her hand. He touched her wrist, examining the gold chain. "You wear this always."

She nodded and swallowed. "Now that I know that my mother—my birth mother—gave it to me, I think that perhaps deep down I knew it was a connection to her. Gives me a sense of comfort when I need it."

He drew his brows together and gently lifted the chain, softly rubbing it and then smoothing it against her skin. "What were you thinking about just now? When you were helping me?"

She shrugged again, feeling self-conscious and awkward. "Just wishing for you to be well." She looked away and tried to withdraw her hand, but he held it and ducked his head to recapture her attention.

"My mind is clearer when you are present during procedures in the clinic. We've known it for some time."

She nodded.

"Those abilities, combined with a brain like yours—a person might hone some formidable talents."

She laughed and shook her head, and this time when she shifted, he released her hand. "A good memory does not formidable talents make." She rose from the floor and dusted her skirt.

He looked up at her, and she stilled. Her chuckle faded, as did his smile, and they studied each other for a moment.

"Everything about you is gold," he murmured, "from your eyes, to your hair, to your heart."

Her breath caught in her throat. He couldn't look at her like that, couldn't say things like that, because though he meant them as friendly tenderness, she wanted nothing more than to pull him close and hold tight. If she misread even one little gesture, he would unintentionally break her golden heart into a million golden shards.

She forced a bright smile, reached for a nonchalance she didn't come close to feeling. "Well, Doctor, that was lyrical. Perhaps you've missed your calling as a poet."

Something flickered in his expression—disappointment, perhaps—then he cleared his throat and stood, running a hand along the back of his neck with an awkward chuckle. "Thank you for helping me. My apologies for being a burden when I am here to help you."

Eugene muttered something from across the room, where he continued to unpack the trunks and put away clothing.

"What did he say?" Hazel asked Sam.

Sam shook his head and eyed the 'ton warily. "I wouldn't want to guess."

She frowned, studying the servant. "For all that he's supposed to be attuned to your biorhythms, he did nothing just now to aid you."

"I calculated that your abilities to help Dr. MacInnes surpassed mine, Miss Hazel," Eugene said without turning around. He shook out one of Sam's shirts and hung it in the wardrobe. "Short of giving him a sedative, there was little else for me to do."

Hazel shot him a flat look. "For the love of heaven, Eugene, that is no help at all."

The 'ton muttered something inaudible, and Sam rubbed his forehead. "Every day I consider wiping his programing tin. Life with a bland servant would be much simpler."

Hazel's lips twitched. "Where does his name come from?"

"Eugene was my uncle, and the world's nicest man."

Eugene looked over his shoulder. "You couldn't have chosen a more fitting name for me. Sir." He turned fully toward them and eyed Sam from head to toe. "You're decidedly mussed. Should you desire an upper hand with your host, you must freshen immediately and change."

Hazel raised a brow at Sam. "You desire an upper hand with our host?"

Sam's eyes narrowed. "I hadn't verbalized it as such, but yes." He looked at her. "There is something not quite right about him, Hazel. We need every advantage we can get."

Hazel felt defensive—much as she had had for her mother—but wasn't certain why. She'd not known Dravor long enough to feel any kind of loyalty. "Perhaps he is nothing more than my uncle, who has no nefarious intentions."

Sam paused, his silence telling. "Perhaps. My cynicism surfaces now and again, regrettably. We likely have nothing to fear."

Chapter 10

S am followed Hazel down the hallway to the Main Room for dinner and tried to collect his thoughts. Hazel's little trick seemed to be helping. He had nearly succumbed again to panic after she'd left his room, but he'd pinched his fingers together and visualized his happy memory, and his heart rate and breathing had slowed a bit.

He'd allowed Eugene to him dress for dinner, and the 'ton had commented on the peculiarity of it. Sam did not usually require much help—especially since his days in battle when life had been boiled down to its essence of things that truly mattered. He liked to live as self-sufficiently as possible, and he'd only decided to use Eugene as a valet after the 'ton commented on his appearance at the clinic one day about how a helping hand with a cravat was sometimes useful.

Eugene had refrained from any sarcastic remarks after Hazel left, which struck Sam as amazing. Apparently the automaton was advanced enough to know when to keep his thoughts to himself. Sam was sure the explanation was simple enough. Eugene monitored Sam's vitals constantly and would temper his behavior accordingly. If Sam's blood pressure and heart rate were soaring, combined with an elevated rise in temperature and a decided lack of casual conversation, Eugene would know.

Hazel looked over her shoulder at Sam and slowed her step. She smiled, a little uncertainly, he thought, and why wouldn't she be? He'd fallen apart spectacularly, and she'd had to put him back together. It was disconcerting, especially when he'd fashioned himself as her protector.

"Oh!" she said suddenly. "Is Eugene still in your suite?"

"Yes," he said, puzzled. "He should be stationary since I didn't leave him with instructions. Although, come to think of it, that might have been a bad idea."

"Will you wait here? I have something I'd like him to do for me."

He tilted his head. "That sounds mysterious, Lady Hazel."

Her lips twitched. "Wait here." She ran lightly back down the long hall to his door and knocked. Eugene answered, and she spoke to him for a few minutes, gesturing occasionally. She eventually nodded and left, Eugene closed the door, and Sam watched the entirety of it, baffled.

"What business do you possibly have with my 'ton?" he asked when she returned, a little breathless.

She smiled. "None of yours, yet." She gestured toward the double doors. "Shall we continue to supper?"

He inclined his head, glad to see her more relaxed than she'd been since the night of the ball when they'd met her new uncle. He held out an arm to her, and she tucked her hand inside the crook of his elbow, her fingers resting lightly on his arm. She smiled up at him, her cheeks flushed, and for a moment he forgot the subtle vibration of the engines, the strange person they were about to dine with, and the fact that they were farther beneath the surface of the ocean than he'd ever wanted to be.

"You are a ray of light," he said, feeling inane, but meaning every word.

She laughed and nudged him forward. "And you are silly."

As they neared the Main Room, she paused and lowered her voice. "I've not been gracious enough, Sam, and for that I apologize. You've sought only to keep me safe in the midst of all this strangeness, and I've acted quite the spoiled girl. I did not even request time away from the clinic. I merely told you what my plans were without a second thought. I am mortified you have so drastically rearranged your life to accommodate me, but I am grateful you would. You truly are a good friend."

He placed his hand over hers. "It is my honor." Something about her face seemed different to him, perhaps it was the light. When they'd first met, she'd seemed young. She was of courting age, and had been for a couple of years, but the innocence that had been so clearly part of who she was had blinded him to the fact that she was, in fact, a woman.

In the year since, he'd come to rely on her professionally and enjoyed their easy banter. She'd occasionally gone on her mad "bravery" escapades despite his protestations, and perhaps her experiences had instilled some maturity she'd not had before. She even seemed leaner, her jawline more defined. Everything in her face was in clearer focus.

"What is it?" she asked, frowning, and he realized he must be staring.

He blinked. "Nothing. Shall we?"

Employer, employer, I am her employer.

He gestured with his head toward the room where murmured conversation sounded.

She nodded. "I am not surprised to see placards at each door. This place is rather like a hotel."

"'Main Room,'" he quietly scoffed. "That was the best he could do?"

She laughed. "Why complicate things when simplicity suffices?"

He shook his head as they entered. "That would make sense except nothing about this contraption is plain," he murmured.

The hallway bustled with 'tons, going about the business of keeping the giant ship running smoothly. The Main Room also contained several servants who carried in, and prepared to serve, the meal.

Their host was seated to the far right of the large room with his assistant, Renton. The room itself was appointed with lavish rugs, lightly paneled walls, and shelves with books, plants, and mementos from varying cultures. To the left was a large table, set for dinner, and a glittering chandelier hung suspended from the high ceiling, which was adorned with wooden rafters. The room might have been one Sam would have seen in a fine Colonial house in India. The only element missing was stuffed game posed in threatening, snarling positions in each corner.

Hazel exhaled and looked around the room, clearly as

taken in by the grandeur as he was. She blinked, looked at Sam for a moment, and then her uncle.

Petrescu rose from his chair and smiled broadly. "You've arrived!" He gestured toward the table. "I am pleased—you must be famished."

Sam was anything but famished. He doubted he would ever find himself relaxed while on the submersible and wondered if his lack of appetite was due to his discomfort with the mode of transportation or the person with whom they traveled. The air was thick with tension; he figured Hazel noticed it as well, because she tightened her fingers on his arm.

Hazel smiled at Petrescu. "The food smells delicious," she said. "I fear I've not eaten much in the last two days."

Petrescu chuckled and indicated Hazel's chair, which was to his immediate right. "It certainly is not a daily occurrence to meet family one never knew existed." He looked at Renton. "That is all for now. I believe I shall be safe enough while dining with family."

Renton nodded once, made unflinching eye contact with Sam, and then left the room.

Sam held the chair out for Hazel and took the place next to hers. "Is your safety often a cause for concern?" he asked the count.

Petrescu signaled two servers to bring food from a sideboard, and the meal began with a bowl of warm soup. It smelled good, even to Sam's queasy stomach, and he was relieved when he was able to eat it slowly without issue.

"I am not usually in danger, no, but there have been occasions when I've found the presence of a large, brutish guard to be a satisfactory deterrent to any bent on mischief."

They ate in silence for a moment before Petrescu spoke again. "I hope your accommodations are to your liking?"

Hazel nodded. "Everything is exquisite. I would never have believed such a craft existed had I not seen it." She dabbed at the corner of her mouth with her napkin. "Where is your suite?"

"Here on Deck Two, at the bow."

Hazel nodded, and the group lapsed again into uncomfortable silence. Sam fought the urge to fill it, and instead observed Petrescu, who was watching his guests with a shrewd eye.

"Tell me, dearest Hazel, how would you describe your life with Rowena? You seem fond of her, or at least indulgent," Petrescu said, leaning back in his seat, his fingers steepled.

Hazel tipped her head and nodded as she set her spoon down and again dabbed her mouth. She sat up a bit straighter, and Sam wondered if she were stalling. "My mother was very loving—*is* very loving. She has always had a nervous temperament, but I've never doubted her affection and care for me. She had dreams for me, and I don't know that I've fulfilled those expectations to her satisfaction, but I hope to, one day."

"What sort of expectations?" Petrescu signaled to the 'tons to serve the next course.

Sam looked at his host's bowl. Not a drop of soup remained, but Sam didn't recall seeing the man eat. His gaze shot to Petrescu's face, and he narrowed his eyes, looking for something amiss. Everything seemed normal about the man, and yet that was part of the problem. Fiends now hid in plain sight.

"My mother was certain I would be a Medium," Hazel

continued, and leaned back to allow the 'ton to set the next course before her. "She insisted it was in the family, and in truth she did have a cousin who was an effective Medium, but now I realize she must have been making inferences from the information given her at the time of my . . . adoption."

Petrescu nodded. "The midwife told her the family were Light Magick practitioners, which is true. Rowena must have decided your skills would include communion with the deceased. This was a mistake, of course. How would you define your skills?"

Hazel stilled and cleared her throat. Sam fought the urge to snap to in her defense; if he'd learned anything about her in the past year, it was that she was learning to fight her own battles.

"I do not know that I possess many skills beyond an exceptional memory and a desire for knowledge." She smiled and glanced at Petrescu. "I hope I do not disappoint if my blood family is indeed exceptional. I fear I am rather ordinary—perhaps a touch of Healing ability, but nothing extraordinary."

She was hiding the depth of her abilities from her uncle. Sam wondered if she sensed something off about the man, as he did.

Petrescu glanced at Sam as he speared a piece of meat on his plate, cut off a small bite, and deliberately ate it. Clearly the count had not missed Sam's earlier attention to his empty soup bowl. Sam filed the information away for later perusal. To the best of his knowledge, mind reading was not a phenomenon common beyond the closest of family ties, which meant Dravor Petrescu was exceptionally observant.

"I heard," the count continued, "that you had an episode of some concern at Blackwell Manor last year?"

Hazel's fingers tightened on her silverware, and Sam frowned. "How do you know that?"

Petrescu regarded him evenly. "I have made it my business to learn as much as possible about my niece. I am certain you understand my concern that something dangerous happened to Hazel while she was attempting to work magick."

Sam opened his mouth to retort, but Hazel cut him off. "I wasn't attempting to work magick. I was attempting to summon a ghost that was haunting the manor and the Blackwell family. I did not, in fact, summon a ghost. I summoned a vampire." Hazel's smile was tight.

Petrescu leaned forward, eyes focused. "What were you doing? How did you do it?"

Hazel shook her head. "I am mostly jesting. I did not actually summon anything. The vampire had been stalking the family, and I happened to be in the wrong place at the wrong time."

Petrescu kept his gaze on Hazel, unblinking, until he finally sat back in his chair again. A hint of a smile appeared on his lips. "You are too modest, I believe."

Hazel shrugged, a little helplessly, it seemed, but then straightened her spine. "I would dearly love to believe I have some special gift." Her tone strengthened as she spoke. "But the fact is I simply do not."

Petrescu did not respond, but the small, enigmatic smile remained.

There was a predatory element to the man that Sam was determined to uncover. Hazel had initially seemed to hope the count was a benevolent, beloved family member. She'd not known a father in her life, and it could be she would place Petrescu in that role. Sam was unencumbered by sentiment, and therefore more objective.

He grimly thought again of Hazel making the voyage alone, which reminded him they were under the ocean at an unseemly depth, which then boosted his heart rate and made a sheen of sweat break out on his brow.

He fought to maintain control, to avoid losing his first course all over the second, and took a shaky breath.

Hazel's hand crept beneath the table and found his fist, which he'd shoved hard against his thigh. When he relaxed his hand, she placed her thumb and forefinger over his and gently pressed them together.

The motion prompted his memory, and he took a deep breath while moving his vegetables around on his plate with his fork. His hand was pleasantly warm beneath hers, and he noted again her effortless ability to heal. He was unsure if the sensation emanated from her gold chain, which touched his skin, or simply from her.

"Tell me about your homeland," Hazel said to the count. She kept her hand atop Sam's, and if Petrescu noticed Sam's distress, he didn't remark on it.

"It is green," Petrescu said with a chuckle. "Rugged, and incredibly beautiful. Charming villages clustered in valleys and around ancient monasteries, and situated against mountainous passes. My country is filled with a rich history and resilient people. Castle Petrescu is located near Vania, which is a town dating back centuries that has survived differing invasions and rule. The people remain steadfast and unbroken through the generations, despite attempts at subjugation by foreign invaders and despite any number of plagues."

Sounds lovely, Sam thought as he focused on the light touch and warmth of Hazel's hand.

"Your surname is certainly Romanian, is it not?" Hazel continued.

Petrescu nodded. "Places and names in Romania often bear three names: Romanian, Hungarian, and German. We have only ever been known as Petrescu, however."

"And how long has your—our—family been in the country?"

Sam straightened in his seat and tried to focus on the conversation.

The count smiled at Hazel. "Five hundred years."

She nodded. "And before? Do you know where the family originated? I couldn't find any reference to the family name before the 1300s."

Petrescu blinked.

The silence stretched, and Sam watched the count with interest.

Hazel cleared her throat and added, "I read a book on Romanian history last night."

"You read an entire book on Romania's history last night?" Petrescu asked.

"I skimmed over passages," Hazel said. "Perhaps I missed something."

"I'm certain that must be the case," Petrescu said. His smile was cold, like everything else about the man. The light from the chandelier cast shadows on the table, and Petrescu's pupils seemed to obscure any color in his eyes. "Histories of nearly any subject tend to be dry and laborious."

Sam kept his mouth shut. Hazel's verbal retreat had been smart, but he also knew it was untrue. If she said she'd read a book last night, it meant she had truly read the book, and she hadn't missed a thing. Why would Petrescu evade explaining something as simple as the family origins?

Hazel laughed. "So true. I confess, parts of history volumes bore me to tears."

Sam was forced to reevaluate his analysis of Hazel's innocence and vulnerability. She was lying through her teeth, but anyone unfamiliar with her would be none the wiser. Her comment lightened the mood and allowed conversation to naturally flow to other topics. She was much savvier than he'd realized, and at that point he knew his association with her over the past year had done little to illuminate her depth.

Perhaps she didn't need him after all. He'd rushed in, assuming she required rescuing. Her hand still rested over his, and he acknowledged that if anybody had done any rescuing to that point, it had been she.

"Tell me about my sister," she said.

Petrescu's face took on the grave, compassionate air he seemed to have perfected. "Your sister is identical to you in appearance, save hair and eye color. It is as you said earlier: where you are golden-haired and golden-eyed, she is blonde—nearly silver-haired—and her eyes are a unique shade of lavender."

Sam tried to imagine Hazel with her sister's coloring, and found it was impossible. He could only see the gold he had always known.

Petrescu set down his silverware. "I have been forced to consider that, of course, someone may know of you and your sister and of the abilities I believe you both possess." He leaned forward and braced his forearms on the table's edge, his fingers laced loosely together. "You see, my dear, we are a family of wealth with our share of enemies."

Sam wrapped his fingers around Hazel's, which she had tightened into a fist. She glanced at him, and he gave her hand a small squeeze. He looked at their host, whose eyes flicked from Hazel to Sam, and back again.

Petrescu watched her for a moment and then relaxed in his chair. This time, his gaze rested only on Sam, and the corner of his mouth turned up in a smile.

Challenge accepted.

Chapter 11

Hazel slowly paced the length of her suite and examined the details within it. It was truly beautiful, and had she been on an excursion of a different sort, she might have found pleasure in it. She'd learned some things about her uncle at dinner tonight, things that cast his truthfulness into question.

She had read the entire book on Romania's history, in less than an hour, in fact, and while she didn't consider herself an expert on the subject after one volume, Dravor had paused tellingly when she'd asked about the Petrescu family history. She wouldn't have given the matter another thought if he'd stated he was unsure or he hadn't found records before the 1300s—there was certainly nothing suspect in that—but something about his expression hinted that he knew something he did not want to tell her.

The sitting area in her suite contained a faux mantel with an illusory flame. Hanging above it was a bucolic painting of a meadow, a stream, and a forest line in the distance—it could have been anywhere in the world. There was nothing to tie it to Romania, and while she appreciated the eclectic value of the ship's décor, it was also unfamiliar and unattached to any one style. She felt adrift, cut off from everything she knew, and an aura of uncomfortable mystery, of half-truths and deception clouded the whole experience, and she knew a moment of truly alarming confusion.

She wandered to the lovely bed and touched a length of the gauzy fabric that threaded around the frame atop the four posts and then draped down each one. She sat down on the mattress, which was soft and decadent, and closed her eyes.

She'd been concerned for Sam. She had known the moment when his fears about the submersible resurfaced and had been gratified to know her gesture helped him reclaim a sense of relative calm. The best moment of the meal, however, had been when he must have sensed her own distress at Dravor's subterfuge and turned his hand over to protect hers. She couldn't reconcile her feelings of guilt that Sam had put his own life aside to help her, and her gratitude that he had, that she had no choice but to be in his company, to enjoy the thrill she felt sitting next to him.

She heard a sound in the maid's room adjoining hers, and she made her way to the French doors that connected them. The glass was frosted, but she saw Sally Tucker's shadowed image within. She knocked quietly.

"You're settling in?" She asked when the girl opened the door.

"Yes, miss—my lady." Sally curtsied and lowered her eyes.

Hazel smiled. "Please, you must call me Hazel. And your hair—I didn't see it before in the dark of the carriage. It's the most beautiful shade of red I've ever seen."

Sally blushed. "My thanks, miss—Hazel."

"Have you been acquainting yourself with the ship?"

Sally nodded. "The count said I should introduce myself to the other servants, and the cook's assistant gave me a tour. I hope I'll be useful to you, but I found myself quite lost while looking for the laundry."

Hazel smiled. "I've yet to see the whole of the craft, but I'm certain we'll manage it together. Is your room to your liking?"

Her eyes widened. "Oh, yes. I've never had my own room before."

"I confess, my accommodations are beyond anything I've seen in some time." Hazel paused. The girl was extremely thin, and very pale. "Have you eaten dinner?"

Sally nodded. "Only just. I'm to take meals and tea with the servants in the kitchen. I quite like it—it's warm in there."

Hazel was struck by the simplicity of the statement, and the knowledge that she had much for which to be grateful. She'd never been cold; Rowena had provided comfortably for the two of them. It had never been extravagant, but it had been more than enough.

"I'll leave these connecting doors unlocked between our rooms. Feel free to access the lavatory just through here."

Sally's eyes widened. "Oh, I couldn't! I'm to use the servants' facilities down one deck."

"That is utter nonsense. I insist we share mine. Agreed?"

Sally's brow pinched, but she nodded. "Thank you, my la—Hazel." She paused. "I've never been a lady's maid, forgive me if I slip in my duties. Shall I help you change clothes?"

"Not this evening, thank you. We'll discuss routines tomorrow. I shall be fine for now." Hazel smiled.

"Very well." Sally curtsied again very properly, and Hazel felt tenderness settle into her heart. The girl was earnest, and more than a little apprehensive.

"Do you have a book to read, or a journal?"

Sally shook her head. "I can read some, but I don't have anything like that."

Hazel held up her finger and crossed the room. She took a copy of *Gulliver's Travels* from her portmanteau, along with a small, blank journal she'd intended to use for sketching once her other journal was filled. She retrieved a spare pen, checked it for ink, and then handed the small stack to Sally, who took it with trembling hands.

"I cannot . . . my lady, I—"

"I insist, Sally. Take them, or my feelings shall be bruised. I find I often sleep better at night after I've read for a bit or written some thoughts in my journal."

Sally swallowed and offered Hazel the first smile she'd seen. "Thank you, I shall treasure them. Thank you."

Hazel nodded, and before she closed the door, widened it a bit and added, "Also, you may come and go as you please. You'll not bother me; I could sleep through a monsoon." That last was a stretch—Hazel was a light sleeper—but Sally would never use the facilities otherwise and would instead make the trek to the lower deck.

Sally nodded and curtsied again.

Hazel quietly closed the door with a smile and released a sigh. She thought of Sam, one cabin over, and wondered if he were sleeping.

She hoped Eugene had been able to follow through on her request while they were at dinner. A quiet knock sounded at her outer door. She opened it, half expecting to find Dravor, but saw Sam instead. He braced one hand on the doorframe and looked at her with eyes that were glossy with unshed tears.

Her heart pounded in alarm. "Sam, what is it? Are you crying?"

He shook his head and scowled. "No, I am not crying. Well, perhaps. May I come in?"

She stepped back and opened the door wider, and he entered. Suddenly, her suite seemed smaller—not unpleasantly so, but he was a big presence in any room.

He ran his hand across the back of his neck. "Hazel, I don't know what to say. I am touched beyond words. Imagine my surprise when I entered my room tonight and found small Tesla bulbs wound cleverly around my canopy. Eugene told me he procured them at your insistence and that the lights are substitutes for stars in the night sky."

Hazel blushed and looked at her feet. Suddenly hearing a grown man verbalize her silly idea made her feel self-conscious in the extreme. "I . . . I didn't assume it would be an actual substitute, but I had hoped you might find a measure of comfort in it." She paused. On further reflection, she wondered if it had been a good idea at all. If he awoke to see the lights, it might serve as an unpleasant reminder of where he actually was.

"It is perfect, Hazel, and I simply do not have the words to express it." He took her hand and pressed it between his. "Thank you."

She smiled. "I simply wanted to help. I am conscious of the emotional imposition this trip entails, and I hoped to make it more pleasant for you. At least less onerous."

He brought her hand to his mouth and placed a kiss on her knuckles. He lingered there, his eyes holding hers, and he slowly lifted his head. His eyes roamed her face, her throat, even her hair that she'd released from its pins. A messy braid hung over her shoulder, strands escaping it to curl in every direction. He swallowed, and a muscle worked in his throat.

He released her hand carefully and backed toward the door. "I am most grateful, and I am grateful for your friendship. Very grateful." He fumbled for the door handle. "Grateful," he repeated, and if the light in the room hadn't been dimmed for the evening, she might have imagined she saw a blush. He opened the door without turning around and stepped out of the room. "Good night, then. And thank you." He closed the door, and a moment later, she heard his door open and close.

Hazel stared at the space he'd just left, jaw slack. What on earth had just happened? In the time she'd known Dr. Samuel MacInnes, and in all the settings she'd seen him, she had never, ever seen him bumble, stumble, hesitate, or exhibit any sort of awkwardness. And he'd certainly never blushed. She reviewed the conversation in her mind, going over every minute detail. He'd said thank you, she'd mumbled something about wanting to help, he'd kissed her hand, and had . . . had . . .

She blinked in delighted surprise. She walked to the lavatory and looked at herself in the mirror. She braced one hand on the edge of the porcelain pedestal sink and covered her mouth with the other. He had made eye contact with her and, then, as though someone had flicked a switch, he'd gone from grateful friend to something different. Something *more*.

She stifled a laugh and looked at her reflection. Her large, golden-green eyes showed the smile hidden behind her hand. Perhaps he had suddenly felt awkward being in her suite. Perhaps he was embarrassed that someone had needed to in-stall night-lights in his room. Perhaps he'd reminded himself she was his imagined younger sister, and her bedtime was long past. She conjured a multitude of reasons for his sudden, awkward departure, but to her surprise, nothing stuck. She couldn't talk herself out of the fact that she had turned the smooth, suave Dr. MacInnes into a blushing schoolboy.

As she readied for bed and hung up her clothing, her smile remained. Even if nothing of significance ever devel-oped between her and Sam, she had the satisfaction of know-ing that, for a moment, she'd rendered him witless.

She pulled out her journal and made notes of the day's events and her observations. She wrote down every detail, drew sketches of the *Magellan* and the rooms she'd seen thus far, and scribbled until she could think of nothing else to add. Then she jotted down a few last thoughts.

I hardly know what to think of my new reality. Now that I know I have a sister, and that she is in danger, I feel anxious. There is nothing more to learn this evening, nothing I can read or examine that will shed more light on this mystery, so I shall go to bed and imagine a world where I am strong and brave and can conquer all.

And perhaps I shall indulge in reliving a splendid memory, a moment just passed, where a certain paragon fumbled a bit in my presence.

Hazel extinguished the lights in her room, and using a handle next to the "fireplace," dimmed the illusion of flames until it looked as though the grate contained only glowing coals. She climbed into the fluffy bed and sighed. She'd not realized how incredibly tired she was, and her body insisted her mind finally rest.

She woke later to a dark room. The image of coals still glowed, and the only noise was the subtle vibration of the *Magellan*'s huge engines. There was nothing to indicate a reason she'd awakened. She was still incredibly tired, her thoughts groggy and her vision blurry as she rubbed her eyes and fluffed her pillow. Something felt different, but it was nothing she could define.

Her ears pricked as she awoke more fully, and she lay very still on the pillow. The light in the water closet remained off, but the outline of the door to it stood ajar. Could Sally be searching for it?

"Sally? Are you awake?"

A rustle of fabric sounded at the foot of her bed, and she forced herself to continue breathing deeply, calmly. She thought of her ray gun, which was across the room in her portmanteau, and nearly ground her teeth in frustration. Isla had told her to always keep it within reach if she were ever away from home or afraid for her safety.

She was being silly. She'd given her maid access to her room, and Sally had simply risen to use the facilities and returned to her room.

The light from the fireplace suddenly went black, and

she sucked in a breath. The same rustle of cloth sounded—so quietly she wondered if she imagined it—and she realized the coals hadn't been extinguished with the turn of the handle. They were no longer visible because someone stood at the side of her bed, blocking her view of them.

She couldn't imagine Sally would stand silently at the side of her bed, but then, she didn't know the girl.

She drew in a deep, shuddering breath and slowly slid to the far side of the bed. She had nearly decided to get up and at least fight for her life when she saw the coals in the fireplace appear again. The figure had moved.

Terrified, she lifted a shaking hand to the Tesla sconce nearest her and turned the knob. A familiar hum filled the room as the light came to life, though she kept it dim to avoid blinding herself. She looked around the room quickly, but whatever she'd expected to see wasn't there. The room was empty, and the only sounds were the hum of the lamp and her own uneven breaths.

Chapter 12

The next morning, as Sam made his way to the Main Room for breakfast, he reflected on how well he had slept the night before. When he had first set foot on the submarine, the idea of sleep had seemed impossible, but Hazel's gift of hanging lights in his room had been the perfect remedy.

He'd been overwhelmed with gratitude for Hazel's thoughtfulness. Which he'd expressed to her repeatedly, like a fool.

He still couldn't say what had happened to him. One moment he had been profoundly touched and charmed, and the next he had kissed her hand and looked at her—truly looked at her—and saw a woman becoming herself, not a young woman whose eyes were a constant reservoir of uncertainty and vulnerability. Somehow, in the last few months, she'd ceased looking so young.

And she had never been more beautiful.

She had quite taken his breath away, and he'd fallen all over himself trying to escape her cabin before he did something foolish, like kiss her. He'd felt the sensation before—that night at her home when Petrescu had stormed into her life; had it been only two days ago?—but he'd dismissed the urge as a strange phenomenon brought about by a desire to protect a friend and the proximity in which he found that friend's pretty lips.

He entered the Main Room to find Hazel and the count already present. He felt his heart lift at seeing Hazel, but then paused. She was subdued, and bore faint traces of telltale smudges beneath her eyes, a true sign of a sleepless night.

"Hazel, dear," Petrescu said, "you seem distant. Are you feeling well?" The count was the very picture of paternal concern, and Sam wished he knew why it rang so patently false.

Hazel cleared her throat and managed a smile. "I slept rather fitfully, but I suspect it is a result of recent excitement. I feel fine, otherwise."

Hazel said little at breakfast, despite Petrescu's innocuous questions and attempts to engage her in conversation.

The count tried another tack, instead asking Sam questions about Eugene's programming and features. Sam explained Eugene's system of tins that controlled his activity and "thinking," all the while wondering if Petrescu truly cared about the latest in 'ton technology. The man's eyes occasionally flicked to Hazel, assessing, and Sam knew Petrescu was as curious about Hazel's subdued demeanor as he was.

"Fascinating," Petrescu said to Sam. "I fear our 'tons at Castle Petrescu are rather basic, and we have a proud tradition of hiring local villagers. Some families have been with us for generations."

Sam refrained from smirking. Hearing Petrescu refer to his home as "Castle Petrescu" made him want to laugh at the absurd arrogance of it. "I find that commendable," he said instead. "Employing people is a preferable choice, of course. Most Londoners who require servants utilize a combination of both."

As the 'tons cleared away the last of the dishes, Petrescu smiled and clapped his hands together once. "Now, how do you both plan to spend your time today? Dr. MacInnes, surely you must have business to attend to, but Hazel, perhaps you will allow me to give you a tour of my ship? I would love to show you the best part of the *Magellan*—the Control Room. You saw it from outside at the docks, but to witness it in deep dive is a thing to behold."

She smiled. "I would love to see it. It certainly was an impressive sight from the outside."

"Excellent." He rose and extended his arm as she stood.

She glanced at Sam and then put her hand in the crook of her uncle's elbow.

"My work can wait," Sam said, though the idea of standing in a glass room so far beneath the surface made his heart pound. He had done incredibly difficult things in his life, from surgery in the middle of a battlefield to saving the life of a friend with a heartclock device he'd created himself. He could look out of a large window into the ocean. He couldn't allow his phobia to prevent him from protecting Hazel.

Petrescu glanced at him with a brow raised in surprise. "Oh, you'll join us, then? Excellent. I am glad."

Sam pursed his lips at the count's dry tone, more determined than ever to not leave Hazel alone with the man.

"Shall we?" Petrescu said, gesturing toward the doors.

Sam's head spun as he followed Petrescu through the massive submersible. Hazel walked with him, her expressive eyes large. The engine rooms required a small army to run. A conservatory boasted comfortable seating, as well as a pianoforte, cello, viola, violin, flute, and harp. There were 'tons at the ready to play, identical in uniform and features befitting their station in that room. Upon Petrescu's request, they performed a delightful musical number.

The ship's library boasted floor-to-ceiling shelves filled with leather-bound volumes, some extremely old, and ladders were interspersed for easier access to the books. 'Tons unique again in appearance and uniform shelved volumes and wiped nonexistent dust from tabletops and chair backs.

The "small" infirmary Petrescu had mentioned was complete with surgical stretchers and medical equipment every bit as advanced as Sam's own clinic at home. Three 'tons were present and wore attire common to medical assistants. Petrescu assured him their programming had been updated while in London with the latest in medical advances and studies.

Sam was handling his anxiety better with each passing hour, and was able to focus his attention not only on Petrescu, but the craft itself. If not for the fact that there were no windows showing the outside world—the *terra firma* outside world—they might have been in a grand hotel or museum.

One element working in his favor was that the submersible was more massive than anything he'd ever traveled in. If he could remind himself that traditional claustrophobia wasn't a problem, he found he could remain upright and not require the use of the infirmary's gurney.

They rode the convenient lift situated next to the Grand Staircase, which was large enough to carry the three of them comfortably, but tight enough that Sam was grateful when the ride was done, and Petrescu led them to a door which he unlocked.

Indicating within, he said, "This is my personal study, where I conduct business affairs. I'm certain the library will suffice should you have need of work space for business affairs." Sam's quick glance inside before they moved on showed a room decorated in dark mahogany, richly adorned with more eclectic pieces that seemed to be scattered throughout the rest of the ship.

"Tell me about your home, Uncle," Hazel said, and Sam followed them from the room. "You've said it has been in the family for generations?"

Petrescu smiled. "Ah, my dear, you will quite adore it, I believe. It is informally called 'Coppergate,' due to the copious amounts of the material our ancestors used in its construction. Some has been replaced and thus has yet to take on the green hue that copper assumes after years of exposure to the elements. I find it a delightful combination of old and new.

"I have fitted it with treasures from my many travels. It is

large, of course, with the elements you find on this ship mul-
tiplied tenfold. The library there, I believe, will be of particular interest to you. We have the distinct honor of housing the
most exclusive privately held collection of first-edition classic
literature in all of Europe. It is a hobby of mine, one in which
I take immense pride. I continue to search far and wide for
rare items—published works and private writings—from the
finest minds and cultures."

Hazel nodded, appearing serene as ever, but Sam noted
her left fist was clenched at her side as they returned to the
lift. "And your pieces here on the ship itself—I note statuary
and artwork from widely varied cultures. Some of the styles
are familiar to me, and others I'm certain I've never seen. You
must have traveled the world over." Her voice sounded light,
engaging, and had Sam not seen the evidence of her discomfort, he would have believed her performance.

"Yes, yes," Petrescu said and opened the lift gate. "Please,
ask me about anything that catches your eye. I am happy to
share my adventures." He smiled. With his white teeth, com-
pelling eyes and features, and thick head of hair, he should
have been handsome, but the underlying currents of something cold surrounded the nobleman like a cloak. "And now,
shall we tour the Control Room?"

Hazel glanced at Sam, concern in her eyes, but he took a
deep breath and nodded.

Petrescu followed Hazel's gaze and spoke to her, though
clearly his words were meant for Sam. "Some people find the
clear evidence of our position in the depths of the sea to be
overwhelming. The windows hide nothing from view, and

the ship's lights illuminate a world entirely different than the one we enjoy on the surface."

Sam held Petrescu's eye contact and remained silent for a long, protracted moment before finally offering a tight smile. "I am sure I'll find it awe-inspiring."

"I would be disappointed otherwise. It really is a most spectacular sight." He placed his free hand over Hazel's fingers. "Fascinating," he said to her, "is it not? That grown adults sometimes develop fears of things even small children can manage?"

Hazel didn't respond but smoothly moved aside for Sam to join them in the lift. She dropped her hand from the count's arm and inched closer to Sam—just a tiny shift in her stance—and the fabric of her skirt brushed his leg. Her nearness was an odd combination of soothing and pleasant discomfort, and by focusing on her instead of the lift's confines, the tight band across his chest lessened.

"Tell me about your assistant, Renton," Hazel said as the lift jerked and then smoothly descended. "He sounds British. Has he been long in your employ?"

"I found Renton in a dockside tavern, years ago, looking worse for the wear, but amenable to gainful employment. He has proved loyal and steadfast. I would be quite at sea without him." Petrescu chuckled at his own pun.

They descended to the lowest level, and Sam exited the lift behind Hazel and Petrescu. He followed them down a long hallway, focusing on the conversation to keep himself distracted.

"You've also given Renton an opportunity to travel, which I should think would be attractive to someone in a position to enjoy it." Hazel paused, waiting for Sam to draw up alongside her.

Petrescu held out his hand toward a wide set of double doors. "This deck contains the engine room, storage room, and maintenance supplies, but I have saved the best for last. My personal favorite." He opened the doors with a flourish. "I do hope you enjoy the splendid view."

Sam stared, openmouthed, at the sight before them.

Chapter 13

Hazel drew in her breath when Dravor opened the doors. The near end of the room was lined with shelves containing charts and sailing instruments. A ship's wheel and periscope dominated the center of the room on a raised dais, but catching her eye and holding it were the front windows that showed the ocean outside the craft as clearly as if there were no glass at all. A peculiar ping sounded in the background, noticeable but unobtrusive.

The submersible moved through the water at an incredible rate of speed, discernible only because of the small fish and particulates that zoomed past the window. Dravor gave one of the five 'tons instructions to gradually slow their speed, and Hazel felt the subtle pull of the engines. She looked at Sam, who stared at the sight, rooted to the spot.

She ventured slowly toward the window seat that spanned the front of the chamber, rested her knee on the cushion, and placed her hand on the glass.

As the craft continued to slow, individual shapes loomed larger and became clearer. She spied a host of creatures she'd never seen before, never imagined existed, and at another soft command from Dravor, a 'ton illuminated the view with an additional set of powerful exterior lights. The beams cut through the darkness, extending into the depths until even their powerful reach was ineffective.

Dravor joined her at the window, and she looked at him, wanting to appear sophisticated and unaffected but knowing her eyes were huge with shock and wonder. He chuckled and nodded toward the view before them. "A pod of whales just ahead." He pointed up and to the right. "Do you see?"

Her breath caught in her throat. They were huge. She'd only seen drawings in books, never imagined she would one day see the actual creature in its habitat. To the left was a strange animal with a bulbous head and tentacles that undulated slowly near a school of fish. "An octopus!" she breathed. They eventually passed the creatures, and she craned her neck to watch until they were out of sight.

She felt a presence at her other side and turned to see Sam, who also stared out in wonder. "I believe I am too awestruck to be panicked," he murmured.

"It is incredible," Hazel told Dravor. "I daresay most people have never seen such a thing."

Dravor nodded. "We are among the fortunate few. You are both welcome to visit this room whenever you wish."

A sound to their right caught her attention, bringing to mind an object being sucked through a tube. Just at the corner of her eye, she spied a fabric sack being jettisoned from the submersible and then floated, suspended in the water, until they passed and it was no longer visible.

"What on earth was that?" she asked Dravor.

"Trash, waste products—things of that sort. I do not care to keep refuse aboard the ship, so we offload as necessary. I also have a small submersible for use in making quick trips ashore when I do not wish to dock the entire *Magellan*. The torpedo tube comes in handy for many purposes."

Hazel frowned. "But to dump all that waste into the ocean—might it harm the wildlife?"

Dravor chuckled. "Sailors have been dumping trash overboard since the dawn of time. The wildlife appears wholly unaffected, as you can see. The ocean is a very big place." He smiled at Hazel and then Sam. "I must conduct some business in my office. Are the two of you comfortable enough to freely wander the ship?"

"We are," Sam answered. "I believe I shall follow your earlier suggestion and work in the library. Will you join me, Hazel?"

Hazel nodded and looked up at him. "I do have correspondence to write, and I was hoping to peruse those beautiful shelves in more detail."

"Excellent." Dravor beamed. "I shall leave you to enjoy the view here and continue your activities at your leisure." He gave a short, courtly bow, instructed his pilot 'ton to resume former speed, and took his leave.

Hazel looked out at the ocean beyond, her feelings a conflicted tangle. "Perhaps his intentions are not entirely nefarious," she murmured.

"I am reserving judgment," Sam said. "He is all things affable for the moment."

"Perhaps he really is nothing more nor less than he has presented."

"That would be a delightful turn of events." Sam's eyes met hers in the reflected window, and his mouth was a grim line. "I would love nothing more than to be convinced his intentions are simple and for your best good."

"Do you truly wish to spend time in the library today?"

"I do." He leaned close. "Perhaps we could discuss this privately."

Hazel nodded. The room was staffed with 'tons, any one of which might be programmed to make a recording of conversations around it. The pull of the craft as it resumed its former speed through the dark increased, and Hazel widened her stance to maintain balance. The ocean's residents again became a blur, the steady ping continued, and Hazel considered for one horrifying moment that all that separated them from the frightening abyss beyond were a few inches of metal and glass.

She clasped Sam's arm. If her mind was taking fanciful tangents, how long would it be before his did? His expression was controlled, but his pallor was worrisome. She tugged him from the window, out of the Control Room, and to the lift.

They rode upward in silence, and Hazel noticed that Sam's breathing seemed more steady now that they were away from the view of the ocean.

"Now," she said as they stepped out of the lift, "what are you hoping to find in the library?"

"Evidence of your family's ancestry." He paused. "You have been withdrawn this morning. Has something happened?"

Hazel took a deep breath. "I thought someone was in my

room last night while I was asleep. It wasn't Sally; I asked her this morning."

They began climbing the Grand Staircase, and Sam stopped in his tracks. "Why did you not telescribe me? Hazel, who do you suppose it was? Is anything missing?"

"No," she said and nudged him to resume the ascent. "I do not know who it was, and nothing is missing. I was horrifically tired, so perhaps it was my imagination. Regardless, I felt uneasy, and I hardly slept afterward. I am weary today, hence my reserve."

"I want your word that you will sleep with your scriber close at hand."

"I promise," she said with a smile.

They reached the top deck and made the short walk to the library doors. The room lifted Hazel's heart. Even having seen it before, she doubted she would ever tire of the sight. Three 'tons were in the room, one shelving an armful of books and the other two dusting.

The 'ton holding the books smiled and said, "We are happy to help you find anything you need."

"Thank you, that is much appreciated." Hazel wondered if they ever tired of repeating the same tasks. It wasn't as though the library was regularly used by a large population. But of course 'tons didn't tire; they weren't human. They could dust the same shelves eternally, stopping only when a charge was necessary.

"I'll need to delve deeper into the country's history," she admitted quietly to Sam, not wanting to ask the 'tons for help, knowing Dravor had access to the information recorded on their tins. The count would assume she would be looking for more information on the family history, but she saw no need to prove it easily. "He is very thorough by nature, so I would assume the books are organized by subject. I will begin searching for anything relating to the Petrescu name over here. Perhaps you'll take the other end?"

Sam nodded, and Hazel began tracing her finger along book spines, moving from shelf to shelf, climbing atop ladders and examining titles. Some of the volumes were so old she felt she ought not touch them with anything short of gloves. The pages smelled divine. Flowers were beautifully fragrant, certain desserts made her mouth water even from a distance, but the smell of old books, old paper, was her favorite by far.

Several minutes passed, and she was forced to admit a cursory review of the collection was not going to yield any information on the Petrescu line. She felt a measure of relief when the 'tons left the room for their scheduled charging time.

"I could just ask him," she mused aloud.

Sam shook his head. "Not yet, if you don't mind. Let's see if Oliver finds any new information."

Hazel put a hand on her hip and looked at Sam, who stood across the room, flipping through the pages of an old book. "You told Mr. Reed to gather information—*more* information?"

Sam looked up, his expression changing from interest in the book to wariness. "Yes," he admitted slowly. "I did not think you would object to learning as much as we can from whatever sources we have at our disposal." He crossed the room toward her. "You'll forgive me if I overstepped my bounds, I hope."

Hazel scowled, feeling churlish. "I do not mind, of course. I suppose I had hoped . . ." She bit her lip, uncertain of her own wishes.

She climbed two rungs on the ladder and replaced a book she'd taken from the shelf. Sam leaned a shoulder against the bookcase, and because of her position on the ladder, they stood eye-to-eye. He looked at her, his expression unreadable, until she finally huffed, "Well, what!"

"Accepting help from others does not mean a person is weak or lacking. It means that person is wise and uses the resources available." He raised a brow. "I'm certain you would agree, if you were offering counsel to anyone other than yourself."

Hazel released a quiet breath and looped her arm around the ladder. "There is no disgrace in holding myself to a higher standard."

"There is if it's foolish. You know that's true. And a desire to solve one's problems without accepting help from those who offer it does not constitute a higher standard."

His eyes were so blue, and right there in front of her. If she were the adventurous and experienced sort, she might loop her arm around his neck instead of the ladder. Feeling a keen sense of disappointment that her mad bravery was unpredictable, she contented herself with the fact that the space between them wasn't large at all.

She closed her eyes briefly. "I do want information about this whole affair," she said quietly, waving a hand at the room, "but I find myself wishing he were trustworthy. I need to believe that he is not a fraud when he says he is family and that he cares enough for me and my sister to travel the world and bring me home." She lifted a shoulder. "I have no family except for Rowena, and she has not always been the easiest of mothers."

"Perhaps he is everything he claims to be and has only the best of intentions," Sam said, also lowering his voice. "If we find that to be the case, so much the better. We are not left wondering if there are secrets. But Hazel," he said gently, "you must know there are secrets. There is something, an undercurrent to Petrescu, and I believe you feel it as keenly as do I."

Hazel agreed, as much as she'd like to insist otherwise. She paused, swinging a tiny bit on the ladder. "What are you reading?" she asked, motioning to the book Sam held.

He looked down at it. "Oh, yes. A history on Romania's traditional flora and fauna, as well as early animatronic creations in the region."

"That book looks much too old to contain any information on cyborg animals."

"It's rudimentary, at best," he agreed, "but it also lists regional plants for healing purposes. Might serve us both well, as our fields do tend to overlap."

She laughed. "I do not have a field."

He looked at her again, his expression serious, but the tiny lines around his eyes showed a lifetime of smiles. "You are a Healer, Hazel Hughes, and a very, very good one. With your natural abilities and my training, we make a formidable pair."

Her breath hitched, and she was mortified he stood close enough to note it.

"Would you not agree?" He smiled.

"I suppose," she said, fighting the urge to place her hand on his shoulder and pull him closer. All intelligent conversation fled, and she found herself mentally stammering as he had done verbally the night before. Just desserts, she supposed. She had quite enjoyed his scene of awkwardness and discomfort. But despite her own feelings for him, she'd never stammered or stumbled or otherwise made a fool of herself. Hiding her feelings had allowed her to protect herself. That her awkwardness and insecurities were now making an appearance meant she was either losing control of her ironclad will, or she realized on some level he might be interested in her and as a result had lowered her own guard.

"Never a good idea," she muttered.

His mouth quirked at one corner. "What is never a good idea?"

"Opening one's jacket to reveal the target painted beneath."

"Is that what you've done?"

She bit her lip. "I've no idea, really. I am not well-versed in . . . in . . ."

He smiled. "Flirtation?"

"Is that what this is?" She felt breathless, as if she'd run laps around the submersible.

"Oh, I believe that is most definitely what this is."

"I must find a book on the topic," she said, more to herself than to him.

He laughed, and the delighted sound warmed her heart.

"I'm certain you would make a good study of it from a publication, but there are some things that are better experienced."

Be brave, Hazel.

She placed a tentative hand on his jacket lapel, her palm over his heart. He covered her hand with his and traced his thumb along her knuckles. He watched her carefully, patiently, and simply waited. But she had no idea what to do next. She wanted a kiss but dared not instigate the contact on her own.

Noises sounded in the hallway—a stumble, a crash, a scream.

Sam released her hand and tossed the book onto a nearby table. Hazel jumped down from the ladder and dashed from the room on Sam's heels. A cacophony echoed up the stairwell from Deck Two, and Hazel ran down the stairs after Sam to see a handful of 'tons and human servants standing beside Sally, who lay unconscious on the floor, having apparently crashed into the medieval suit of armor that stood at attention on the landing.

Renton stood over her, eyes wide, and breathless. "She . . . I . . ."

Blood seeped crimson from a puncture wound on Sally's hip where she'd fallen on the suit of armor's spear.

"Your 'ton—" Renton managed, pointing at Sam. "He tried to kill her!"

Chapter 14

Renton bent over Sally, who was still sprawled atop the suit of armor, and placed both hands around the hilt of the spear buried in her hip.

"No! Don't pull out the spear!" Hazel shouted in horror, just as Sam lunged forward and stopped him.

"We must get her to the infirmary." He looked up at Hazel. "Please, retrieve my medical bag from my suite. Eugene will find it."

"That thing tried to kill her!" Renton's face was an angry red.

"Impossible," Sam said to him grimly. "I left Eugene in my cabin." He looked at the iron spear that extended from Sally and then gingerly placed his arms beneath her small, inert form.

Petrescu descended the stairs. He took in the scene, looked at Hazel's shocked face and clenched fists, and fury flashed across his features.

Hazel took an involuntary step back, uncertain where his anger was directed.

"What has happened?" he asked in a low tone, which was somehow more frightening than if he had yelled.

"I must get her to the infirmary," Sam said.

"I . . . that automaton . . ." Renton looked up at his employer and swallowed.

Hazel watched the exchange in amazement. Renton was easily the larger, stronger of the two men.

"What are you suggesting?" Dravor asked him. "Did he stab Miss Tucker with that?" He gestured toward the spear.

Renton swallowed, then muttered, "Chased, chased her . . ."

Hazel held her breath as the count regarded his assistant for a moment. His features gave no hint of his emotions. "We cannot have a 'ton running amok in the ship," he said to Sam.

"I shall address the 'ton," Sam snapped as he lifted Sally carefully in his arms. "Be useful and open the lift."

Hazel bit her lip. Sam had no use for inefficiency during an emergency. In that moment, she figured he could easily take both men single-handedly. Anger flowed around the scene like a palpable thing.

Her uncle raised his brows high, but opened the lift.

Hazel took in the whole, strange scene, trying to understand what hadn't been said. She would stake her life on the fact that Eugene had certainly not tried to kill Sally. She looked at Renton, who straightened his lapels and smoothed back his hair. The calm, calculating look on his face chilled her, and she wondered if he were the sort to protect himself at all costs.

She rushed over just as Sam was entering the lift. "What is Eugene's neutral code?"

Sam frowned. "'Halt.'"

"Original," Hazel muttered and dashed past Dravor, who entered the lift with Sam and Sally. She ran past Renton, down the hallway, coming to a breathless halt at Sam's door. She knocked loudly. "Eugene! It's Hazel."

The door opened. "Miss Hazel?" He held one strand of the delicate twinkle lights and another draped around his neck. "One of the bulbs is out," he said.

She shoved past him and slammed the door shut, locking it. "Did you have any interaction with Sally just now?"

He frowned. "I did not."

"Did you hear anything unusual?"

"I detected movement in your cabin, but reasoned it was your maid."

"Did she say anything?"

"There was a murmur of voices, but nothing detectable."

"A deep voice?"

Eugene paused. "Yes. Why? What has happened?"

Hazel swallowed, seeing Sally's still, pale face. "We must take Sam's medical bag to the infirmary. Miss Tucker has met with an accident." She paused. "Renton said you tried to kill her."

Eugene frowned and set the strands of lights on the bed. "That is untrue. I did not attempt to end her life. I've been nowhere near her for at least three hours."

Hazel nodded, but couldn't help the twitch of a relieved smile. "I did not believe you did. Your programming is un-paralleled. Where is the doctor's small medical bag?"

Eugene crossed the room. "This is the smaller of the two." He handed it to her. "I'll carry the trunk."

Hazel nodded. "Before we leave, however, I must tempo-rarily neutralize your advanced programming. Dr. MacInnes has told me your neutral code, and it should take no time at all to examine your history tin to show you did not assault Miss Tucker. I do not want anyone accusing you of a crime and insisting you be permanently discharged."

Eugene nodded. "I am fully compliant, so you needn't bother with the neutral code. I'll caution you, however, that should you forget to replace that which you remove, I'll be boring. My simulated thought patterns and uncanny sense of humor will be absent, and I'll not resemble at all the enter-taining, nonhuman companion the doctor has come to know and love." He lifted a shoulder in a shrug, and Hazel, despite the sense of urgency, laughed.

"Eugene, that would perhaps be the most tragic thing this world has ever known," she said, rummaging through the medical kit for the small tool used to open the access panel to Eugene's programming.

"The saying goes, 'Sarcasm doesn't become you,'" Eugene said, "but I would submit that sarcasm becomes you nicely, Miss Hazel."

"That is because excellence at sarcasm is surely the most prominent feature of your programming, thus you've an above-average appreciation for it." Hazel smiled and finally found the tool. "Come, then. We must hurry. And you have my word, I'll examine the tins straightaway. You'll not be bor-ing for long."

Eugene frowned and unbuttoned his shirt. "Suppose the doctor prefers a bland Eugene to a witty one." He slipped his shirt from his shoulders and turned around, giving Hazel his back.

She located the access panel, stunned at the material that housed the cyborg. It was warm, and felt as much like skin and muscle as any person she'd ever touched. "I am most certain," she said as she opened the panel, "that the doctor adores 'witty Eugene.'"

Eugene sniffed. "I am not certain that is true."

"Put your fears to rest. Doctor MacInnes appreciates your personality, and you have my word I shall restore you to your full, sarcastic glory."

Hazel ran her finger along the multiple tin slots behind the panel, gently pulling the correct ones from their slots. The quality was excellent, and she sincerely doubted Eugene had malfunctioned at all, and certainly not because of faulty hardware.

"Eugene," she said after closing him up and gathering the supplies Sam needed, "please follow me to the infirmary, and bring the doctor's large medical chest."

Eugene nodded. "Yes, Miss Hughes." His movements were still smooth and fluid, but there was a flatness to his tone. What a funny thing it was, Hazel mused, to miss a simulated personality.

She led Eugene to the Grand Staircase and down one deck to the infirmary, where Sam had already washed his hands, donned a clean smock and gloves, and was in the process of sedating Sally.

Dravor stood to one side, watching with detached curiosity, and it bothered Hazel. She turned her attention to Sam, who motioned to her with his head.

"Set the small bag here, please," he said to Hazel. "Eugene, place the trunk over there for now, and then clean your hands and dress in that smock by the sink."

"Yes, sir." Eugene did as he was told, and Sam paused while checking Sally's breathing.

"What is wrong with you?" he asked the 'ton.

"I am functioning properly, sir. An initial diagnostic test indicates an absence of errors."

Sam looked at Hazel.

"I pulled some tins." She set the medical satchel on a tray near his elbow. "I shall examine his history to determine any potential involvement in this accident with Sally. I also re-moved the advanced personality programming until we have better answers. If there is cunning or independent thought involved, we are better served having him neutralized for now." She glanced at Dravor, whose face showed a flash of annoyance.

"We shall identify the problem, Uncle," she offered, again wondering at his irritation. "I do not believe Eugene inten-tionally caused Sally harm or distress."

"You believe Renton to be lying?"

Hazel blinked. "I believe Renton to be mistaken."

Sam cursed, and Hazel looked at the source of his dis-tress. He was preparing to remove the spear from Sally's hip, and blood pooled around the wound in alarming volume. Sam barked a few technical questions at Eugene to test the remaining knowledge base. Satisfied, Sam instructed the 'ton to stand near his side and assist.

"I need you here," Sam said, glancing up at Hazel.

She nodded, already crossing the room. She pulled a

gown from the shelf and removed her form-fitting jacket, glad she'd donned a short-sleeved corset blouse that morning.

Sam again probed Sally's wound. "Eugene, what is her heart rate?"

Eugene was quiet for a moment. "Fast. One hundred thirty beats per minute."

"Pulse strength?"

Eugene placed two fingers alongside Sally's throat. The soft click of gears sounded as he processed information. "Weak, sir."

"Blood volume insufficient, surely."

"Initial scan shows significant internal bleeding." Eugene's voice lacked the quality that had made him so lifelike.

"Prepare to quickly hand the stack of cloths to me," Sam said. He glanced up at Dravor. "She will need a transfusion. Do you have a blood supply aboard? I noticed a cooling box."

Dravor shook his head. "It holds elixirs and medicines. I fear I cannot donate, as I have a blood condition that would harm her as efficiently as that spear."

Sam glanced up, and Hazel knew what he was thinking. The count was likely unaware that one person's blood did not necessarily match another. Sam and Hazel, with Eugene's analysis, had only just discovered it themselves.

And more to the point, what sort of "blood condition" did he have?

Hazel frowned as suspicions crowded her head. "Sam, I can help. When we conducted our experiments on blood interaction with several samples under a microscope, my blood was consistently compatible with each different sample." She spoke over her shoulder as she scrubbed her hands and arms.

Sam hesitated. "I remember. I would rather not, but it appears we have no choice." He finally nodded. "Eugene, please set up the second gurney."

Eugene complied, and Hazel pulled on the gown, then climbed atop the makeshift table next to Sally. Sam instructed Eugene to collect supplies from the large trunk. While he did so, Sam looked at Dravor. "I'll need three of your medical 'tons. I'll have one of them alert you if I require additional help."

"You'll not play irresponsible with her health, I presume."

"The wound is severe, Petrescu, but I shall do everything in my power to save her."

"I speak of Hazel."

Hazel looked at her uncle. Sam must have been equally surprised; his pause was telling.

"Naturally, I would never put Hazel in harm's way. Her role, however, is not one that poses significant risks. I'll perform the procedure myself to insure it goes as planned."

"And your intimacy with her as a close friend will not impede your skills?"

Sam requested a length of tubing and needles from Eugene. "It has not been an issue, to date. I saved her life once, and I have repaired broken bits and pieces ever since."

He looked at Hazel, but his smile was fleeting. He coated her arm with cleansing fluid from a corked bottle while still speaking to the count. "I confess, I thought you would be more concerned with Miss Tucker's welfare. I understand she is not family and Hazel is, but Sally is, by far, in greater danger."

"I have every confidence in your surgical skills." Dravor's glance flicked from Sally to Hazel.

Sam measured a length of tubing and draped it across Hazel's midsection so he could prepare Sally's arm for the other end of the transfusion tubing. "Eugene, the patient's pulse strength?"

"The patient's pulse is weaker, sir," Eugene said.

Sam hurriedly ripped Sally's sleeve along the seam and then prepared the final steps for the transfusion. He put his hand on Hazel's arm. "You are ready?"

"Be quick." Hazel looked over at Sally. "She does not appear to have much time left."

She ran her fingertip along the gold chain at her wrist. As always, the soothing warmth made its way through her, and she relaxed.

Sam made quick work of the needle insertion, first on Hazel, and then Sally, and connected the tubing. He glanced at Hazel several times as if to assure himself of her continued stability while continuing to receive updates from Eugene regarding the patient.

Hazel closed her eyes and imagined sharing her sense of calm with Sam, wishing she were somehow clairvoyant.

Sam quietly instructed Eugene and the three other 'tons as he began treatment for Sally. They worked efficiently and well. Sam seemed calm, and expressed irritation only in the smallest of terms when Eugene did not anticipate his needs.

"We've done this sort of procedure before," Sam said to Eugene as they worked. "Do you not remember?"

"I remember, sir. I do not have the capacity to act before you instruct."

"I am now giving you permission to act before I instruct."

"My sincerest apologies, but that is an impossibility."

Sam rolled his eyes as he stemmed the flow of blood from Sally's deep wound. "Never in a million years did I think I would miss . . ." he muttered. He stabilized the bleeding, told one of the 'tons to maintain pressure on the wound, and removed the tubing from Hazel's arm. He held a cloth to the pinprick, and when she brushed his hand aside so she could hold the cloth herself, he smiled.

"Do you know yet if the damage is extensive enough to require deeper procedures?" she asked.

He lifted a shoulder. "Not certain, yet, but I am hopeful the solution will be relatively simple. Please remain on the table for now and rest. You'll experience light-headedness for a time." He instructed one of Dravor's 'tons to retrieve a cup of tea for her.

"Do not look so worried, Sam, I am perfectly well."

He glanced at her with a distracted smile. "Using you as an emergency blood donor is not something I would choose."

Dravor had remained a silent observer; Hazel had nearly forgotten he was in the room. She turned her head on the gurney to look at him, and he smiled. "A relief to see you well."

"Thank you, Uncle." She paused. "I was unaware of your blood illness I am sorry to hear of it."

He smiled. "A token from a mentor, but one man's plague is another man's gift."

She frowned. "Perhaps Dr. MacInnes might know of a treatment."

"Ah, if only. There is no cure for my malady, but I have altered my life accordingly."

The 'ton returned with a cup of tea for Hazel, and she sat up on the gurney. She was light-headed, but none the worse for wear.

Sam suddenly swore, focusing even more intently on Sally, and his jaw clenched. Sweat dotted his brow, and though his movements remained steady and sure, Hazel felt a ripple of unease. "Assess vital measurements," Sam barked at Eugene.

"Pulse weak. Oxygen levels depleting."

Chapter 15

Hazel set her cup aside and shifted to the edge of her gurney. Sally's face was obscured by the operating mask, and Hazel felt a moment of panic. Eugene appeared to be proficient enough, but Hazel wondered if she had been right to pull his higher-level tins so quickly. Her eyes filmed, and the image before her blurred. She knew little to nothing about Sally, but it was clear that she must have been terrified before this strange string of events unfolded.

She reached over and took her limp hand, uneasy at the cold feel of her fingers. She focused her thoughts and envisioned Sally's full return to good health. She imagined the bruised and broken blood vessels healing, the internal organs responding to Sam's care. Her gold chain bracelet reflected a soft, subtle glow of light. She touched the metal to Sally's hand, wishing she could impart the warmth she felt to the stricken young woman.

Desperate to help, wishing she could do more, she rested her head next to Sally's arm and closed her eyes. She was tired and was fighting alternating waves of fear, dizziness, and light-headedness. She slowly found herself in that strange space between consciousness and dreams.

Marit was watching her with wide eyes. She reached for Hazel, but couldn't grasp her hand. She sang a soft tune in a language Hazel didn't understand. Romanian—of course it would be Romanian. Hazel had studied German and French.

She breathed in, her eyes still closed, and tightened her fingers gently on Sally's. As she floated in the space between Marit and the infirmary far beneath the ocean waves, the words of the song found their way into Hazel's thoughts, and she quietly whispered along.

She was barely aware of her surroundings. She distantly heard her uncle's voice, and Sam's sharp command for the man to stay back.

Her eyes fluttered open, and she sensed Sam's attention on her for a fraction of a moment. His demeanor had relaxed by small degrees, his jaw unclenched and the creases between his brows smoothed.

"Vitals," he said to Eugene.

"Improving, sir."

Hazel breathed a sigh of relief, wary of premature celebration, but feeling her spirits lift. She closed her eyes again and kept her fingers clasped around Sally's. *Warmth and light . . . golden bright . . .* She envisioned every good, miraculous thing she could think of, then deepened her breathing and imagined she was breathing for the two of them—for herself and for Sally, who now shared her blood.

She lost track of time, and she was surprised when Sam gently removed her hand from Sally's. She opened her eyes to see Sam's, so close to her own she thought she might drown in their depths.

Eugene and the other 'tons quietly moved Sally behind a curtain that they closed for privacy.

"What . . ." Sam shifted his hip against Hazel's gurney and ran his hand through his hair and over his face. He looked exhausted. "What did you just do?"

Hazel swallowed. She glanced at the closed curtain, and her heart thumped. "Did I do something? I . . . What did I do?"

"I don't know," Sam said. "Whatever it was, I felt it. My mind grew clearer, and the patient began responding well to the procedure. The whole room felt calm."

Hazel thought for a moment. "I meditated, envisioned a good outcome. I saw . . . I saw Marit; I heard her. And I sang something she was singing." She shrugged, suddenly very tired, and her eyes blurred with tears. "I don't know."

"It was a good thing," Sam said, his smile wry. "I believe perhaps your healing gift aided Sally just as you helped me earlier when I was out of my head." He paused. "Do you speak Romanian?"

She shook her head. "I do not." She frowned. "I do know what I said, though. Something about warmth and light, a poem."

He smiled again and leaned in, kissing her forehead. "Think about it later. Right now, I suspect you could use a rest. I know I could." He removed his surgical smock and balled it up, tossing it in a corner bin. "Petrescu sent word that dinner will be available whenever we are ready."

"What time is it?" Hazel fumbled for her pocket watch.

"Late." He took her hand and helped her down from the gurney. "The 'tons will take the patient to a post-operative bedroom next door, and I'll check her recovery periodically."

"Are you willing to put her in the room next to mine? I would rather keep her close."

"I suppose so. I'll instruct the 'tons to clean the room, and we'll move her soon." He paused. "Hazel, she was floundering. I feared I was going to lose her. I don't know I could have done this successfully without you."

Hazel blushed and scrambled to turn attention away from herself. "Uncle Dravor is pleased, I assume?"

Sam rubbed his eyes and held the infirmary door open for her. "Who would know," he muttered as they skipped the Grand Staircase and opted instead for the lift. "He seemed quite pleased at your involvement, that was evident."

"My involvement?"

Sam nodded and closed the lift gate. The gears engaged and lifted the cage upward. "When he saw you holding Sally's hand, meditating or praying, he seemed almost euphoric. Wanted to come closer. I finally ordered him out of the room, though he returned two more times that I noticed, peering inside the room. He seemed focused on you, rather than Sally."

Hazel tapped her finger restlessly against her leg, wary of the fact that her uncle seemed to know so much more about her than she knew of him. "Marit was here." She tapped her forehead. "In here. He must have known, or suspected it. Perhaps he is hopeful that I might find a cure for her madness."

"What exactly do we know about your birth mother?"

Sam asked as they exited the lift and made their way down the hall to their suites.

Hazel shrugged. "He has said only that she was his sister, gave birth to me and another baby girl, and then the midwife sold me to Rowena. Our mother died shortly after we were born, followed soon by our father."

They reached their suites and stopped. "Oh!" Hazel reached into her skirt pocket and closed her fingers around a stack of cold metal rectangles. "Eugene's tins. I didn't have an opportunity to run them through the reader in the Tesla Room. I don't believe for a moment he attacked Sally, or chased her." She lowered her voice. "Renton is involved, I'm sure of it, and he is trying to deflect his guilt onto Eugene."

Sam took the tins from her. "I'll analyze these myself right now. Where is the Tesla Room in this death trap?"

She couldn't help but smile, and pointed upward. "Deck One, just off the library. Would you like me to join you?"

"No, you freshen up and rest. I'll come to you when I finish."

Her lips twitched in another smile. "Eugene was concerned you would prefer him 'bland and boring.' I gave him my word I would have him restored to his proper glory, so do make haste."

"Never thought I'd miss him, but he's right. He was bland and boring, and I didn't much care for it." He paused. "Hazel, again, thank you. Today was . . . You were . . ." He brushed his thumb across her cheek and dropped his hand. "I'll return straightaway. Lock your door, yes?"

She nodded, and as she locked the door behind her, she heard footsteps receded. She released a breath and rubbed her arms, which were suddenly chilled. She retrieved her ray gun and a small knife from her trunk and placed them within easy reach of her bed. She might not be as competent as Isla, but she could do some damage to an opponent, should one decide to visit. She was certain of one thing—she wouldn't surrender without a fight.

She rose from the bed, awakened from sleep by a sense of despair that nearly overwhelmed her. She walked around, and around, and around, never finding the door, never able to see beyond the world outside her single window. The room turned slowly, continually, offering her a glimpse of the world from every angle, but never an escape. She loved the room, and she hated the room. It was her prison and her sanctuary.

She read so many books; he always brought her things to read, and she never forgot a word. She learned languages, histories. She learned of places and people and things, yet she was trapped! Eternally trapped! She imagined a life outside the room, a life with people to meet and things to do. She lived it all in her head until she felt mad, evermore increasingly painfully mad . . .

Around and around and around the room, and now the other direction. Perhaps the woman in the mirror would visit again tonight, the woman who looked just like her. The woman who could go and do and be, the one she loved and hated . . .

If she moved faster, if she ran in circles, around and around and around, maybe something would change! She would laugh and sing! She would see the world and all of its treasures, instead of spinning and spinning and hearing her own voice scream

inside her head that she wanted to get out! Out of her head, away
from the room, into the trees! Out! Out!

"Hazel!"

Her head hurt. She collapsed to the floor, clutching fists
of her hair close to the roots, her fingers tightening until her
nails sank deeply into her palms. A scream echoed around the
walls of her room, followed by frantic sobs that escaped her
throat. She touched her forehead to the floor, welcoming the
feel of the textured carpet that helped ground her in reality.

The low hum of the *Magellan's* engines vibrated through
the floor, quiet, rhythmic, comforting. An insistent pounding
on the door was jarringly at odds with the sound.

"Hazel! Open the door!" Sam's loud voice was muffled by
the locked door.

She inhaled deeply, trying to calm her racing heart. Her
throat hurt, and her head pounded, even when she forced her
fingers to relax their painful grip on her hair. Sam pounded
again on the door, and she heard him murmuring something,
probably to Eugene. She shoved herself off the floor and
stumbled to the door as the sounds of scratching on the lock
indicated an attempt to open it.

Light from the hall arced into the room by degrees as the
door swung wide. Sam rushed inside. He grabbed her shoulders and looked into her eyes, from one to the other, and
then at her arms, her torso, down the front of her nightgown.
His fingers tightened. "What happened? Hazel!"

"I don't know . . ." She looked at him in fear, and then
slowly around her cabin. Her portmanteau had been knocked
off its perch on her travel trunk. Her journal, books, and

toiletries were strewn on the floor as if swept aside by a flailing arm.

She drew in a shuddering breath. "I do not know! Sam . . ." She clutched his shirtfront, terror creeping into her throat. "I do not walk in my sleep, I— This is not me!"

"Shh, I have you." Sam pulled her close against his chest and wrapped his arms around her, gently rubbing her back. He said something quietly to Eugene, and she heard the door click closed.

She kept her eyes squeezed tightly shut. Tears seeped from the corners and fell onto Sam's shirt. He held her for a long time until she finally calmed, her racing heart slowed, and she was able to draw a stable breath. He guided her to the settee near the hearth and pulled her down next to him. He kept an arm around her and reached for one of her hands, which he held securely, rubbing his thumb softly across her knuckles.

"Are you hurt anywhere?" he asked quietly.

"My head." Hazel sniffled and dabbed at her nose, looking uselessly for a handkerchief.

Sam gave her one from his pocket and then took her hand again.

"Did I awaken you?" she asked. Another thought struck. "Did I awaken Sally? Is she here? She must be terrified!"

"No, she's still in the infirmary. I've been sitting with her—she's become feverish. I analyzed Eugene's tins after checking on her—and thankfully, the results exonerate Eugene from any wrongdoing—and then came up to change into fresh clothes; I heard you crying and then screaming. I assumed you were asleep." The corner of his mouth lifted. "And you were."

"I was in her head, Sam. In Marit's head. Or she was in mine." She shrugged miserably. "I must speak with my uncle. She is trapped somewhere, and it is driving her insane." She looked at Sam, her eyes widening. "Do you suppose he has her locked somewhere? Is he keeping her captive?"

He frowned. "I wouldn't think so, however . . ."

"However?"

"Perhaps he has restrained her movement for her own protection? He says she's ill, but you've maintained all along that she's slowly been going mad." He rubbed her back between her shoulders as if he could soften the blow.

"She's been going mad because she's trapped! What is he doing to her? What does he want from me? And a blood disease? He said he has a blood disease!" Her voice rose, and she heard her own manic fear. "Is he a vampire? He could be taking Assimilation Aid!"

"Shh, steady, there." He squeezed her hand. "First things first. I know you have questions, but for now I think it best he has no knowledge of your connection to Marit. Until we can ascertain his motives and the reality of Marit's situation, we're better to hide what we know. Would you agree?"

She hesitated. Logically, he made sense, but enough raw emotion still bounced around in her head to make her want to argue. "What is he doing to her?" she whispered.

"Hazel, she may indeed be mad. Perhaps what you saw through her eyes is not an accurate reflection of reality." He paused. "And if she is indeed locked in a room or a home, it might truly be for her safety or the safety of others. It would also explain why he continually digs for information about you, about your 'gifts.' When he witnessed your healing abilities today with his own eyes, he was extremely satisfied."

"Are you defending him?"

He chuckled. "Not in the least. I still do not trust him an inch. His motives, however . . . If your sister is losing her sanity, I can understand the necessity for restraint."

"You do not believe that. We've argued with other doctors about inmate treatment in asylums!"

"Asylums, yes. Barbaric care that is only now coming to light, yes." He paused. "Do you believe Marit is in an asylum?"

Hazel frowned and rubbed her forehead. "No, whatever I saw, it is the same as what I've seen in dreams all my life. The vibrancy has faded, though. The paint is no longer fresh. The room feels . . . old. Sad. She is losing hope." Her eyes burned. "And she hates me, because I am out here."

Sam looked as though he might question that, but held his tongue.

Hazel dropped her hand and looked directly at him. "Sam, she hates me."

Chapter 16

The following day and night were blessedly uneventful, and Hazel was grateful for small mercies. During the day, she spent time in the library, ate awkward but benign meals with Dravor and Sam, and she and Sam worked on patient notes and a few files he'd brought from the clinic. She had difficulty focusing, however, which was not usually an affliction that plagued her. She couldn't shake the memory of walking in circles in that endlessly turning room, desperately looking for a way out and knowing it didn't exist.

The effort to remain cordial and objective with her uncle was more difficult than she'd imagined. She heard his claims of a "blood disorder" constantly in her head and knew she would feel better if she could at least find some Vampiric Assimilation Aid in his office or cabin. Then she would have proof. Gaining entry to either room would be a challenge, of course, and she'd have to evade Sam, which might be the hardest part of all. Since her dream the other night, he'd watched her like a hawk.

The perfect moment arrived shortly after breakfast, when

Sam returned to the infirmary to check on Sally in preparation for moving her back to her room, and the count responded to a summons from the Control Room. She made her way quickly down the long corridor from the guest suites to her uncle's room. She passed three 'tons on her way, each of which nodded to her. As she reached the count's door, she looked back over her shoulder to see all three 'tons watching her.

She forced a smile at them and turned with purpose, making a show of knocking on the door. She didn't look back, but wondered if they were still there. She knocked again and was surprised when it swung open. Renton towered over her, scowling. She saw the moment he must have told himself to be pleasant, because he smoothed his features and managed a parody of a smile.

"Lady Hazel?" The insolence in his tone was unmistakable.

"Hello, Renton." She straightened her shoulders. "I was hoping to speak with my uncle. Is he in?"

"He is not. Tell him you called, shall I?"

She smiled, narrowing her eyes. "I'll find him." She didn't trust Renton at all. She suspected him of involvement in Sally's accident, though one bright spot in the aftermath had been exonerating Eugene from all responsibility. His tins corroborated his version of events during the time Sally had been frightened enough to run for safety.

Renton tilted his head to the side. "Remarkable."

Her heartbeat increased. "And what is that?"

"How much you resemble her."

She paused, knowing he was baiting her, trying to make her nervous. "My sister? Stands to reason, as we're twins."

"Lacks your sass, though."

"Probably a result of being locked away her entire life with nobody but herself for company." She tossed the comment into the air and hoped he would confirm or deny it.

He looked at her for a long moment and then slowly smiled. "I wouldn't know."

"Yet you know enough to recognize our similarities." She folded her hands together tightly—clearly a sign of stress—and when his eyes followed her movement, she wished she hadn't.

"How fares Miss Tucker?"

"She has yet to awaken from surgery."

"Pity. She's not been able to explain her accident, then."

"No, but Doctor MacInnes is the best in his field, so I have every confidence she will awaken soon."

His eyes flickered, something angry passing through them. "We'll hope for that."

"Good day, Mr. Renton."

"Good day, my lady."

She made her way back down the hallway with a concerted effort to keep her movements deliberate but unhurried. She didn't hear the door close and wondered if he watched her as the 'tons had. When she turned the corner, she picked up her pace, heading down one deck. Irritation, born of fright, settled into her thoughts, and by the time she reached the infirmary she had very nearly convinced herself to turn around and demand Renton explain his vague implications, his knowledge of Marit.

She found Sam seated at Sally's bedside, tapping a pencil against a journal he used for sketching medical devices. The pages were blank, however, and he stared at the wall above the bed.

"Hello," she said quietly and gave a light knock on the open door with her knuckles.

"Oh!" He pushed up on the chair to stand, and she waved him back down. "Where have you been? I thought you were joining me here directly following breakfast."

She chewed thoughtfully on the inside of her cheek. "I paid a visit to my uncle's cabin."

He raised one brow and said slowly, "He isn't in his cabin. He was called down to the Control Room."

To confess or not to confess? Hazel weighed her options. "I had hoped to gain access to his cabin. I wanted to look for Assimilation Aid."

He stared. "You want to find evidence that he's a vampire."

"Yes. His 'blood condition' is suspicious, wouldn't you agree? And there's a strange feeling in the air whenever he's present, and that could well be the reason."

"How were you planning on gaining entrance?" he demanded.

"Isla taught me how to pick locks."

He closed his eyes and leaned back in his chair. "The fact that you're here and not there suggests you did not meet with success."

"I never had the chance to try. Renton was there."

His eyes flew open. "He caught you skulking around his master's door?"

"I was not 'skulking.' I knocked to be certain nobody was there. Well, and to put on a show for the 'tons. I'm relatively certain they've been programmed to spy on us, or at least gather information about our movements aboard the ship."

He regarded her without comment. "Hazel," he finally managed, "are you feeling well?"

"Of course, I am. Are you concerned I'm channeling my mad sister again?"

"You must admit, breaking into a man's locked room isn't exactly in keeping with your character."

"My boring, staid character? Perhaps my acts of bravery in recent months have been unconscious efforts to toughen my hide."

"Or perhaps they have been a result of Marit's influence."

She pursed her lips. "My actions are my own."

Sam tapped the pencil to his lips, thoughtfully. "You mentioned earlier that you've felt a 'compulsion,' I believe you called it. A drive to try dangerous things you actually had no desire to experience."

Her irritation rose. "What are you suggesting, Sam?"

He pinched the bridge of his nose. "I am suggesting— I am *begging* you to be sensible. Cautious."

"I am being sensible. Nothing about this situation is normal, and my customary reserve will get me nowhere. You must agree."

"I'll agree that our circumstances are odd, but I will not agree that you should feel justified in throwing caution to the wind! Reckless behavior leads to missteps and mistakes."

"What do you suggest, then?" she repeated. Somewhere during the conversation, her fingers had planted themselves on her hips and he'd risen fully from his chair to stand nose-to-nose with her.

"I suggest we exercise a modicum of reason!" The color in his cheeks was high, and Hazel realized she'd never seen him agitated with her before.

So be it! After all, her own frustration was climbing by leaps and bounds, though she was unable to put her finger on exactly why she was upset. Everything he said mirrored sentiments she'd have expressed herself less than a week ago, before reality had shifted beneath her feet.

"I am perfectly reasonable, but I am tired of being acted upon. I need to *do* something, not sit idly by while my life erupts. We are *trapped* here, like rats on a sinking ship, so I shall make good use of my time by determining the true nature of my uncle's 'condition.' Seems like an excellent time to investigate, as my schedule is clear and I have no pressing commitments."

"Hazel, we do not have the luxury of being impulsive! You mustn't do anything else without consulting with me first."

"I am not a child, and you are not my keeper!" Heat rose in her cheeks, the hue probably matching his.

He threw his arms wide. "I am not claiming to be! I am your partner in this, however, and your actions will not affect you alone!"

Frustrated and slightly confused, she looked away from him, took a deep breath, and searched for calm.

Her gaze landed on Sally, who lay pale and motionless on the bed. "Why has she not awoken?" she asked.

Sam blinked and then looked at Hazel for a long

moment. Assessing, ever assessing. She knew what he was thinking, how his mind worked. "I'm at a loss," he finally said. "You and I both know she ought to have been conscious yesterday." He frowned. "I worry the ether dosage may have been too high."

"I've never known you to miscalculate dosage."

He looked at Sally and lifted a shoulder. "Perhaps this marks the first."

"Or perhaps my Healing skills are not as strong as I'd hoped." Hazel frowned. "She is so pale. More than usual, considering the transfusion."

Sam paused. "Her blood volume is low," he admitted. "I had Eugene analyze it."

"Why would someone's blood volume be low?" She bit back another sarcastic comment and told herself to relax. "A vampire attack would be one possibility."

Sam eyed her flatly. "I thought of that, but she bears no puncture marks on either her neck or pressure points. She may be anemic."

Hazel nodded reluctantly. Anemia wasn't uncommon, and living in poor conditions as the Tucker family did, Sally was probably unaware there was treatment for the fatigue from which she likely suffered.

"Not all vampires utilize pressure points." Hazel tenaciously clung to the idea that her uncle was undead. It would explain so much that was strange about him.

"Hazel." Sam glanced outside at passing 'tons and quietly closed the door. "Your assumption is that Petrescu is a vampire, and from his wealth and stature, one might assume a very old one. Possibly not," he added, holding up a hand, "but that would be my guess."

Hazel pursed her lips, refusing to speak.

"We know an inexperienced vampire tends to make a mess of things, often not bothering with pressure points or the bounty of the jugular vein. Do you, for one moment, imagine the count behaving in such a way? Even if he were turned only yesterday, I cannot see, with his measured and cold personality, his behavior as anything other than . . . tidy. Efficient."

She sighed. "Sam, I am not wrong." She rubbed her forehead. "Perhaps it is not vampirism, exactly, but I know there is something about him that is not . . ."

"Not quite right? I believe that wholeheartedly. And he may be a vampire. All I ask is that you not go alone on a crusade to prove it. That is not an unreasonable request."

"Then what shall we do? I need a plan, steps to follow, something to study."

His lips quirked. "Ah, there she is. That is the most Hazelish thing you've said since entering the room."

She scowled at him. "You've never seen me under duress, Samuel MacInnes. I am allowed the odd fit of temper."

"Of course, you are. You've spoiled me, though. In the past year, I have seen you perform in emergency medical situations without batting an eye. To see you flustered, or angry, is something new."

"I suppose every person has a breaking point," she admitted quietly.

"Of course." He smiled. "Your back holds strong longer than most."

Silence filled the short distance that separated them. She remembered the warmth she'd felt when he'd pulled her to him after her nightmare. She'd been too traumatized to fully appreciate it at the time. Her irritation ebbed away, and in its place crept the familiar yearning, the self-conscious awareness she always experienced around him. She found it hard to believe she'd been shouting at him moments before.

She looked at the floor, the patient bed, anywhere but at him. "I apologize for being quarrelsome."

"Do not apologize. I am not sorry in the least. I found it enlightening." He offered a half-smile.

"In what way, exactly? In a 'Hazel is actually combative' sort of enlightening?"

"In a 'We can disagree and still maintain civility' sort of enlightening. I am glad of it." His smile grew. "We've never argued before. I suspect it has happened now in part because you have finally realized a fundamental truth."

She smiled. "What would that be?"

"That you and I are equals."

She couldn't conjure a response, witty or otherwise, and she felt a blush creep upward from her neck.

"Now that we have moved to a different plane, I expect a fair round of shouting at least weekly."

She laughed. "I shall try to think of reasons to be irritated."

"If the well runs dry, I shall manufacture some for you."

She extended her hand, and he took it. "Agreed," she said.

"Agreed." He held her hand for a long moment, only releasing it, slowly, when a knock sounded on the door.

"Hazel, dear?" The count's voice sounded from the other side.

Hazel released a sigh and opened the door, allowing Dravor to step into the room. "Uncle, hello."

"Renton informed me you sought an audience with me?" His voice was deep, resonating in the small room. His accented English was clear and precise.

Hazel nodded. "I wondered how long it will be until we surface near Greece. I'm anxious to send a telegram to my mother."

"Eighteen to twenty-four hours." He frowned, the very epitome of paternal concern. "Renton told me you seemed agitated. Is anything amiss?"

Curse that Renton! Aside from her hand-wringing, she'd presented a calm facade!

"No, nothing is amiss." She sighed, knowing he would see through the flimsy lie. "I am simply anxious to send a message to my mother, as I said. And to meet my sister. And I am worried about Miss Tucker. I can't imagine who is responsible for her accident, since it clearly was not the doctor's 'ton."

Dravor frowned. "Yes, Dr. MacInnes informed me of his findings after analyzing the tins. Have you any suspicions?"

She pulled her brows together in faux thought. "I haven't a clue. I thought it odd that Renton was on the scene so quickly, but he was clearly closer than we were."

"Mmm. Clearly." Dravor settled his hand on her shoulder. "I shall be on Deck One in my office, should you have need of me."

The count nodded to Sam, gently squeezed Hazel's

shoulder as if they were affectionate relatives, and left the room. Hazel watched his progress through the open door as he crossed the hall and headed up the Grand Staircase.

"Did you notice?" she said to Sam as the count disappeared from view. "He didn't once ask after Sally's welfare."

Chapter 17

Hazel paused outside the Main Room before dinner. "Table is still being set," she told Sam, looking over to where the count sat with Renton.

Sam glanced in the room, appearing to make a mental note of the number of servants. "I'll go check on the patient. I've postponed moving her from the infirmary because I'm concerned about her continued unresponsiveness. I would rather have her close at hand for safety's sake; Eugene will carry materials up, and we shall create a makeshift infirmary in her cabin."

Hazel nodded, then a thought struck, and she swallowed. "If I have a mad spell in my sleep, it may not be safe to have her close to me." The notion made her ill.

"We can trust Eugene, and we can keep him at her bedside. You'll rest easier, and Sally will be protected day and night." He frowned. "If she doesn't awaken soon . . ."

She watched Sam descend the stairs to Deck Three. He had been preoccupied the entire day, instructing Eugene to run diagnostic tests on Sally, who lay as unresponsive and cold as ever. Hazel offered another transfusion, but Sam preferred to wait.

She turned her attention to the duo in the Main Room, swallowed a sudden knot of nerves, and then forced a smile. The men rose when she approached, and Renton sketched a quick bow. "I'll leave you to your dinner."

The count nodded at him and indicated an empty seat near the hearth for Hazel. He sat opposite her with a smile. "We've a few minutes before dinner. Perhaps you'd like a drink?"

"No, thank you, but I would enjoy some conversation." She smiled. "In fact, I have a question. I am curious why you would employ a human servant or assistant when 'ton programming can produce something more efficient."

"Ah, there are some duties best performed by an actual living, breathing person. I could never utilize an impersonal machine as my personal assistant."

She wondered if that was a subtle dig at Sam, but didn't comment on it.

"Tell me more about my mother," she said impulsively.

His brows lifted in surprise. "Your mother? Hmm. Your mother was a beautiful woman, truly striking. She was kind and generous, even as she lay dying."

It was an odd thing to remark upon, and Hazel felt a sudden chill.

A 'ton quietly appeared at the count's side with a drink. Dravor took a sip, his eyes closing in pleasure. "When one goes for a time without simple pleasures, experiencing them again is all the sweeter."

She shook her head. "Have you known times of destitution or loss, then?"

He smiled and swirled the liquid in his glass. "I simply mean when away from home. I did not bring an adequate supply of my creature comforts from the *Magellan* to my new London house." He took another sip. "You are the very image of your mother, and it haunts me."

Hazel hoped she managed an appropriately sympathetic expression at his declaration, but her heart skipped a beat. There was a ring of truth to his words, and Hazel had no doubt that, if nothing else, she reminded Dravor of someone he'd lost. "You were fond of her, then?"

"I was. Her death was untimely and cruel."

"It would be natural, I suppose, to hold some level of resentment toward me or my sister because of it."

He frowned. "Why would I do that?"

"She died due to complications in childbirth, yes?"

He dipped his head in acknowledgment. "I certainly would never blame you and Marit. You were innocent victims. If anyone is to be held accountable, it would be the midwife."

"Do you suspect nefarious intent?"

"Ineptitude."

"What happened to her? The midwife?"

"She met with a mysterious illness not long after your mother passed. Strange thing that circulated through the village. It took her husband, as well." He spoke with no inflection, no overt malice, but Hazel still shivered with unease. There was simply no emotion in his voice at all.

"You expect I should feel some remorse, I suppose?" His mouth lifted in a half-smile.

Hazel realized her guard was down, and her thoughts were likely written on her face. "I would assume not, as you hold her responsible for both my mother's death and the abduction."

He nodded.

"Tell me about your parents."

He seemed surprised. "What do you wish to know about them?"

"They are my grandparents, after all. Unless they're still living, I'll never meet them."

He chuckled. "No, they are most definitely not still living."

"Did they succumb to the same illness that swept the village?"

"No." He set his glass of brandy aside. "My father murdered my mother."

Hazel swallowed.

"He then met with his own violent end. Eastern tradition would define it as 'karma.'"

"How long ago did this occur?"

"Long before you were born."

"And you and my mother were the only children?"

He inclined his head.

Hazel was digging for information but had no idea what she was looking for. He shared only bits and pieces, threads, and they were barely connected. Far from giving her a satisfactory picture, she had nothing even resembling a discernible image. Mulling over the things he'd just shared, she wondered if she had the stomach to hear much more. Her family history was not shaping up very prettily. Life with Rowena was taking on a rather rosy hue.

She regarded him with what she hoped would pass for sympathy. "You've been alone for some time, as an adult, at least."

"I do not mind solitude."

"You've never been tempted to marry?"

He smiled. "I was unable to find a woman who shared my interests and passions."

"Surely in the village or countryside there existed a woman who wouldn't have minded the title of countess?" She smiled, wanting him to believe she was only making small talk but feeling like a mouse darting in front of a cat.

"Ah, again," he said, steepeling his fingers, "there has never been a creature noble enough for that lofty title. In fact, there has not been a countess at Castle Petrescu since my mother."

A possible chink in the armor? "You loved her very much."

"I did. She was a gifted Light Magick witch who was much too gentle for someone like my father."

"She protected you from him," Hazel guessed.

He smiled and picked up his glass of brandy, swirling the liquid. "Are you painting a portrait of me in your head, my dear?"

"You must grant me some level of inquisitiveness. I've only just discovered my true ancestry and have much to learn."

"And learning is your forte." He tipped his head. "I wonder if that, perhaps, is the most significant of your gifts."

She smiled tightly. She was not prepared to discuss her talents with him. "It is my only gift."

"Ah, I disagree. You forget, I observed your actions in the infirmary. Miss Tucker would certainly have died if not for your help."

"Sam had the situation well in hand."

He raised his brows. "'Sam.' Not 'Dr. MacInnes,' as you would have had me believe at first."

"Of course. I did not know you, was not familiar with you in the least. The level of my friendship with anyone was none of your concern." Hazel decided to add "Antagonistic Back Talk with Frightening Man" to her list of brave accomplishments.

"What is the level of your friendship with the good doctor?"

She smiled. "Are you perhaps painting a mental portrait of me?"

He chuckled. "Oh, I had obtained a fairly complete portrait of you before we ever met. I am merely now finding levels I did not expect."

Her heart thumped hard again. "And how did you paint this portrait of me before we met?"

"My dear, I have helpers everywhere."

Sam returned, and Hazel was glad for a natural end to the conversation. Dinner progressed formally, stiffly, and the count was pensive, less conversant than usual. They finished quickly and said their good nights.

Sam had also been quiet, and she turned to him as they left the Main Room.

"What is it?"

He frowned and led her by the elbow to the stairs. "I've had two 'ton medical assistants sitting with Sally when I've not been there. They insisted they never left the room, but a bruise has appeared on Sally's throat, and they claim ignorance of it."

Hazel's heart skipped a beat. She lifted her skirt and followed Sam quickly down the stairs. "Have you seen anything like it? Bruises that spontaneously appear?"

He shook his head. Eugene stood outside the infirmary but moved aside as they approached. "Has anyone attempted to enter?"

"No. It has been quiet." Eugene opened the door to reveal Sally, still sleeping.

Hazel entered and turned up the lamp next to the bed. Sally's beautiful red hair reflected the light and was a stark contrast to her skin.

Sam wiped his hands on a clean cloth and gently turned Sally's chin to the side. "Here." He pointed to a faint smudge on the young woman's neck.

Hazel frowned and leaned closer. "There are several bruises, rather like—" She sucked in a breath, and her heart beat hard, once, and then raced. "Like this." She demonstrated with her hand, hovering over Sally's throat. "Fingers. They are finger marks."

Sam's jaw clenched, and he moved to her side. He pulled the lamp closer and illuminated the dark stains against the pale throat. He held his fingers next to the marks, and Hazel saw his line of thought. She held hers open next to his.

"Someone with small hands did this." She paused. "There are very few women aboard. I might suspect one of the medical 'tons, but their strength is immense. Her throat would have been instantly crushed."

"Unless she was interrupted."

Hazel looked again at her own hands. She backed up, horrified, and held her hands out from her, examining them as though outside herself. "Did I do this? Did I walk in my sleep, last night, perhaps?" She looked up at Sam, who straightened and shook his head.

"No, Hazel, no."

"You cannot know that! I didn't dream last night, but that doesn't mean I didn't wander, didn't come down here—"

"Hazel, I instructed Eugene to stand watch in the hallway outside your door all night."

She stopped, her mouth falling open. "You did?"

He nodded. "If you left the cabin, I wanted to know. Everything was quiet. You didn't leave, didn't make a sound. Besides, these marks were not here earlier in the day. They didn't appear until just before dinner, so it must have happened fairly recently."

Sam removed the infirmary telescriber from the wall and punched in a message. "I want the medical 'tons' this immediately."

"Are you requesting it from Dravor?"

"Yes."

"Whoever tried to kill her doesn't want her to awaken." She bit her lip and looked at Sally's inert form. "What if the initial accident had nothing to do with an attempt on her life?"

Sam looked at her.

"What if someone was looking to steal a kiss? Or worse?"

He rubbed the back of his neck. "And she ran. Fell or was shoved, landed on the spear."

"Renton." Hazel bit the name out and felt a surge of anger. "He was there, he stammered all over himself when we appeared, and then he blamed Eugene."

"The count wasn't far behind." Sam raised a brow.

She shook her head. "I don't believe he's guilty—of the initial attack, I mean. He seemed wary, and then furious." She frowned. "I don't wish to defend him, but he was . . . he wasn't surprised."

"Renton would have access to the 'ton programming tins. Does he possess enough knowledge to use one of the nurses to kill her?"

"I don't know. I find him boorish, but that doesn't mean he can't punch in a simple code."

"Doctor, shall I check the Tesla Room records to see who programmed tins today?" Eugene waited for Sam's reply.

"Yes, and check yesterday, also."

Hazel frowned and used the connecting door to enter the operating room. She crossed to the equipment and looked at the ether delivery machine.

Sam joined her by her side. "What are you thinking?"

"I am wishing we had a method of determining whether this has been used on Sally since the surgery."

Sam sighed lightly. "Too many of us have handled it since. After I finished, Eugene handed it to one of the medical 'tons, and they were tasked with cleaning and storing the machine and mask . . ." He shrugged.

Hazel looked over her shoulder at the other room. "Who else besides the 'tons would know how to operate it?" she asked quietly. "Renton? Doubtful, but possible. My uncle? I would think so."

"We do not even know if this happened."

"Why else would she have never regained consciousness? She is still asleep!"

"I haven't a clue." Sam shook his head, his brows drawn. "We must move her tonight."

Chapter 18

His telescriber pinged, and Sam rolled over in bed. After two unsuccessful attempts to grab the thing, he finally made contact and closed his fingers around it. He squinted and read the message from Eugene.

Miss Hazel is leaving the cabin. I cannot stop her. I must remain with Miss Tucker.

Sam cursed and sat upright. He shoved his legs into the trousers he'd discarded only an hour before and searched for a shirt. He'd had trouble falling asleep, and now he figured he shouldn't have even bothered.

He abandoned the search for yesterday's shirt and instead yanked a fresh one hanging in the wardrobe. His gut was in knots, and he wondered if he wouldn't be mad himself before too long.

His worry for Hazel had reached new heights. The night he'd interrupted her nightmare and broken her odd connection to her twin, he'd been afraid. Afraid he wouldn't be there soon enough next time, afraid that if her trancelike sleep repeated itself, it might be worse. He'd given Eugene instructions to alert him to any unusual activity concerning Hazel during the night, and was grateful for the foresight.

He managed a few buttons on his shirt, and shoving his feet into his shoes, pulled open the door.

The hall was dimly lit; the sconces had been turned down for the night. The *Magellan*'s engines remained a steady, constant hum, but otherwise, all was still. Hazel was nowhere in sight. He tried her door and found it unlocked, but when he entered and saw only Eugene and Sally, realized she must have moved quickly.

Where would she go? If she were dreaming, connecting somehow with a woman who was locked in a room, whether literal or figurative, what would she want to see?

He knew a moment's panic. Marit considered herself trapped, captive. She would want to escape. There were mechanisms in place that would prevent Hazel from opening the submersible's top hatch, but would she have the capacity to instruct a 'ton to do so?

He could only hope Petrescu's programming safeguarded against it. To be safe, he ran up the stairs to Deck One and then the length of the corridor to the short series of steps to the top tier and the hatch that opened to the outside world.

Which was empty except for one 'ton who stood guard.

He turned and sprinted for the Tesla Room. He didn't know how much of Hazel was present when Marit visited her dreams. Marit might not know how to code tins for automatons, but Hazel certainly did.

To his relief, the Tesla Room was also empty of human activity, with only two 'tons on guard and three others against the wall, charging. He ignored one who asked if he needed assistance and made his way down the hall, checking the library and the conservatory. He even tried the count's door, which was locked.

He descended to Deck Two, glanced in the Main Room, which was eerily empty and dimly lit. Perhaps she might have gone to the infirmary? He jogged down the steps to the next level and checked each open door.

Frustrated, he stopped long enough to plug into the scriber attachment in the infirmary and asked Eugene if Hazel had returned to her cabin. When he received a response in the negative, he took a deep breath and made for the bottom deck.

"Hazel, where in blazes are you?" he muttered under his breath.

He checked the maintenance room, which was locked, and the engine room, which contained only 'tons. That left the Control Room. If she wasn't there, he would awaken the count and instigate a search.

He held his breath and opened one of the two adjoining doors. The room inside was dim, lit only by the instrumentation readings glowing in greens and yellows. The exterior lights had been switched on, illuminating the depths outside the window, and before the glass panels stood a figure in a white gown, curls hanging down her shoulders and back.

Her hands pressed against the glass, and she had rested one knee atop the cushioned window seat.

He leaned against the doorframe, weak with relief.

He lifted a hand in greeting to Winston, the 'ton at the controls, and quietly crossed the room to the windows. He sat on the cushions near Hazel and looked at her face, which glowed a pale green from the reflected lights.

Her eyes were huge, and her smile was one of pure joy. His throat suddenly ached, and he swallowed past the lump that formed there.

She murmured something, and he leaned closer, trying to hear. It was an odd smattering of English and what he assumed was Romanian.

" . . . seen all of these in my books . . . the most beautiful sight . . ."

She occasionally shook her head as if confused, and then a pained expression crossed her face. She leaned her forehead against the glass and closed her eyes. When a tear slid down her cheek, he decided he'd seen enough.

"Hazel," he whispered. "Hazel, love, can you hear me?"

She turned her head, and her eyes flew open. She stumbled away from him with a string of Romanian and fell to the floor.

"No, Hazel, I'll not hurt you—" He reached for her, crouched down on the floor, but she scooted backward until she was up against the window seat.

She whispered incoherently, terrified, and looked at him with blank eyes.

"Marit?" he whispered. He tried again, using the rolled *R* he'd heard the count use.

She stilled, her posture relaxed. She continued watching him, wary, but calmer.

He wished Eugene were there—he was programmed with a multitude of languages.

"Marit, I need Hazel." He doubted she understood, but took a spark of hope from a flicker of recognition in her eyes.

"Hazel? Will you awaken? I need you here."

She blinked repeatedly, then cried out softly again in Romanian and rubbed her forehead. She pushed the heels of her palms into her eyes and shuddered. With a quiet gasp, she lifted her face and stared at him.

"Hazel? Please, please be Hazel."

She looked around and slowly sat up straight. She shoved her hair back from her face and gathered it at the nape of her neck, holding it in place as she twisted around and looked at the windows.

She released a shuddering sigh and looked back at him. "Sam, what is happening?"

Chapter 19

Hazel looked around the Control Room with a strange sense of knowing she'd gone there but unable to remember how. Bits of images flashed through her mind, combinations of Marit's room and the *Magellan*. She'd been driven to explore, had known what Marit would like to see, but the rest was a muddle until she heard Sam.

"I am afraid," she whispered, hating that she felt it so keenly, hating to admit it aloud. "I am afraid."

He extended his hands to her, and she scooted over to him, still on the floor. She pulled her knees up and hugged them tightly. He wrapped his arms around her, smoothing her hair, and she rested her head against his shoulder.

"What am I going to do?"

"Do not fret, love. I will help you. Yes?"

She nodded, bumping her head against his chin. "Yes." She paused, her eyes burning with tears. "I am so sorry." She caught her breath on a sob. "Sam, I am so very sorry! What have I led you into?"

"Shh, none of that. I'm not sorry, not in the least. I would choose to be here with you, again and again. No apologies."

"But this is a disaster. I may never sleep peacefully again without having to share my brain with a madwoman!"

She felt him smile, but still knew exactly how his face would look. "We'll reach her soon, and then help her. When that happens, she'll no longer need to see the world through your eyes."

"I am simply not going to sleep. I will remain awake until we reach her."

"As your physician, I advise against that course of action."

"Sleeplessness cannot possibly be worse than this."

"Believe me when I say it is. I've seen soldiers go for days on end without sleep. I cannot recommend it in good conscience."

She felt a smile creep up, which surprised her. She'd been convinced only one minute before that she'd never smile again. "I suppose I shall devise another plan, then."

"That is a much better idea." He slowly, softly brushed her hair away from her eyes and rubbed his thumb against her temple.

She was becoming warmer by degrees, and she wrapped her arm around his. His muscle was firm beneath her fingertips, solid, smooth, and secure. She closed her eyes and placed a kiss on his arm, hoping he didn't feel it but knowing she would expire if she didn't do it.

She loved him with her whole heart. She always had. She didn't know the extent of his affections, if he would ever think of her as more than a cherished friend, but while he held her close and smoothed her hair, she could pretend. She sighed, and despite everything, wished she could remain in that moment forever.

He seemed content to indulge her unspoken wish, but she knew he was probably sore from sitting so long on the floor. She slowly lifted her head and offered him a tremulous smile. He was so close, his mouth inches from her temple, and she held her breath, wondering if he would place a kiss there in return for the one she'd given him.

He looked at her for some time, and then finally, as if having made a decision, shifted the slightest bit. "Not when you're vulnerable." He whispered it so softly she wasn't certain she'd understood.

He stood with a small grunt, putting his hand at the small of his back as he stretched. She took his offered hand and quietly left the Control Room with him, grateful when he encircled her again with his arm to chase away the chill. She shook her head when he indicated the lift, and they climbed the stairs instead. She didn't want the noise of the lift to alert any more 'tons. She didn't want to contemplate the number that may have seen her running through the halls, out of her head.

Sam walked into her cabin, made a cursory check of the water closet and of the adjoining room, where Sally slept and Eugene kept a faithful vigil. He urged her to bed and tucked the covers around her as one would a child.

"I'll sit here until you sleep again." He indicated the chairs by the hearth, which were comfortable, but not for sleep.

"Sam, no. I am fine now. You go back to your bed. You're

the one who provided a lecture on the evils of sleep deprivation."

"Did I forget to mention those rules apply to everyone but me?" He paused, then kissed his fingertip and touched it to her nose. "Close your eyes."

"I—"

"Hazel. Go to sleep. Should I need to stretch out, this carpet is thicker than most cots I slept on in the military."

He sat in one of the chairs and leaned back, his long legs stretched in front of him.

Now that she was lucid, she was mortified. "Sam, please—"

"Hazel, I'll not say it again. As your doctor, I am ordering you to sleep."

Her lips twitched. "You cannot do that."

"I can and I am. Not another word out of you."

She decided to save her breath. She turned to her side, facing him, and pulled the duvet close under her chin. If she hadn't loved him already, by now she was well and truly sunk.

Her eyes drifted closed, and she felt her body relax. Bless all things holy, Marit must have also gone to sleep. Perhaps she would get a few hours' rest before breakfast.

When she awoke later, she checked her watch. She'd overslept by an hour, and her head ached. She needed some tea. When she sat up, she noted the empty chair in the sitting area. She smiled. Her protector had stayed long enough to see that she was resting peacefully.

On the nightstand to her left sat a cup and saucer, tendrils of heat rising from it. She felt tears threaten as she carefully lifted the cup to her nose. Her favorite breakfast tea, steeped to her preference, and contained in her favorite teacup from the clinic. It was ivory china with delicate yellow flowers and twisting green vines, and she wondered if by some miracle, the *Magellan* carried the same pattern she happened to love.

She took a sip and closed her eyes in bliss before looking carefully at the rim near the handle. There was a tiny chip, so small as to be invisible at first glance. No, this was *her* cup, which meant Sam must have packed it for her, just in case.

She indulged herself in the softness of the bed and the warmth of the tea for a few luxurious minutes before facing the day.

It was time to make a plan.

Chapter 20

Hazel climbed the staircase to the top level of the *Magellan* to beard the lion in his lair. The *Magellan* would reach Romania soon, and Hazel had decided she would not travel one foot in any direction other than home without some answers from her uncle.

She had been stewing over Marit's welfare, convinced her sister was being held captive, and she wanted confirmation from the count. Though she still believed he might be a vampire, she wasn't concerned for her safety. Dravor had specific reasons for taking her to Marit, and he couldn't hurt her until his purposes—whatever they were—had been accomplished.

In addition to her concerns for Marit, the issue of Sally's "accident" and continued unconscious state, not to mention the bruising on her neck, had not yet been addressed. She did not trust Renton and wanted Sally to confirm his identity as the man who had caused, even inadvertently, her injury.

She was exhausted from a night filled with cries for help echoing through her head, and then an unexpected adventure to the Control Room. Even now she felt trapped, as though she were also locked away, unable to get out or speak to anyone. Stirrings of desperation flitted in and out of her thoughts, and she fought to remain calm. Panicked, racing heartbeats struck intermittently without warning, accompanied by waves of horror.

She paused at Dravor's study door, nerves stretched taut. She wanted to speak to him without anyone else around. Sam was big and protective, and his hostility toward their host was thinly veiled, if at all. She wanted Dravor's unfettered comments and would judge for herself if he was telling her the truth.

Besides, between bouts of possible insanity, she was all aflutter after her embrace and almost-kiss with Sam the night before. She'd told Sam she needed some time alone in her suite this morning, and when he'd headed for the infirmary, she'd made a beeline for the stairs.

She knocked firmly on her uncle's study door. She heard nothing inside, but she knew Dravor often worked there after breakfast.

Deciding Dravor had lied or was otherwise detained elsewhere, she turned to go. Then the door opened, and her uncle stood at the threshold, brows raised in surprise.

"Hazel?"

She swallowed and turned back on her heel. It wasn't difficult to pretend she was nervous. She wanted him to believe he had the upper hand with her, always—and frankly, he did—because she knew any civil relationship with him depended on her ability to keep her hostility and mistrust hidden.

"Have you time for a word with me?" She folded her

hands in front of her though she felt the urge to wring them and pace. Nervousness was one thing, but she needn't show abject fear. She did have her pride, after all.

His smile transformed his face, and she noted again the handsome visage that should have been welcoming, but it was as though something skeletal and rotted shifted beneath the surface. Her heart hammered in her chest. Before she could decide if her eyes were playing tricks, his appearance was normal—nothing out of the ordinary.

"Certainly! I always have time for you. Please, come in." He stepped back and held the door open as she entered.

She'd caught the barest glimpse of the room from the tour he'd given her and Sam initially. She took in the details now, with an interest she hadn't expected. The room was large, richer in tone than the rest of the *Magellan*, and aesthetically beautiful. She guessed the wood paneling and rafters to be combinations of cherry and oak, and a large desk situated on the opposite wall was a substantial piece of mahogany. A smaller side table sat in a comfortable seating area in the right corner, flanked by two chairs. The room itself was dim until Dravor turned the knobs on a few elegant sconces and lamps.

To her left, built-in shelving housed items that showcased the count's widely traveled past. A small item caught her eye, and she moved to the shelf, delighted in spite of herself. "This is an ancient American totem! Isla has one, but I suspect hers is a newer replica. This one appears quite old." She looked at Dravor, who watched her with satisfaction.

"I procured that piece last year in Port Lucy. I am quite proud of it, I do not mind admitting. I've searched for years to find it, tracking it from the American states. How it found itself in a small voodoo shop on the isles is anyone's guess."

She looked in wonder at the rest of the collection, noting extremely old statuary, bits and pieces of broken medallions, and artifacts representing a multitude of cultures.

"You recognize many of these items, I presume?" he asked, standing just behind her.

She jumped at his unexpected nearness and glanced at him, forcing a smile. "I do. I read voraciously, and histories of cultures and peoples specifically hold my interest." She paused and looked back at the shelves. "These are very old. I daresay many are original."

He nodded.

She waited, but he didn't elaborate, and the silence between them stretched. Rather than ask why such items were in an obscure nobleman's personal collection rather than in a museum where all could admire them, she opted for a benign observation instead.

"You must derive great pleasure in owning them. I cannot imagine a student of history or the arts who would not wish to see them." She paused and confessed, "I am in awe. They're beautiful."

He smiled and indicated a chair in the seating area. She took it as he went to a small mahogany bar near his desk. "A drink? Something mild—grape juice, perhaps?"

"That would be lovely, thank you."

He poured two glasses of light liquid and offered her one before taking the other chair. "From the purest white grapes on earth. I own a small vineyard in Italy. We shall visit sometime, if you like."

The words should have been lovely and full of warmth. Yet every time he said something socially appropriate that, coming from anyone else, would have sounded normal, she felt something was off, like dissonant notes in her ear. The utter lack of emotion in his voice when he spoke was the most chilling part of all. He smiled, he laughed, his voice paused in all the right places, rose and fell depending on the sentiment behind the statement—there just was no sentiment behind the statement. As much as she looked, intentionally watched for it, she knew he did not care about her welfare for her sake. He wanted her for some purpose she had yet to divine.

She was struck with a sudden pang of yearning, a wish that he would have filled the gap that she had always felt when she watched other people's interactions with their fathers. Her interests overlapped Dravor's; the things they had in common should have brought them closer together, but she found herself unable to make a connection with him.

Why could he not have simply been what he claimed? She would give the world for a father like him, and yet, she knew to her soul he was not all he seemed. Perhaps she was truly going mad after all. When she looked at him now, she saw nothing out of the ordinary, certainly not skull bones or decaying flesh.

She sipped the juice, which was light, crisp, and sweet. She clasped the glass with two hands in her lap while her uncle took a drink and then settled likewise.

"Now, Hazel, dearest. How may I be of service to you?"

She took a quiet breath and steadied her nerves. "I am worried about Marit."

He wrinkled his forehead but then smoothed it again.

"Why is that? You have concerns beyond the things I've told you?"

"But therein lies the problem. You've told me very little about her, and if there is something I can do, something to learn or study that might help her when we arrive, I would very much like to do that." She dared not tell him Marit had been visiting her, that she felt her presence more keenly with each mile that brought them closer together. She didn't want Dravor monitoring her sleep, hoping to witness one of Marit's "dreaming visits."

He watched her carefully before saying, "Your sister suffers from delusions, I fear. She seems to have lost her grasp of reality. She paces; she mutters nonsense." He lifted his shoulders. "I am at a loss. Short of institutionalizing her, I do not know how to help her."

She was impressed he'd finally told her the truth. "I see. I'll use your library to research illnesses of the mind—I believe I saw a volume or two on the subject." She paused. "Is she— Is Marit . . . Does she live with you in your home?"

"Oh, yes. Her entire life. I've provided her with every comfort, have seen to her every need." He frowned, affecting a look of concern. "That I have been unable to help her has troubled me greatly."

"You said it seems she has lost her grasp of reality. Does that mean she once possessed it? Was she clearheaded before and only now exhibiting signs of illness?"

He nodded. "The changes began just over a year ago."

She filed the information away for later use. Perhaps something had happened a year ago, perhaps not. She needed to think, to make some notes. "One more issue troubles me. I am concerned about my maid, Sally."

"Ah. The poor girl. I am concerned she remains unresponsive." His brows drew together. "Naturally, I am ultimately responsible for her welfare, and when we surface, I shall telegraph her mother to see if she would like Sally returned home."

"In an unconscious state?"

"My dear, if she does not awaken, there is little anyone can do for her. She may as well be with loved ones."

Hazel's fingers tightened on her glass. "I would very much like to know who hurt her."

He tipped his head. "Whom do you suppose would have reason?"

"Perhaps someone who found her attractive? Or easy prey?" Did she dare name Renton as the man she suspected?

"I ought to have considered it earlier, but there may have been 'tons that day who were in close proximity and recorded the events. Perhaps we might glean information from those records. It will take some time, but I'll instruct the Tesla Room operators to begin preliminary work." He paused. "Will that be to your satisfaction?"

She nodded. "And to yours, I hope. I am certain you wish to solve this mystery, eradicate any danger, as quickly as possible."

"Of course. I do appreciate your concern for Miss Tucker. You're kind to show such attention for a servant." He took another swallow of his juice, watching her over the rim of his glass.

She was able to twitch a smile, barely. "My life has not been so different from hers."

He nodded gravely. "I cannot tell you how it pains me that so much time was lost before I found you. You've been noble since birth, yet have been forced to live well below your station."

"My life has been a good one. Rewarding and filled with love. My mother worked diligently so I might go to school and acquire skills."

He watched her for a moment before smiling and lifting his glass. "Indeed. To Rowena Hughes."

A chill chased down Hazel's arms. "To Rowena." She sipped her juice and then changed the subject. "Tell me what brings you the most joy in your collections." She indicated the shelves across the room.

He took a breath and released a sigh. "Hazel, you are of magick blood. Thus, you know there are elements of life bound in earthly science and other matters that take on an ethereal quality. Some might define them as 'unexplainable.'"

She nodded. "I've found most people tolerate the idea of magick, even while wary of the power behind it."

"That power is as real as the gravity that anchors us to the ground, or the air we breathe."

"Yes."

"Has it been your experience that magick can tie itself to physical objects? That whether by natural means or spells commanded by a gifted witch—Light or Dark—earthly items can absorb and contain a power of their own?"

She glanced at her gold chain encircling her wrist.

"Exactly." His voice rose in conviction. "That is exactly

my meaning. Your mother charmed that length of gold, and through it, gifted you with an affinity to gold in general." He placed his glass on the side table and leaned forward. "That simple piece of jewelry"—he pointed at her bracelet—"has become a physical manifestation of magick." He sat back in his chair. "Healing magick, I believe."

She followed his logic and turned her eyes to the shelves holding priceless antiquities. "Do you mean to suggest the pieces you collect possess magical properties?"

He nodded once. "Precisely."

They were silent, and she realized the glass in her hands was slick from her sweating palms. She carefully placed it on the table and turned her attention again to the far wall, her imagination now lending the inanimate objects a life of their own.

"Hazel, my dear," he said. "I would like to show you something. Look at that wall." He indicated with a flick of his finger to her right.

She leaned forward and gasped. A portrait hung there, a woman with a child at her knee, and it was large enough that she should have seen it immediately upon entering. Yet it had not been there a moment ago. The colors were vibrant, the subjects arresting, lifelike, but what stopped her cold was the woman's face. It was the very image Hazel saw each morning in her mirror.

Chapter 21

Hazel pushed herself slowly from the chair and took a few steps forward to examine the portrait fully. It was as though the artist had seated Hazel and a child only that morning and painted their likenesses with incredible skill. The only disparity between Hazel and the woman was the clothing—the clothing style in the portrait had been worn in the Middle Ages. The dress was a long sheath with a braided rope around the waist, and her long curls were parted in the middle, with a circlet adorning her head. The painting itself and its frame, though, showed no age.

"What is this?" Her voice was hoarse.

"That is a portrait of my mother and me."

She felt her uncle's eyes on her as she stared at the picture. "Surely now you accept the truthfulness of my claim. If you doubted before, here is proof of our relation."

Still, she stared. "Why did you not show this to me before?"

"I did not see the need. The proof was evident enough

in Rowena's reaction and your own birthmark that matches mine." He rose from the chair and stood beside her, studying the portrait dispassionately. "You knew I spoke the truth from the first moment. You will not admit it, but it is true."

She lifted a shoulder, confirming his statement by not admitting any such thing.

"I was prepared to show you and your mother this, if necessary. It is rather cumbersome, so I had hoped to avoid carrying it around London."

Her heart thrummed steadily. The image unnerved her, although it wasn't unreasonable for her to resemble her own grandmother. "Your mother had an affinity for the Middle Ages?"

"Yes. We periodically sat for her favorite artist, and each time she chose a different era for our clothing. This one is my favorite."

She studied the child, features that showed a very young Dravor Petrescu, one hand on his mother's knee. There was a softness to the mother's face, and the sense of affection she felt for the child was evident in the slight angle of her body toward him. Protective.

Hazel swallowed. "Why did I not see this when we entered?"

"Because I hid it."

She finally tore her eyes from it and looked at him. "I never saw you move it, and there is no curtain or panel to obscure it."

"Look again."

She looked, and the portrait was gone. "What magick is this?" she demanded.

"I funded a recent excursion to the polar regions. My scientists recovered an odd ship buried in the ice, one that had settled deep below the surface. Among several mundane pieces of pottery and various supplies, they found this." He pulled his hand from his pocket and held it out to her. Sitting in his palm was a flat stone, perfectly round, and translucent white. "Take it," he urged.

She touched her fingertip to the stone, which was smooth and cool. She glanced up at his face, which bore a pleasant mask, and with reluctant curiosity, took the stone. "To whom did this belong?" She examined it, nestled in her palm.

"A Nordic tribe, predating even those we consider ancient. One of their practitioners of magick—legend does not identify who—created a spell that would render an object invisible to an enemy. That object could be a person, an animal, an entire ship. The spell was tied to this stone, and the bearer controls it."

Hazel turned the stone over in her palm. "Any bearer?"

Dravor chuckled. "Very astute. No, only one of magick affinity."

She frowned. "What are the mechanics of it?"

"The spell?" His voice rose in surprise. "It works as any spell does."

She shook her head. "All magick has its roots in science. One cannot simply defy laws that govern physical properties. What seems magical to the lay person is actually an extension of principles we already know. I do not understand how all spells work, but I do know I cannot create something out of nothing, nor can I make something become immaterial."

He smiled. "Energy, which is what you use to heal. Displacement of the elements that form the physical makeup of the object." He indicated the portrait. "Close your fingers around the stone and envision the portrait melting into the wall behind it."

She followed his instructions and felt waves of energy stretch between herself and the painting, the kind of waves she saw during hot days outside. The portrait shimmered before her, translucent and hazy, but not entirely gone from her view. "I still see it."

"But I do not."

She looked at Dravor, who raised a brow and nodded. "Truly. It is gone from my view."

Hazel regarded the shimmering portrait for a moment and then released the image. It returned to the wall as before, real and solid.

"You learn quickly. But patience is a virtue with these objects. You must understand that proficiency with bigger items and living objects requires a fair amount of practice. In fact—"

Hazel held an image of herself in her head and closed her fingers around the cool stone.

Dravor abruptly stopped speaking, and then he muttered a short Romanian word, probably a curse, under his breath.

She looked down at her own arms, which now shimmered, ghostlike. Her heart skipped a beat at the oddity of the phenomenon, but also at the ease with which she had commanded it. She released the spell, and her form returned.

Dravor watched her, his gaze stoic and calculating, and then finally turned up a corner of his mouth. He held out his hand. "You've more talent than I realized."

She placed the stone back in his hand. "Why did you hide the portrait from me?"

He nodded his head toward it. "Had you noticed it immediately upon entering, your visit's purpose would have been forgotten, and I was curious to know the reason you would venture here alone, without your doctor or his 'ton for protection."

Her head spun as she looked at the shelves full of artifacts. "Am I to understand that each of those objects is bound to a spell?"

He followed her eyes and shrugged. "Some of them. Not all."

She felt cold. "And do you have a purpose behind your ownership of these magical tools?"

Dravor sighed and put his hand on her shoulder, subtly guiding her toward the door. "Ah, my dear, the world is a chessboard, and while I do appreciate a good game, my purposes behind my collection are innocent. I simply enjoy owning them. I have no grand plan involving their use." He smiled and opened the door. "I must finish some correspondence, but I am so glad you visited. It has been enlightening."

She stepped into the hallway, and he inclined his head in a bow, closing the door. She leaned against the wall and took a deep breath, staring down the hallway at a few 'tons, her brain still spinning. What on earth had happened? She'd come hoping for answers but had exited with questions and more than a few concerns.

What sort of power did Dravor Petrescu have at his disposal?

She pushed off the wall and made her way quickly to the stairs. By the time she reached the main level, she was skipping steps, and she ran the last stretch of hallway to her cabin, which she hastily unlocked, entered, and slammed the door. Her notebook sat on a bedside table, and she grabbed it and her pen.

Flipping to a blank page, she began sketching each item Dravor had on his shelves, closing her eyes periodically to see them again clearly. She'd skimmed over each shelf, looked at least briefly at every artifact, and she was able to draw the setting exactly as she remembered it. Once all items had been rudimentarily drawn, she wrote the culture or country of origin beneath all the artifacts she recognized. The items had originated from various points around the globe, and while the general regions were clear on many, specifics evaded her.

She snapped the book closed, grabbed her pen, then left her cabin and made her way up the stairs to the library. The whole experience had been odd. Witnessing magick spells at work often felt like watching a stage magician at work. She might have been tempted to believe her grape juice had been tainted if not for the fact that she had produced magick of her own with the Nordic rock.

Her mind felt that familiar fever of having a puzzle to work out. She was grateful beyond words that she now had somewhere to turn, something to focus on instead of feeling as though the walls were closing in and her mind was fracturing.

Her purpose in the library was threefold: research methods and rules for tying spells to objects; discern the cultures of origin for the items in Dravor's study; and uncover Dravor's ulterior motives, of which she was certain there were some.

Hazel entered the library and saw Sam at a table, absorbed in work and tapping a pencil against his well-traveled, thick notebook, the pages nearly all used. He looked up as she pulled a chair close and sat opposite him with a flourish.

"This will be good news, I hope?" His pencil stilled, his expression wary.

She leaned forward. "My uncle has a magical rock that makes things disappear."

He frowned, brows knit. He opened his mouth, then closed it. He tried again. "I'm not entirely certain what to do with this information."

She shook her head, wishing she could just open her brain and show him everything she'd seen. "He collects artifacts that are tied to spells. Ancient items, old and powerful magick." She huffed out an impatient breath. "I must read." She stood and crossed to one of the tall bookcases. She slid a ladder down its track and climbed up one rung, running her finger along several titles until she found the one she sought on elemental spells.

"Yes," she whispered, and returned to the table. She noted two 'tons in the room, dusting shelves and watching her.

In her periphery, she saw Sam glance at the door and then back to her. "What does that mean?"

"I am not certain. Yet." She flipped through the book until she came to a section on casting and utilizing physical objects as aids. "I've not seen much casting, just a few times in the Dark Quarter."

"What sort of casting—" He paused, then leaned toward her. "When were you in the Dark Quarter?"

She ran her finger down the page. "A few months ago, researching Isla's curse."

He sat back in his seat, and she finally looked up at him. She recognized the tightened lips and slight flare to his nostrils. "Do I even need to say it?" he demanded.

"No." She looked down at the book and continued turning pages. "I did what needed to be done. If I hadn't learned about the permanence of the spell, Isla would be sleeping like the dead, and Daniel Pickett would still be a disgruntled bachelor."

"The Dark Quarter, though, Hazel. Of all the places in London—I would have accompanied you." He paused again. "You thought Daniel Pickett a disgruntled bachelor?"

"That was my assessment, yes." Movement at the doorway caught her eye, and Eugene entered with a sheaf of papers.

"Your patient notes," Eugene said and handed the stack to Sam.

"So, you knew him well then? Daniel?" Sam took the papers from Eugene without looking.

Hazel shook her head as she continued looking for specific

information that proved frustratingly elusive. "Everybody said that about him. Do you never read the society pages?"

"I should say he does," Eugene said and pulled up a chair. "Every morning at breakfast, even before he reads the more serious news one would think a physician of some renown would find more relevant."

"I did not instruct you to join us," Sam told his automaton.

Hazel glanced up with a quick smile, glad his full personality and programming had been restored. "Perhaps he might be of use." She stopped her scanning and looked at Eugene. "My uncle"—she lowered her voice, leaning forward, causing Eugene to lean in as well—"has in his possession several ancient artifacts I believe may be cause for concern."

Eugene pitched his voice to match hers. "What manner of artifacts?"

"Ancient."

Eugene nodded. "So you said."

She frowned, preoccupied. "I need to know what sort of spell is tied to each object."

"Interesting." Eugene's brows pinched together. "I am finding it difficult to follow your thought process given the amount of information you've offered to this point."

"Finally," Sam muttered, "I am the superior intellect. She is saying Petrescu is in possession of ancient items which have been imbued with certain magical elements via spells, but there is no rhyme or reason as to the pairing of spell to item."

Hazel nodded. "Yes. Precisely. And they range in origin from numerous cultures, many I cannot identify, though he has a Nordic relic that renders objects invisible to the human eye."

Eugene's cogs whirred.

Hazel stream of thought continued. "Which I believe is a random coincidence. I would not think ancient Nordic cultures have enjoyed a particular talent for rendering things invisible any more than any other group of people."

"Ah." Eugene nodded.

Sam sat back in his chair, one arm stretched on the table, tapping his pencil absently. He watched Hazel with speculation, and she tensed. "You told me after breakfast you wanted to rest in your suite for a time," he said, eyes narrowing.

Drat. She sighed. "I have every right to speak to whomever I choose."

"Of course you have the right. That doesn't make it wise, Hazel. You shouldn't have spoken to him alone."

"I wanted his honest reaction to me, not the flippancy he would affect in your presence."

"And did you get it—an honest reaction?" There was a subtle bite to the question.

"Honest may be the wrong word. Different, I suppose. He showed me that stone, demonstrated it on a portrait of himself as a child with his mother. I do not think he would have done that if you had been there, or Eugene."

Sam pursed his lips. "Did Petrescu confirm that each item has some sort of magical property?"

She frowned, thinking, and flipped open her notebook. "He said some of them do. But even knowing which culture they represent, that doesn't offer clues as to the type of spell they contain." She studied her own sketches for a moment.

"May I?" Eugene offered.

She slid her notebook across the table to the 'ton. He nudged Sam's paperwork aside. Sam glared and gathered the pages, stacking them together while the 'ton placed his finger on one of Hazel's drawings.

"Islands of the Pacific," he said.

She raised her brows in surprise. "Truly? The fossil?" She handed him her pen, and he wrote the identification beneath the small sketch as she had done with others.

Eugene continued labeling sketches Hazel had left blank. He settled fully into his task and elbowed onto more of the table space.

Sam scowled and shifted his chair a few inches away from Eugene. "Hazel, what do you know of this Nordic artifact?"

Hazel shrugged. "Dravor funded an expedition to a polar region where a ship was found, buried in ice. The stone was among the items recovered."

"Could be the recent discovery of the Icemen Expedition, perhaps. I read about it in *The Times*." He cast a pointed glare in Eugene's direction.

"I did not say you never read anything of substance," Eugene said, cogs still whirring and pen still scratching.

Hazel shook her head, trying to focus. "What of this expedition?"

"The initial supposition is the crew was attempting to evade detection by a herd of polar saber-mammoth. The ice froze around the ship, and they were stranded without cover or means of escape."

Hazel sat back in her seat and folded her arms. "The sort of instance when a shield of invisibility would be beneficial."

Sam nodded, leaning on the table and tapping his pencil against his notebook. "And would have been effective had they not been facing an adversary who detects prey through scent as well as by sight."

"Did the article mention human remains at the site?" Hazel asked.

"A few scattered bones."

They fell silent, and the only noise in the room was the ticking of a clock on the wall and the quiet hum of Eugene's gears and scratch of his pen.

Hazel released a slow breath. "How in blazes am I to discover the origin story behind any of these objects? I suspect that will be the only way we will learn what sort of spell binds them."

"What do you hope to do with the information when you have it?" Sam asked.

"I want to know what sort of magic Dravor has at his disposal," she said quietly. "And if any of the spells can be reversed, or eliminated, or destroyed without destroying the object itself."

"Would you remove all of the spells?" Sam asked. "Perhaps some might be useful."

Hazel rested her elbows on the table and rubbed her temple. "I've no idea. Perhaps none of this is of any consequence. Why is he so interested in magick? Why am I so concerned with what he owns or what he does?"

"Because he is 'shady,' as my father would say, and we all recognize it. Your instincts propelled you into action and led you to this." Sam pointed at her notebook. "I've found that the times my brain and instinct are at odds, the best course is to follow my instincts."

"I would prefer to follow my brain," Hazel said. "Knowledge is power."

The corner of Sam's mouth lifted in a smile. "And you wield it well."

She rubbed her forehead, frustrated. "I cannot wield it if I do not have it."

"I can offer details about these items in a matter of hours," Eugene interjected without looking up. "Assuming they have been documented in professional journals or articles during the past two hundred years. Though, you may be interested to know that my preliminary findings suggest a trend."

Hazel and Sam looked at each other.

"What sort of trend?" she asked.

"Prolonged life."

Hazel looked at Sam, baffled. Perhaps her vampire theory had indeed been faulty all along. As a vampire, he would have access to prolonged life and wouldn't need to find it via magick artifacts.

"He's looking for prolonged life," Sam said quietly, "and you are a Healer."

She shook her head. "My skills are basic, at best. I cannot imagine the two are related. Aside from that, there are artifacts on that list that likely have nothing to do with prolonged life."

"We all know he has some purpose for you, something he wants from you." He spoke quietly, his blue eyes holding hers. "I would wager your safety with him will eventually expire."

"I appreciate your position. You see yourself as my protective faux-relative."

He leaned both elbows on the table, and with a half-grin, murmured, "Do you honestly believe my inclinations run in the 'relative' vein?"

She felt the blush on her cheeks and bit her lip to hide her smile.

"I can affirm his biorhythms do not indicate fraternal affection," Eugene said, turning a page in Hazel's notebook and jotting notes as his processors continued to spin.

Sam sighed and pressed the heel of his hand to his eyes.

Hazel smothered a giddy laugh, lovely warmth furling from her abdomen to her extremities. For months, her fondest wish had been for Sam MacInnes to regard her with something other than brotherly affection, and the fates were finally smiling upon her. If not for the fact that they faced unknown peril, life would be rosy and sublime.

She motioned to Sam's notebook. "What are you working on?"

"Transplant designs."

"May I see?"

He hesitated, and she tried not to feel hurt. "Yes, but you know my methods are unconventional." He nudged his notebook toward her, and when she turned it around, she knew the reason for his reluctance. Social convention frowned upon the use of cyborg implants in people, and his drawing of a heartclock included elements that were often fabricated for use in 'tons.

"This is incredible, Sam, and will save lives."

He lifted a shoulder. "There are many who have moral objections to the notion."

"Until they have need of such a thing for themselves or a loved one, I imagine."

He shook his head with a rueful smile. "I once presented at a conference where a potential donor told me she would rather lose her husband or child than have them live as unnatural, fabricated, soulless creatures."

Hazel's mouth dropped open. "That is ridiculous."

"I suppose it speaks to the larger question," Eugene said, "which is 'What constitutes a soul?'"

Hazel chuckled, but Eugene looked up from his work without a smile, or even a twitch of one. She cleared her throat and nodded. "Yes. Well, of course. Humans certainly cannot lay proprietary claim to soul ownership." She glanced at Sam, who merely shook his head.

"In less-philosophical observations, at least our time aboard the *Magellan* draws to a close in only a few days." Sam placed his palms together and looked heavenward with gratitude.

Hazel smiled. "It will be cold where we're going. You may find yourself missing the comfort of this nautical home."

"I cannot begin to express how poor circumstances will need to be for me to prefer this thing over travel on land. I am glad we are nearly done."

She nodded wearily. "As am I." She glanced over her shoulder at the 'tons, who wielded feather dusters but turned their attention intermittently toward her and Sam.

He gathered up his notebook, then paused. "Your

telescriber is set to my scribe name? You have only to send the message."

She nodded. "I will remain in here for a time; I have reading to do. I also need to peruse one more topic."

"Which is?"

"Psychological illnesses." She drew a breath. "Madness."

Chapter 22

After a few hours of study, Hazel returned to her cabin to change and freshen up. She was still restless, though, her brain animated, and she desperately wanted to walk.

The beautiful expanse of luxurious carpet stretched down the long corridor outside her cabin. She walked from one end to the other and back again before circling around to the other side of the Main Room that sat like an island in the middle of the deck.

Now and again a 'ton passed by with a nod to her, carrying clean linens and supplies. She was torn between being comforted by their presence and being uneasy at the eerie feel they elicited with their ever-watchful eyes.

She made her way to the kitchen, which housed a quiet hum of activity. The human chef was busy, but his 'ton assistant worked alongside four others.

"Might I trouble you for a cup of tea?" she asked.

"Of course," the 'ton answered, and another assistant poured her a cup from a pot that steeped on a stove. All four 'tons paused to look at her, processors whirring. She was accustomed to Eugene's mannerisms and movements, but for some reason the deliberate pause in their activity was unnerving.

She took it with murmured thanks, and left the kitchen, deep in thought.

She wandered to the steps with her cup of warm tea and slowly descended, not thinking about where she was headed until she reached Deck Four and found her way into the Control Room. The *Magellan* cruised along at its normal quick pace, and she nodded to the 'ton at the controls.

"Hello, Winston," she said.

"Lady Hazel," the 'ton answered. "Would you care to have the bright lights switched on?" The other 'tons in the room paused briefly, nodded to her in greeting, and resumed their activities.

"That would be lovely." She took her tea to the window seat, where she relaxed, sipping the warm beverage. She leaned her head against the window and let herself be mesmerized by the view of marine life blurring past the large window like shooting stars.

She finally finished her tea and stood. Thanking Winston, she wandered out of the Control Room. She collided with a 'ton and dislodged the large load he'd been balancing on his shoulder. It was a garbage sack, made in the same thick, black fabric she'd seen jettisoned from the torpedo chutes.

"Oh!" Hazel gasped. "I apologize! I was not paying attention at all." She reached down to help, but her fingers just brushed the fabric as he hefted the bag away from her and back onto his shoulder.

"Please do not concern yourself, my lady," the 'ton said.

"No harm done, and at any rate, it is merely some laundry."
He smiled. His load was bent in the middle, one half hanging
down his back. "The cleaning machines are just there." He
pointed to the next door down the hallway.

She smiled, something nagging at her. "I won't keep you,
then. And again, my apologies."

"Think nothing of it." He touched his fingers to an imag-
inary hat, and they went in opposite directions.

As she reached the stairs, Hazel turned back as the 'ton
put his hand on the door handle, effortlessly balancing his
bundle of laundry. He paused and looked at her, as though
he was waiting for her to leave before opening the door. He
smiled and nodded again, door still closed, hand still in place
on the handle.

She put one foot on the bottom stair, and returned the
smile. She thought she heard a clicking sound amidst the
quiet whir of the 'ton's processing unit. It might have been
her imagination, though, because the engine room was also
located on that level and provided a steady thrum not as easily discernible on the rest of the ship.

As she finally turned away, she heard the door open, and
she peeked around the corner in time to see the door close
behind the 'ton. She slowly climbed the stairs, wishing she
had taken the lift instead. She couldn't reason through why
the encounter with the 'ton nagged at her, until she reached
her room and the realization struck.

The bundle he carried, whatever it was, had not been
laundry. It had landed heavily on the floor with an odd thud.
Even in memory, the sound made her wince. She was certain
that bag had not been full of fabric.

Something else nagged at her, and she checked her timepiece. She had a few minutes left before dinner would be called. With a quick glance through the partially open doors leading to Sally's room, where she saw Eugene standing guard, she ran out of the room and down the stairs one deck to the infirmary recovery room.

The bedding had been changed, and she chastised herself for not thinking to check the room earlier. She walked around the bed, checked the emptied wastebasket, and finally bent down and lifted the plain, thin bed skirt.

An object lay on the floor directly beneath where Sally's head had lain. Hazel reached for it with a combination of triumph and dread. It was a small sachet, and she lifted it to her nose. She sniffed and immediately held it away from her face, recognizing the sleeping agent within it. She could also detect traces of eucalyptus oil, a product often used when casting spells.

Someone with an affinity for magick and spells had cast one over Sally, keeping her unconscious since the surgery.

Hazel's blood ran cold. Who but her uncle would have the knowledge and resources to do such a thing? After all, the man had a room full of magick-infused artifacts only two decks above her. He'd mentioned that his mother had dabbled in Light Magick, and his sister—Hazel's mother—had as well. He might have learned enough from them to cast spells on his own.

She imagined him touching his finger to the oil on the sachet and then tracing it lightly along Sally's forehead, murmuring words in Latin as an incantation to complete the spell.

She slowly stood and exhaled, wondering why her uncle had wanted to keep Sally unresponsive.

A quiet bell sounded, signaling dinner, and she considered replacing the item in case Dravor looked for it, but instead she wrapped the sachet in a handkerchief and put it carefully in her pocket.

She thoughtfully climbed the stairs to Deck Two and stopped just outside the Main Room. Harsh, hushed voices sounded within, and she stilled, straining to hear.

The count was angry, speaking rapidly in Romanian, and she looked down the hall, wishing Eugene was available to translate. The corridor was empty, save for Sam, who was just stepping out of his cabin and locking his door. He turned to her cabin door, but she waved her arm at him, capturing his attention. She beckoned him forward.

A second voice chimed in on top of the count's, and she immediately recognized it as Renton. Part of his response was lost, and to her frustration, all she heard was " —handle the matter!"

Sam drew near, and she put a finger to her lips. The men inside had moved away from the door; however, she still heard a murmur of sound. They must have headed toward the hearth.

She quickly showed Sam the sachet and explained in a whisper the snippet of conversation she had overheard. "Something's happened," she finished. "I wish I understood what the count was saying."

Sam frowned. "All is well with Sally and Eugene?"

"As of ten minutes ago, yes. I saw Eugene as I left my cabin. I was going to put this away in there, but now I want to see what they're doing." She motioned to the Main Room with her thumb.

He took the sachet and rewrapped it, tucking it into his trouser pocket. "I am famished," he said loudly and took Hazel's arm as they entered the room. "And something smells delicious." He paused. "Are we ascending?"

The count and Renton stopped talking, but Renton still held the expression of a stampeding bull.

Dravor straightened his lapels and managed a smile. "We are nearing Greece. I have cargo to unload, and then we will immediately dive again. I also must alert the castle to make arrangements for our arrival." He took a breath, and his shoulders relaxed. "If you wish to go ashore, a small boat can shuttle you back and forth, but we are pressed for time. I am most anxious to return to Marit." He cleared his throat, turning to his assistant. "That will be all, Renton. See me in my office in an hour."

Renton offered a light bow to the count, and then to Hazel and Sam. He left the room in quick strides as the others made their way to the dinner table.

The count was once again the consummate host. Hazel could hardly focus on the conversation and did little to hold up her end. Sam spoke with the count in general terms about his time in the military, and they discussed the beauties of Greece. All the while, Hazel envisioned the sachet in Sam's pocket, and wondered if she could unravel her uncle's intentions before they reached his castle.

Chapter 23

S am stood atop the *Magellan's* deck near the stern of the submersible. The lights of the Grecian shoreline twinkled in the darkness, the only signs of human life amidst the panorama of melded ocean and sky. Stars filled the dome above, and he breathed easier for the first time since boarding the cursed craft.

Hazel had returned to the library immediately following dinner, and he'd have joined her if Petrescu hadn't announced they'd surfaced. He took another deep breath of the fresh sea air.

Rising from the depths of the abyss was like being reborn, and he loathed the thought of submersing again. Beyond his aversion to dropping into the depths of the ocean, a darkness had settled into the craft since their departure from London. Hazel mentioned again that the 'tons seemed unduly observant, and interaction with human staff had become extremely limited. A sense of eerie disquiet followed him down the long hallways and into each beautifully decorated room.

The door opened behind him, and Hazel joined him on

231

the narrow deck. "Would you like to go ashore? Dravor said his business will take no more than an hour, so we have that long to stretch our legs." She smiled, but it was tight and strained.

"I need to check for communications from Oliver," Sam said. "Will you join me?"

She nodded. "I assume the telegraph office operates under late hours."

"Yes. Petrescu confirmed it." He glanced at Hazel. "I notice you do not refer to him as your uncle now."

"Only to his face, to maintain pretenses," she muttered. "I do not want him to think I believe anything other than what he tells me."

"Did he and Renton go ashore?"

She nodded. "They used the self-contained capsule docked beside the Control Room and went via the torpedo chute."

"I told Eugene to lock the cabin door and check the Tesla Room for any communication that may have come directly to the ship." Sam narrowed his eyes against the wind and scanned the shoreline. "What do you suppose Petrescu's real motives are?"

"I wish I knew." She turned to face him. "I must confess, I've wondered if we wouldn't be better served to get off this thing here in Greece and go back home, but I cannot afford the risk to my sister." She cleared her throat. "My dreams of her grow darker, and I cannot shake the sense that she is being held against her will in a place haunted by tragedy. I feel her distress so acutely, I begin to wonder if I am also going mad. I do not pretend to assume we will be the best of friends, or even that this journey will end well, but I can't leave until I know she's safe."

She turned back to the water, and the soft breeze blew curls from her forehead.

He looked at her, and a knot tightened in his gut. He wanted a reason to put his arm around her shoulders and pull her close to his side, but he couldn't use the weather as an excuse. It was balmy and beautiful.

Something had simmered between them since that moment in the library, early in the voyage, when he'd teased her gently about flirting, and she'd ventured beyond her own reservations to place a tentative hand over his heart. They had been interrupted by Sally's accident, but the sense of intimacy had begun to creep back into their relationship the night he'd found Hazel in the Control Room.

It had taken every ounce of willpower he possessed to refrain from kissing her right there on the floor. She anticipated it, and he felt she would have welcomed it, but he wouldn't do her the disservice of confusing consolation with intimacy when she was under such stress.

She must have felt him staring, now, because she glanced his way and then back to the shoreline, a light blush staining her cheek, visible even in the semi-dark.

To his knowledge, she'd not entertained serious suitors or seemed to have set her cap for anyone, and he definitely found himself wanting to move into that role. He'd never been shy and had done his share of socializing through the years, but he had never met a woman he wanted to spend a lifetime with.

Hazel interested him, always had. Conversation with her

was enlightening and funny, and her subtle sense of humor surprised him constantly. She was reserved, so her wit slipped in unnoticed until he thought for a moment about what she'd said.

Now that he'd begun to notice her—really notice her—it seemed too good to be true that someone who fascinated him on an intellectual level would also be someone he found physically stunning. He glanced at her again and shook his head, smiling to himself. His friends would fall all over themselves in laughter to see him stumbling to summon the charm that usually was so effortless. It was probably good for him to be humbled; he'd never doubted his desirability to women, never wondered if he'd attend a ball and not find a soul who would dance with him, or a soiree where he'd be unable to secure pleasant conversation for the evening or a stroll in moonlit gardens.

The *Magellan* continued its slow approach to the shoreline, and Sam leaned on the railing, his arm next to Hazel's hand. He considered remarking on the beauty of the overhead blanket of stars, or the pleasant smell of salt air, but the words lodged in his throat, and he was truly at a loss.

"It's a beautiful night," he finally managed, and fought the urge to smack his hand to his forehead.

"It is," she agreed, glancing at him and then at the shoreline, holding the railing and leaning back. She swayed slightly back and forth, releasing the railing but hovering her hands over it to stop her fall when she leaned back too far. "The stars are lovely," she added, looking up. "They must be quite a welcome sight to you."

"Very much so." He was glad she was able to manage the conversation.

Her curls were arranged in knots and braids and twists in a beautiful coiffure, and the strands at her temples lifted in the gentle breeze. She was always polished. She valued her good appearance, and she took care with it, from choices in clothing to hairstyles to hats. He suddenly wanted very much to remove a few of her hairpins and let all those curls spill downward in a golden cascade.

She turned her attention from the stars to him. He was still leaning on the railing, not towering above her as usual. Her eyes were bright, and the corner of her mouth lifted in a smile. "A penny for your thoughts," she said, repeating a phrase he'd used on her the week before.

He was going to kiss her. It was inevitable.

She swayed infinitely closer, possibly unaware she even did so. He smiled. Or possibly not.

The moment hung suspended in the air, with her hands still on the rail and his arms still braced against it. Once he moved, everything would change. His heartbeat quickened, and he exhaled quietly. He'd never in his life wanted anything more than to kiss this woman, and he'd never in his life worried so much about ruining a friendship. He'd never had a friend like her, and the thought of losing her because of his growing attraction was a calculated risk.

He knew she expected the kiss, saw it in her eyes, and he felt a moment's pause. She wasn't one to play the coquette, but did she view him as someone she might spend a lifetime with?

The thought of another man courting her made his

stomach churn. He didn't want to imagine her directing that look of awareness at someone else. He knew her better than anyone, knew what made her laugh, knew what frightened her, knew how hard she worked to prove her own mettle to herself without realizing that, by facing her fears, she was already head and shoulders above the rest of the population.

She was everything he wanted. She was his Hazel.

He straightened slowly and turned to face her directly. She followed his movements, leaving one hand gripping the railing. He placed his hand over hers and registered the taut knuckles, the tight grasp of her fingers on the metal. Her focus on him was direct and anticipatory. The air around them thrummed with possibility, with promise. His thumb brushed across her gold bracelet, which was warm to the touch against her skin. He lifted his other hand to her face and trailed his fingertips along her jaw. She exhaled a quiet sigh, and her long lashes blinked slowly across those expressive eyes.

The door opened behind them with a grating squeal, and a figure stepped into his periphery. He released Hazel quickly, and she sucked in a breath, looking at the new arrival. Eugene stood in the doorway, one brow raised, and the tableau stood frozen for a long moment.

In the future, the interruption would be funny. In the present, it was not.

"Yes, Eugene?" Sam growled.

Eugene lifted a shoulder in a shrug. "Even with my superior sensors, I am unable to discern your activity from behind a closed metal door. Perhaps next time you desire intimacy you'll inform me in advance, although I understand many cultures prefer spontaneity in such liaisons, and—"

Sam held his hand up, palm out. "Stop."

Eugene shut his cursed cyborg mouth, and Hazel cleared her throat. Sam closed his eyes, feeling a moment of true regret. She would be mortified. When he finally braved a glance in her direction, he was surprised to find her biting her cheeks as though holding back laughter.

She schooled her features into seriousness, which she promptly ruined by pressing her lips together in amusement. She hadn't been entirely unaffected by the moment; color was high in her cheeks, and she knotted her fingers together. She shifted her weight from one foot to the other before anchoring herself to the spot and allowing the smile to fully appear.

"Eugene," she said crisply, "what may we do for you?"

Eugene inclined his head in her direction. "I confess, I would have supposed the doctor to be the more cavalier of you both, yet your quick recognition of the humor of this circumstance far exceeds his." Eugene raised a hand conspiratorially to his mouth and added, "His heart rate is increasing as we speak, and it was already quite high when I opened the door—"

"Eugene!" Sam moved closer to the 'ton. "What do you need?"

Eugene held his hands up as though backing away from an irrational combatant. "I was coming to inform you that I've wired the telegraph office, ashore through use of the Tesla Room below, and there are no messages awaiting either you or Miss Hughes. I thought to save you the time an excursion to shore would require. The sooner we reach Romania, the better, for Miss Tucker's sake if nothing else."

"Are you certain you wired the correct telegraph office?"

Sam looked longingly at the shore, weighing the benefit of avoiding the quick excursion against enjoying the luxury of feeling solid ground beneath his feet. "We are close to shore, and the Tesla Room's reach should cover a wide area, but perhaps we are not close enough."

"There are three telegraph offices within range. I wired each of them, and each returned a negative response. Shall I run the requests again?"

"Please," Hazel said to Eugene but looking at Sam. "Nothing is lost by being certain." All traces of mirth had fled, and her brows drew together.

"I expected word from Oliver," Sam said to her. "Had you anticipated a message from someone?"

She shrugged, frowning. "I left word for Isla and Lucy, and I gave my mother the itinerary before we left. Emme knew I was going. I thought someone might have a message for me before we reach Romania."

He felt a stab of pity for her. Her friends were her true family, and he knew they adored her. If they hadn't sent word to her, it wasn't because they couldn't bother to take the time. "Check one more time, Eugene," he said.

"Very good." Eugene turned and left, closing the door behind him.

Sam scratched the back of his neck, knowing the intimate moment had passed. "Hazel—" he began.

She held up her hand. "Please, no apologies."

He quirked a half-smile. "I was not going to apologize."

"Good." She blushed and looked down at her hands, which she'd twisted again, probably subconsciously. "And of course, Eugene is correct. There is something to be said for spontaneity."

"And something very frustrating about ill-timed interruptions."

Her blush grew, and she nodded with a small laugh.

Hazel's presence was a tangible thing he was coming to recognize as soothing. Well, he amended, among other things. He couldn't say he'd felt particularly soothed when he'd been about to kiss her. As he looked at her now, with a smile and a quick touch of his thumb to her chin, he felt that if he wrapped her in his arms and held her close to his heart, all would be right with the world.

"There is a book I'd like to retrieve from the library," she said, with a shrug that looked very much like regret. "Shall we?"

He nodded and opened the door, and contented himself with the luxury of placing his hand on her back as she reentered the huge submarine. As consolations went, it was extremely insufficient, but then she looked over her shoulder at him and gave him a flirtatious wink.

He grinned and followed her down the stairs, back into the depths of the ship.

Chapter 24

Hazel's heart was thumping out of her chest. But for Eugene, she would have just enjoyed a very lovely moment outside with Sam, in the fresh ocean breeze. She was proud of herself for being brave enough to wink at Sam, and alternately amused and irritated with Eugene.

She and Sam walked down the corridor, passing the conservatory with its idle 'tons, and entered the library to see the same automatons as always, dusting the same corners and watching their entry with the same vacant smiles.

"I'll be glad to be done with this," she muttered to Sam. Even as she spoke, the *Magellan* tilted at a gentle angle, signaling their descent.

His jaw tensed, and she saw him pinching his thumb and forefinger together.

"I believe the count said we will not need to dive as deeply this time. We're almost there." She paused. "I'm sorry, Sam."

He shook his head and managed a tight smile, and then

took her hand. "Let's find your book, and go somewhere that spying eyes are not."

The tables were bare, so she walked Sam over to the shelf where she'd originally found the book, and rather than retrieve a ladder, he reached up and withdrew the title she indicated. They left the library quietly, and he still retained hold of her hand. It was the one bright spot in a moment fraught with worry; his claustrophobia had returned, and the night was upon them, which meant Hazel would go to bed and dread falling asleep.

They had reached Deck Two and were just outside the Main Room when the count and Renton emerged from the deck below. Hazel's heart tripped, and she dropped her book. A sudden cacophony of sound and terror filled her mind, and she shoved Sam to the side, trying desperately to get them both away.

She sucked in a breath, sobbing without tears, and she distantly heard her voice producing words she didn't understand. In flashes, the *Magellan* disappeared, and she was in Marit's room, despair and madness floating around her like a palpable thing. The faded rug, toys, chipped paint on the shutters, the smell of dust—the visceral details overwhelmed her.

Her gaze tore from the count to Renton, and the scream building in her throat finally escaped. She pressed her hands against her ears and strained against Sam's arms. He must have gathered her to him at some point, but she had no memory of it.

"Hazel!" Sam's lips were near her ear. His warmth enveloped her, and she inhaled deeply, finding her footing in the scent of his soap, the smell she loved so much that was uniquely him. It was the smell that pulled her back. "Hazel, what is it?"

The noise in her head ceased. The flashing, unsteady combination of Marit's room and the corridor slammed into clear focus, and her sister's room disappeared completely. She drew in a trembling breath and removed her hands from her head. She blinked, dizzy, and took in her surroundings.

The corridor was still, and only the faintest traces of her scream echoed before fading. Her uncle and Renton stood, rooted to the spot, and stared.

"My dear?" the count said, slowly approaching her as one would a frightened creature. "What has upset you so?"

"I . . . I . . ." She shut her eyes and pressed her fingertips against them.

Sam subtly shifted her back a step.

She opened her eyes and exhaled. "I . . . Apologies, I felt ill for a moment. Likely the *Magellan*'s movement, diving again."

Sam paused and looked at her, his blue eyes close to hers, and moved his hand up between her shoulders to rest on the back of her neck. He touched his fingers to the side, and she felt her pulse beat quickly beneath them.

"Dearest, you were speaking Romanian." Dravor's focus on her was complete, and she realized he knew she had been sensing Marit's presence.

She had felt her sister's terror. Marit had seen the two men through Hazel's eyes and experienced deathly fear. But for the first time, it had happened while she was awake.

"Doctor MacInnes," Dravor said, "bring Hazel to the

Main Room. We shall sit a moment, have tea until her nerves calm."

Sam hesitated, but then asked, "Hazel, would you like some tea?"

She nodded. She needed time to think. "Yes, tea would be lovely."

Renton looked at her with one brow raised, and then turned on his heel and left.

Sam guided her into the Main Room with her uncle, and the three of them sat near the hearth. The lights were low, and the room was comfortably warm.

At the count's signal, a silent 'ton poured tea from a pot that was kept eternally warm and full. She accepted it with shaking hands, and slowly sipped the chamomile.

Her uncle made light conversation, the words flowing around them until she gradually began to relax. She felt calm, and wondered why she'd ever been concerned. She and Sam were safe, and Uncle Dravor loved her and Marit so much that he'd gone all the way to London to find her and bring her home, to gather them together as a family, and all so she could help heal Marit.

She looked at Sam, who seemed to have shed both his earlier anger with Dravor and his anxiety for her, and was enjoying his tea. Gratefully, Hazel turned her attention to Dravor, who watched her intently, unblinking, and smiled.

Once before, she had seemed to see a darker shadow beneath her uncle's expression, and she experienced that same sensation again. This time she saw his smile was artificial. All of it was artificial. The sense of peace, of submission—it all felt fabricated. As though her soul had tried to warn her that all was not well, but had been smothered by a blanket of false assurances.

She pushed her way to the surface, shoving through webs and lies and tangled thoughts until she finally gasped and blinked.

Sam placed his hand on her shoulder. "What is it, Hazel? Are you well?" His eyes were cloudy, and he blinked.

She took another sip of tea, as well as a deep breath, and rotated her head on her shoulders. She glared at her uncle, heart thudding, and experienced a surge of anxiety and worry, as though the feelings she'd suppressed had been dammed up and suddenly released.

Dravor watched her, reluctantly impressed, as though she'd executed a chess move he'd not expected. He lifted his cup to her in salute, and she breathed in slowly through her nose and out again.

"I doubt it will surprise you that I have been experiencing a connection with my sister. It has only increased the closer we draw to our destination," she told her uncle. "I expect before long I shall understand her quite well."

Dravor looked at her with unsurprised eyes. "This makes me happier than I can ever express."

"What, truly, do you want of me?"

He frowned, the picture of concern. "I need your help, Hazel. *Marit* needs your help. You are a Healer, and—"

"Where is her room?"

He blinked. "Her room?"

"Where do you keep her?"

"At the castle. I've told you this."

Hazel narrowed her eyes, relieved to know that the sense

of calm settling over her was her own sense of peace, not something fabricated by her uncle. For the first time, she felt a sense of her own strength.

She glanced at Sam, who seemed to be listening intently, though he didn't say a word.

"The strangest thing happened the first night aboard this ship," Hazel said. "Someone entered my cabin while Sally and I slept. In light of her later accident, I wonder if the person who hurt her was also the same one who snuck about in the dark, interrupted only because I awoke."

Her uncle raised a brow. "I wish you had told me of this event. It is unacceptable for an intruder to enter your cabin."

"When I switched on the light, the room was empty. Tell me, Uncle, who else has access to your invisibility stone?"

The look of surprise on his face was genuine, but was gone in an instant. "Nobody has access to my property, dearest, though I suppose someone might have slipped it away in an unguarded moment."

"Perhaps the intruder hid in the lavatory until I fell asleep again. I failed to look in there. I was afraid."

"Such strength of spirit you have acquired in such a short time. I do not imagine you would be afraid to look now, would you?"

"I would still be afraid. But I am coming to realize something. You were entirely correct; Marit does need me." Hazel remembered the terror, the madness she'd felt when she, but more importantly Marit, had seen the count and Renton. She suddenly understood the fury a mother might feel when protecting her offspring.

Dravor chuckled. "You're exhausted and overwhelmed. The mind does play tricks on one in a vulnerable position."

Sam was still quiet, and she suddenly realized the count was holding him under his thrall while conversing with her, fully engaged.

She inhaled quietly, trying to maintain the calm she'd managed to achieve. "How old are you, Uncle?"

"An odd question, my dear. I am forty-seven." He set his tea on the table next to him and crossed his legs. "I do not understand how that pertains to our present discussion."

She thought of his collection of enchanted artifacts designed to prolong life, and it was on the tip of her tongue to ask him how *long* he had been forty-seven, but she held back the question. He was likely quite old, and with longevity came strength and power.

And his ability to hold Sam, a strong-willed man, so effortlessly, was definitely cause for concern.

Hazel put her hand on Sam's knee and dug in with her fingernails until her hand hurt. He coughed and jerked his knee up, and looked at her, eyes wide, stunned. She could almost see the moment the film was wiped from his eyes. He blinked and recovered quickly, setting his teacup and saucer on the table.

"Apologies," he said, "I thought I felt something brush against my leg."

Hazel tensed. She needed to speak with Sam before Dravor lulled them into a false sense of security again. She wondered if Dravor had a small relic in the pocket of his dinner jacket that allowed him hypnotic suggestion over multiple people.

She stood, and Sam rose with her. She took his arm and said, "Thank you, Uncle, for the tea. Please forgive our abrupt departure, but I am quite fatigued. I believe I shall relax for a time with a good book and retire early."

Dravor placed his hand on his chest. "Of course." He inclined his head. "I shall meet you again in the morning for breakfast."

Hazel pulled subtly on Sam's arm as she turned toward the door. "Until morning," she said over her shoulder, though she didn't breathe easy until she had him into the hallway and well away from her uncle.

"What just happened?" Sam murmured. "And why does my head ache?"

"What do you know of palistocin?" she asked him grimly.

"The memory herb?"

"The benefit is not only to help one's memory. A small daily dose is rumored to build both mental resilience and determination in thought and behavior. Your approach to medicine is more clinical than mine is," she continued, guiding him to her door and unlocking it, "but for the sake of my peace of mind, will you put a pinch of the herb in your tea each morning?"

He frowned. "Of course, Hazel, but I am confused."

"I know you are," she said, closing the door and locking it. "We have just been under a heavy blanket of hypnotic suggestion." She turned to him, hands on her hips. "You were fairly swimming in it until I gouged your knee with my fingernails."

His brows drew together, and he paused, shifting his

weight. "I wouldn't say 'swimming in it' is a fair assessment," he protested. "Are you suggesting you were immune?"

"Not at first," she admitted. "It was insidious. Dravor spoke until we forgot about my fit in the corridor, forgot about everything."

He looked at her, and his gaze sharpened. "Has Marit visited during waking hours before?"

"Never." She rubbed her forehead. "We are closer than ever to her, and I am quite tired. What I've learned tonight is that she is terrified of our uncle, or Renton. Or both."

Sam sat on the arm of a chair and regarded her carefully. "The count is more dangerous than we thought. Than *I* thought."

She lifted a shoulder. "I agree. I think we are facing a deadlier foe than the undead. More calculating, which I wouldn't have thought possible."

He nodded slowly. "Either way, given this information, I'm happy to garnish my tea with your palistocin. I suggest we remain alert, find your sister, and return to London as quickly as possible."

Hazel nodded and, as she opened her box of medicinal herbs, added, "Until we find her, we won't know exactly how to help her." She paused. "And I have no resources in Romania." She selected the correct container from the box and tipped a good portion of the contents into a paper packet. "I don't even speak the language, unless Marit is tromping around in my head." She sealed the packet securely and handed it to him, wondering how she would be able to communicate with her sister in person.

Sam took the packet but held her hand fast. "Hazel."

She looked up at him.

"All will be well. We will pool our talents and finish this thing safely." He lightly shook her hand back and forth. "Yes?"

She nodded and managed a smile. "Yes. And thank you."

He tugged on her hand and stepped closer, and suddenly her only thoughts were of him, the smell of him. The face she had adored for weeks, months, was so close. He didn't waste time with words, but gently tunneled his fingers into her hair and lowered his mouth to hers.

The sensation of his lips on hers was everything she'd imagined and more. He took his time, softly, as though they hadn't a care in the world, and she lost herself in the luxury of the feel and taste of him. His arm encircled her body and pulled her close against him. She wound her arms around his neck, tentative at first, and then bravely tested the feel of his hair against her fingertips.

He softly ran his thumb along her jaw, cradling her head and subtly guiding her as they explored the sweet intimacy of learning another's touch. He finally, slowly, lifted his head, and she sighed.

"Sleep well," he whispered, touching his forehead to hers. "Scribe me immediately if you suspect something is wrong."

She nodded and tried to catch her breath. Had he not still held her close, she suspected she'd have wobbled and fallen over. She wished she had a better sense of how to manage sophisticated situations. What did a woman say to a man who had kissed her senseless, robbed her of coherent thought, and stolen her breath away?

He slowly released her, and she missed the warmth

instantly. As she withdrew her arms from around his neck, her fingers trailed down his jacket lapels and paused on the fabric, as if to hold him there. He would leave, and she would be alone. She was anxious again, completely at sea in more ways than one.

"I can sit by the fire again and read while you sleep, if it would help relieve your worries," he offered quietly. "I would even bring in Eugene to act as chaperone and vouch for your protected reputation." His lips twitched.

"Eugene, lovely timing, that one." She glanced at the adjoining room, hidden by the closed doors. "He probably needs to charge, no?"

She crossed the room and cracked open one of the doors, and then pulled it wide. A single light was on in the small space, and it illuminated an empty bed in an empty room. Her heart thudded in her ears, and she had to remind herself to breathe.

"Sam?"

"Yes?" He was studying the label on one of her herb packets.

"Sally and Eugene—where are they?"

Chapter 25

S am took one look in the adjoining room and cursed. Hazel, heart pounding, followed as he ran from her cabin and entered the one he shared with Eugene.

"Where is she?" Sam asked Eugene, who was reading a book on the history of Romania.

"Hazel?"

"No," Sam bit out. "Where is Sally?"

"I received your message that you moved her back to the infirmary."

"I never sent you any such message." Sam ran his hand through his hair, the other planted on his hip. He looked around as though if he willed it, Sally would appear.

Hazel braced herself against the doorframe. "Eugene, when did you receive this message?"

"When you were at dinner with Count Petrescu."

"That was ages ago!"

Eugene paused, his processors humming. "Odd, it appears there is a four-hour gap in my data."

Hazel closed her eyes. Sam pulled her fully into the room and closed the door.

"Who neutralized you?" Sam demanded of Eugene. "Review the last segments before you received the message."

Eugene's cogs whirred. "I do not have a visual record . . . someone entered the room behind me . . . my neutralization code is spoken . . . that's the last until your message. Processors reinstated just as you started dinner."

She swallowed a sob. "What have they done with Sally?"

Sam looked at her, and his face paled. "We must find her." He grabbed his scriber. "I will start on Deck One. You and Eugene start on Deck Three?"

She nodded. "I'll get my scriber." She hurried back to her cabin and grabbed it from the nightstand.

Sam and Eugene joined her in the corridor, and they quietly made their way to the stairs. They passed three 'tons, all of which paused and stared at them. "How long do we have until they inform their master that we are out and about?" A soft click sounded from the 'tons behind them. "I believe they may also be recording images," Sam muttered as he took the stairs at a jog.

Hazel and Eugene descended and checked each unlocked room up and down the corridor. 'Tons charged in most rooms, but the human chef answered their knock sleepily and said he hadn't seen Sally. They checked both the examination room and the recovery room where Sally had stayed before they took her upstairs.

The room was just as Hazel had left it earlier after she'd found the sachet beneath the bed. She stared at the bed, pinching her lip in thought and fighting the sting of tears. She didn't know what she'd hoped to find.

"Something is wrong, Eugene." She gave the room a long, slow look. "It's as if they've erased every trace of her." Perhaps they had her stashed away in their quarters.

She reached over the bed to switch off the lamp and noted a single hair, bright red, caught just behind it. She carefully pulled it up, the long strand curling around her fingers.

"Where is the rest of Miss Tucker?" Eugene asked as he studied the hair.

The rest of her . . . the rest . . . Images washed over Hazel in a sickening rush, a memory of her collision with a 'ton outside the Control Room, the heavy thud of his falling laundry bag, his quick retrieval and subtle movement away from Hazel's outstretched fingers, his clear dismissal and the way he lingered outside the supply room until she climbed the stairs.

"Oh, Eugene." Hazel put her hand over her mouth. "Sweet, sweet mercy." She tore from the room and ran for the stairs, dashing down to the bottom deck. If she didn't keep moving, she would either collapse or vomit. Possibly both. She rounded the corner, nearly tripping herself over the swirling fabric of her skirt.

She ran past the Control Room doors and grasped the supply room door handle. It was locked. She clutched the handle with both hands and pulled, her practical mind knowing she couldn't open the door, but panic overrode her common sense.

"Miss Hazel!" Eugene reached her side. "Hazel, the door is locked."

"I know!" Hazel's eyes burned. She pounded on the door and yelled. "Open this door! I know you are inside, you horrible 'tons, open it!"

Her fist hurt from pummeling the solid surface, enough to give her pause. "Eugene," she panted, "open this door. Immediately, open it."

Eugene complied, giving her a second and third glance as he manipulated the lock.

"Sally is in there." Hazel choked back a sob.

"Why is she in the supply room?" Eugene asked as the lock clicked open.

The Control Room doors opened, and two 'tons entered the corridor from down the hallway.

Hazel ducked inside the supply room and took in the sight of enormous clothes-washing machines, shelves of supplies, and automaton pieces. Two 'tons were exiting the room to the right, from which a cold blast of air emerged with a smoke-like haze.

Hazel darted to the right, intent on seeing as much as possible before the 'tons physically hauled her from it. The cold room, a freezing compartment by the looks of it, was dark, but light from the main room shone in, illuminating a set of shelves that contained bags like the "laundry" the 'ton had been carrying.

Her brain quickly processed what her horrified senses did not want to acknowledge. She dashed around the pair of 'tons, who called out to her sharply. She ran to the heavy door of the freezing room and caught it before it swung shut. There were four laundry bags, full of something, laid out on shelves. Tags attached were labeled "Chute," identifying their final destination.

"No, no, no . . ." The cold furled around her like fog, her fingers growing numb where she clutched the doorframe.

"Miss Hughes!" One of the 'tons grabbed her hand, and she tried to pull away, stumbling backward when Eugene clobbered the 'ton from behind, knocking it to the ground.

"Intruder!" the other 'ton shouted, and mayhem erupted as time seemed to slow to a crawl.

She lunged into the room and clutched the end of the nearest bag. A drawstring cinched it closed, but a small opening remained. The fabric was stiff and cold, so cold her fingers hurt. The door began to close behind her, dark encroaching by degrees, but then suddenly was yanked wide open, and light shot across the shelves.

A rough hand grabbed at her even as she tightened her grip on the bag, shoving her fingers inside the opening and pulling with all her might.

"No!" Her scream echoed through the icy room as her assailant closed arms around her with automaton strength. The bag slid along the shelf, but her numb fingers were unable to maintain their grip on it. The bag hit the floor with a loud thud, even as she was dragged from the room, the breath squeezed from her midsection so tightly she feared a rib would crack.

"Let go of her!" Sam's shout echoed through the chaos, and the pressure around her middle eased.

She gasped and collapsed, but Sam caught her before she hit the floor. Voices around her rose in anger, an alarm sounded, and the room swirled in her vision until she was certain she'd be sick. A sob rose in her throat, and she clutched Sam's shirtfront as he picked her up and carried her through the noise, his occasional shouts mixing with the others.

He lifted her high against his chest, and when she put her arm around his shoulders, she noted the long, red strands of hair entangled in her fingers.

Chapter 26

Hazel's world was a blur as Sam reached Deck Two, still carrying her while trying to gather information from Eugene. Chaos surrounded them as 'tons climbed the stairs beside them, the alarm still ringing from the bottom deck.

Her breath came in shallow gasps, and she tightened her fist around the strands of red hair, the ghoulish evidence of Sally's demise. Her sense of guilt at having failed to protect the young woman was thick in her throat, and she berated herself bitterly.

"What is the meaning of this chaos?" The count's voice echoed down the hallway, and Hazel turned blurred eyes to see her uncle approach with Renton at his side.

"You!" She pushed at Sam until he set her on her feet, and then she ran at Renton, blind fury coursing through her. "You killed her!" She launched herself at the man, raking her nails down the side of his face and drawing blood. His head snapped to the side, and she shoved his chest, taking advantage of his shock to knock him hard against the wall. She pounded on his chest, his arms, his face, a torrent of sobs and angry words nearly choking her as she attacked him.

Suddenly, Hazel felt hands on her shoulders and someone pulling her away. She struggled, certain a 'ton was going to squeeze her breathless, but slowed when she realized it was Sam who held her firmly.

Renton recovered himself, his eyes hardening and his breathing ragged. He straightened his lapels as he glared at her.

Sam dragged her away from the scene, barking at her uncle to have Renton restrained and then join them in Hazel's cabin.

"You will hang for this!" Hazel's scream echoed down the corridor.

Eugene unlocked Hazel's cabin, and Sam ushered her across the threshold, setting her down on the bed.

Her sobs continued as she doubled over, coughing. Sam instructed Eugene to wet a cloth in the lavatory.

Hazel felt the cool, damp fabric on her face and forehead.

"There, love. There," Sam murmured as he gathered her hair and pulled it aside. He continued to dab her tears from her face.

She cried until her tears were gone, then her breath shuddered out in a ragged sigh and she sniffed, clutching the cloth. She looked at Sam, then, and tears burned anew. If she weren't so devastated, she might have been embarrassed he'd witnessed her uncharacteristic mania.

The grim set to his jaw was a mirror of her own emotions, however. She tried to say something, but her breath caught.

He seemed to know what she was thinking, because he placed his arm around her shoulders and pulled her against his side, guiding her head to his shoulder where her hot tears continued to flow, quietly this time, down his neck and onto his collar. His hand slowly rubbed her shoulder, the other clasping her fingers that rested limply on her leg.

He simply held her, occasionally murmuring soothing words, until her breathing slowed again and she felt some control over her emotions. She heard him sniff, and she raised her head to see his own eyes suspiciously bright.

"I am so very sorry." He cradled her cheek, brushing tears from Hazel's eyelashes with his thumb. "I ought to have known. As soon as Eugene joined us on the surface, I should have realized something was amiss. I was distracted, and—"

She shook her head and squeezed his hand. "It is not your fault, Sam." Her voice was scratchy, and her head felt stuffed with cotton. "Renton did this. I would not be surprised to find my uncle complicit, but I know, I *know* that wretched assistant killed her. He assaulted her, or tried to, she ran away, nearly died then, and to keep her quiet, he silenced her permanently."

"I am responsible for Miss Tucker's death," Eugene said quietly from where he stood by the lavatory.

"No," Hazel said.

Sam shook his head. "Renton neutralized you, Eugene. You weren't aware until you performed a diagnostic review of the afternoon. We shall immediately adjust your programming to correct that problem."

A quiet knock on the door pulled her attention toward it, and at Sam's nod, Eugene opened it. He stood aside to allow

Petrescu to enter, and then closed the door quietly behind him.

"Dearest Hazel, I am beyond horrified by Renton's actions." Her uncle stood before her, his bearing straight, but his expression held distress and underlying anger. "He has been placed under lock and key, and when we are in range, I shall alert the authorities to meet us at the docks. He will pay for his crimes."

Hazel managed a nod and tried to swallow the lump still lodged in her throat.

"He has confessed, then?" Sam asked.

The count's eyes flicked to him and back to Hazel. "He has. Apparently, he was indeed the cause behind the young woman's flight that led to her accident with the suit of armor. He'd expressed . . . interest in her that she was disinclined to return. He knew I would be angry, as this is not the first time such an incident has occurred."

"And still you kept him in your employ," Hazel noted.

"Regrettably, I was unable to hire a new assistant and train him before embarking on the journey to retrieve you. Renton gave me his word that his rash and impulsive behavior was an anomaly. Clearly, that was a lie."

Hazel wondered if Renton's "impulsive behavior" was indeed a recent development, but she let the matter rest.

"Was Renton responsible for Miss Tucker's unconscious state following her surgery?" Sam asked.

The count nodded. "He procured a spell and the accompanying ingredients from my office upstairs. He confessed to that as well, just now."

"And then we moved the patient here, and he no longer had easy access to her," Sam said.

Petrescu nodded. "He attempted to permanently dispatch her once before you moved her. He had programmed one of the nurses to do it, though I interrupted the act unwittingly when I checked on the young woman myself. Once you moved Miss Tucker, Renton took matters into his own hands and disabled your 'ton long enough to move her and—"

"Kill her," Hazel finished.

"I would do anything to spare you this ugliness, my dear, and I am pained that you are distressed because of someone who worked for me." The count shook his head. "He can never truly make amends, but he will be brought to justice."

Hazel nodded. She was drained of energy, but beneath her fatigue and horror, a steely thread of resolve formed. The time had come to fully embrace not only her gifts, but her brain. Her uncle was not what he claimed, and she would learn his secrets one way or another. Something wasn't right about Marit's madness either, something Hazel couldn't divine, but she would. She hadn't been able to save Sally, but she would save her sister—or die trying.

The count turned his gaze on Sam. "Have you medicine that will help her rest?"

"I have herbs of my own," Hazel said.

Sam ducked his head and scratched his nose, and in her periphery, she caught the twitch of a smile on his lips.

Petrescu's brow arched, but he inclined his head. "I'll instruct the kitchen to deliver fresh tea, if you'd like."

She nodded and forced her spine to straighten. "That would be lovely."

Petrescu nodded once more and withdrew.

Eugene closed the door behind him and cleared his throat in what she recognized as purely a human affectation. He had no actual throat, of course, but it was one of the many things that made him less machine and more human.

"I will remain here through the night," Eugene said. "If you will permit me, Hazel."

She nodded. "I would appreciate that very much."

Sam touched her hand. "If you will permit *me*, I would like to sleep in Sally's room tonight. I'm reluctant to leave you alone, even in Eugene's capable company."

It was on the tip of Hazel's tongue to insist that would be unnecessary, but then she looked at the open door into Sally's room and sighed. "Perhaps it would be best. Should I go wandering off again in my sleep, there will be two of you to corral me."

Sam pulled her close again and kissed her temple. "Shall we send for someone to help you change?"

She shook her head. "I can manage." She lay a hand on his knee. He was solid and comforting. "Thank you, Sam. I was quite out of my head."

"You were magnificent." He tucked her hair behind her ear. "Even in the face of such horror, you were well on your way to dispensing justice of your own."

She managed a smile, but it felt sad. "A moment longer and he'd have had me by the throat."

"And I'd have removed his." He kissed her temple again and stood. "I'll retrieve my things, and Eugene will wait in the hallway for the tea."

He paused, looking down at her, and she reached for his

hand. He grasped her fingers and sandwiched them between his hands before finally closing his eyes and placing a kiss on her knuckles. "We will solve this— whatever it is. Then, we are going home."

Chapter 27

S am pulled his collar up against the wind. The air in
Romania had a sharp bite, and the scent of winter
enveloped the train station. Hazel stood next to him,
quiet, and he clasped her gloved hand in his. Her appearance was impeccable as always, and the only signs of the
trauma from two nights before were light smudges beneath
her eyes.

A strange entourage waited to board. Renton had just
been taken into custody by local officials. Dravor had rained
down fire and brimstone upon him and the *Magellan*'s staff
and crew. Renton would pay for his crimes, Petrescu declared, and he vowed to dismantle the female 'ton who had
attempted to kill Sally.

Sam had wanted desperately to call Petrescu a liar, but
Hazel's insistence that they let the matter alone for the moment had held him back. She was more determined than
ever to find her sister, and she was convinced the most effective way was to play her uncle's "game of chess." She'd been
quiet for most of the final leg of the journey from Greece

to Romania, and he watched her closely. She was pale, still upset, but clear-headed in her resolve.

Petrescu conducted business for the group, translating for them and obtaining tickets, guiding them through the passport checks, and facilitating a seamless transition from one spot to the next.

Eugene remained either at Sam's side or hovered behind, blissfully quiet. Sam wondered if Eugene still "felt" remorse for his inadvertent part in Sally's demise. The 'ton also remained close to Hazel, as though protecting her from further distress. Sam understood that desire; he wished he could take her back to London, where she would be safe.

Sam had used his full strength to pull Hazel off of Renton when she'd attacked, although he would dearly have loved to let her continue. The man deserved every scratch and bruise Hazel had inflicted upon him, and had the man not been a hair's breadth from shoving Hazel through the opposite wall, Sam might have waited another moment or two before restraining her.

Petrescu handed them their boarding passes with a sympathetic, paternal gaze at Hazel. "I am aghast that something so horrid would happen in my realm, and sorrier still that you were frightened and harmed."

Wind blew a curl of hair across her eyes, and she moved it aside with her fingertip. She was beautiful, and so incredibly sad. Sam swallowed, fighting his own emotion, and figuring he would do her little good if he were weepy. What he truly wished he could do was punch her uncle in the throat.

"Thank you, Uncle." She took the ticket with a gentle smile. "I cannot express how grateful I am that you contacted the authorities when we arrived. It gives me comfort knowing they are seeking justice for Miss Tucker. Will you keep me apprised of their progress?"

"Of course, dearest. Board the train, now, and warm yourself."

Hazel released Sam's hand and embraced her uncle. Sam didn't know who was more stunned, himself or Petrescu. It was the first time Sam had seen the man genuinely taken aback. His arms closed around her, and he kissed the top of her head.

Hazel pulled back and offered Petrescu a faint smile, then turned to Sam and motioned toward the train. "I would like Eugene to ride with us, not in the 'tons' car," she told him. "I find comfort with him close by."

Sam watched her climb the stairs into the train car. "Eugene, you heard the lady. It seems you've received an upgrade."

The train whistle blasted, and Sam extended his hand to the count. "My thanks for the ticket."

Petrescu's grip was swift and crushing. Sam wasn't a small man, and he had always been athletic, strong, and fit, but the pressure the other man exerted had Sam fighting a wince. Sam vowed he would live aboard the blasted *Magellan* for the rest of his life before giving Petrescu the satisfaction of acknowledging the other man's brute strength.

"It is my pleasure to welcome you to my corner of the world, Doctor." Petrescu held his grip on Sam's hand. "I wager you will enjoy it so much you will never want to leave."

"As long as Hazel remains, so shall I." Sam smiled, but squeezed back, refusing to be cowed.

Petrescu finally loosened his grip, indicating for Sam to enter the train car. "I shall be right behind you," he said. "I must see to it that trunks from the ship have been transferred."

Sam managed a tight smile and entered the train. It was lavishly appointed, appeared new, and promised to provide comfortable travel. Sconces with visible filaments glowed warmly, and appointments and fixtures in gleaming copper and brass adorned the corridor. He found Hazel in a semi-private compartment that contained two high-backed benches opposite each other and a small table by the window with a stuffed ottoman beneath it. He sat next to Hazel, and Eugene settled opposite them.

The train sounded a long, loud whistle and rocked on the tracks as the journey began. Hazel lifted the corner of her mouth in a half-smile and said, "Was it too much?"

"When—with your uncle?"

She nodded. "I want him to think I trust him."

"How are you feeling?"

"Angry."

"Justifiably."

She'd removed her snug-fitting overcoat to reveal breeches, boots, a white collared shirt, a dark vest, and a gentleman's tie. She now removed the matching gloves and hat, placing them on the seat beside her.

Hazel met his eyes again and must have seen something there, because she blushed, but her lips twitched in a smile.

"Would you like to see the sketches I've added to my book?" Hazel asked, indicating the leather-bound journal that contained her drawings of Petrescu's artifacts.

"Absolutely."

She moved closer to him and flipped to the pages she and Eugene had written on. She pointed to some of the additions Eugene had made regarding the artifacts' regions or cultures of origin. "You'll notice the incorporation of elements from the Orient, as well as from as far away as New Zealand."

She turned the page and showed him Eugene's neat handwriting detailing the story behind each artifact's history. Beneath each anecdote, he had written a few suggestions for spells or powers that might have aided the party involved in the artifact's discovery.

Sam took the book from Hazel's hands. According to Eugene's list of "Informed Suppositions," Petrescu possessed items that could potentially levitate an object, facilitate speed in running, freeze an opponent's movement for a short time—"Likely no more than ten seconds"—distort sound waves, and render an object invisible.

The remainder of the objects on the lists all involved some sort of life preservation or the ability to add time to one's life. One object, a relic from the Caribbean, contained symbols that hinted at Reanimation of lifeless organic creatures, and Eugene's final note regarded an aquatic fossil, found along the South American coastline. The animal that had left the impression was reputed to contain elements of *amorterium*, a substance that was most potent when added to an elixir with other specific elements derived from a plant called *fiserate*.

Hazel tapped her finger on the words. "Fiserate is rare. Found anciently on the African continent, but supposedly extinct." She chewed on her lip and glanced up as one of the count's 'tons walked through the compartment, pausing to offer a deferential head bow.

"What is it used for?" Sam asked quietly. "The elixir?"

Hazel hesitated. "It is said that it could infuse an unborn child with Resurrection skills."

"An unborn child? What has he been doing?" Sam considered the implications. "What has he *done?*"

Had Petrescu somehow manipulated events concerning an unborn child? Or *children?* Perhaps even—twins?

Sam had never seen an actual Resurrectionist at work— their activities were greatly restricted in modern cultures— and he had only heard exaggerated stories about the zombies they produced, stories meant to scare children at bedtime. As a physician, he had encountered the history of the practice, but precious little documentation was available.

The most he had been able to ascertain was that a true Resurrectionist could reunite a deceased body with a shade of that person's spirit. The body itself would reanimate for a time and appear whole, but the mind was at the mercy of the one who ordered the act, behaving as a puppet until the body collapsed forever.

The compartment door opened, and another 'ton entered, offering a light tea, which she laid out on the side table under the window. With a soft whirring of her processors, she looked at each of them, then left the compartment.

"Her recording is visual as well as auditory," Eugene said. He looked at the fixtures in the compartment, adding, "There may be listening devices in here."

Sam nodded. He knew Petrescu had watched their every move through the 'tons aboard the *Magellan*, and he wouldn't be surprised to discover the count's eyes and ears would follow them on land.

He flipped the page back and looked at a drawing of the rebirth item. "Egypt," he murmured.

Hazel nodded. "I suspected, but Eugene confirmed it."

"May I add something to your notes?"

She handed him a pen, and he scrawled, *I hate to jump to conclusions, but some of these make me wonder . . .*

She nodded. "Yes, I agree." She met his eyes, and hers were wary, concerned.

Supposition only, though. Eugene is theorizing.

She smiled and took the pen, underlining the words "Informed Suppositions" Eugene had written at the top of the page.

He rolled his eyes. *What could an untrained Resurrectionist produce?*

She grimaced. *A menace. I've never seen it done, but supposedly the zombie is uncontrollable, and the body doesn't regenerate.*

Sam had seen his share of death and stages of decay both during the war and in his work. His clinical approach had hardened his nerves over time, but the thought of the deceased walking and wreaking havoc wasn't a pleasant one. He frowned and wrote, *How long does a zombie "live"?*

She twisted her lips in thought. *If the R is skilled and experienced, then a few weeks, I believe. If untrained—hours.*

Have you witnessed the process? Seen a zombie?

She shook her head. *Research only.*

He smiled and took the pen. *What would prompt you to research Resurrectionists?*

Knowledge is power. She shrugged and smiled. *It is the one part of my life in which I've had confidence. I can learn anything.*

He paused, and she arched a brow, which made him smile. A demonstration of ego, no matter how subtle, was uncommon for her. *You have many, many gifts that lend themselves to confidence. You ought to be the most conceited person of my association.*

She rolled her eyes and took the book from him. Then she smiled, and leaned back against the seat. He settled close to her, resting his arm and shoulder comfortably against hers, their legs on the seat aligned. She crossed her leg over her knee, bringing her booted foot nearly up against his shin.

He'd never been more comfortable or uncomfortable in his life. He wished he had a magical artifact that would clear the train of people and automatons. He gave her a side glance and a grin, which she returned, but as one they seemed to remember Eugene. They looked across to see him studying them, mouth pursed in contemplation.

"Well," Hazel said and cleared her throat. "Thank you for your insights, Sam. I'll just . . ." She put her journal in the portmanteau, then pulled out another book and gestured at it. "I believe I'll read for a time." She paused, her expression clouding.

He wished he could say something useful. Something that would fix everything.

He reached for her hand and gave a little squeeze instead before also retrieving a book. He tried, and failed, to focus on it. He was too distracted by his concerns, and as the train carried them deeper into the heart of the country, farther away from anything familiar, he considered the cold, foreign land rushing by outside the windows and felt a definite chill.

Chapter 28

Hazel propped her legs on the ottoman in the train compartment and wondered if she'd ever again have a regular night's sleep. She fought napping the entire day, despite the comfortable rock of the train that was perfect for lulling one into oblivion.

Throughout the day, her uncle had been in and out of the train car. Hazel was still angry with him and strangely hurt that he wasn't someone she could come to love. She'd known instinctively from the beginning that something was wrong. Dravor was secretive, he seemed to have an agenda that served only his own interests, he collected objects imprinted with magical spells, and he practiced group hypno-control. Clearly he was a person who was untrustworthy and quite unlikable.

But she had still wished desperately for it to be otherwise. Hazel sighed.

The sky outside was darkening, and the tall, thick trees on either side of the tracks would soon be invisible. The interior of the car showed in the window reflection, and she saw, behind the pale image of herself, Sam appearing from yet another foray around the train. He was restless and had paced the train cars multiple times over the last several hours.

Eugene was charging in the 'ton car at the train's rear, so Sam sat down across from Hazel on the vacant bench. He leaned forward and rested his arms on his knees and tapped her booted foot, which still rested atop the ottoman. "A pound for your thoughts," he said.

She rubbed her forehead and chuckled. "A pound now, is it? My goodness, Dr. MacInnes." She sighed. "My thoughts are swirling, and I very much wish they would settle." She looked out the window, but the world outside was too dark to see.

Sam reached up and turned a knob on the wall sconce nearest them, dimming the interior light, and in the moonlit night, she could see the trees as they traveled farther into the countryside. They occasionally slowed to pass trains traveling in the opposite direction, and just before the engines again resumed their former speed, when the loud sound of train and track was dimmed, the mournful cry of a wolf could be heard, echoing through the night. Several howls usually answered, and the sound was chilling until finally obscured again by the train.

"Dravor said we would stop for the night, eventually?"

He nodded. "Two hours more, I believe. We will need to take a carriage to the inn for the night, and then depart in the morning for Castle Petrescu," he said, waving his hands theatrically.

She laughed. "Someday I shall have a cottage of my own and call it 'Castle Hazel.' I shall even create a placard with the name for my front garden. When strangers inquire about my life and where I live, I shall say, 'Oh, I live at Castle Hazel, perhaps you've heard of it.'"

He grinned. "And the stranger will be amazed. She will say, 'No! Castle Hazel? You jest!'"

Hazel released a dramatic sigh. "Everybody will be so envious. They will come far and wide just to stand outside the front gates and wish they had so grand a cottage."

He wiggled her foot playfully, and she looked at him, barely restraining a laugh. If someone had told her she would one day enjoy such familiarity with him, she'd have fainted from shock. And then prayed daily for it to be true. He must have read her feelings in her face, because he smiled and winked at her.

"Even facing the unknown, there is nowhere else I would be," he said. "I would have you know that."

"Thank you. There is no other's company I would enjoy more." She cleared her throat. "Perhaps now that I am related to nobility, it would not be unseemly for you to ask me for a dance when we return home."

His brow wrinkled. "It isn't unseemly under any circumstance, not to me. I never asked because you always gave me such a wide berth. I assumed you wanted no part of me in any role other than as your employer. I understood." He paused. "Mostly."

She tried not to stare, but her mouth slackened. "But the other ladies said you do not like to consort with any but those of title or status."

He stared. "Who said this? When?"

She shrugged, suddenly uncomfortable. "A few months

ago, at a soiree, and again the night of Lady Hadley's ball. Some of the ladies there made certain I heard it."

He shook his head, eyes wide in disbelief. "Those are the words of petty, jealous women. Have I ever given you the impression that I desire only high society for company? If anything, I believe I've shown otherwise. My best friends are far from being titled." He shrugged. "Except Miles, and I like him precisely because he isn't like others with his title."

She felt deep embarrassment on so many levels. She'd eavesdropped on a conversation about him, and then believed the gossip. She knew him to be kind, and he had never shunned her in public or private. She had believed the talk because it confirmed her own insecurities.

"My apologies, Sam. To believe such a thing about you was unfair." She swallowed. "I suppose I have admired you from afar at social events for so long that I was willing to believe the gossip. You began to loom larger than life, even though I worked with you daily in the clinic."

He studied her and raised a brow, his hand settling on her foot and squeezing lightly. "I wish I had known. I didn't realize you 'admired me from afar.'"

"You've only recently stopped seeing me as anything other than a child." She felt the heat rise in her face.

"I've never thought of you as a child." He smiled. "Naïve, perhaps, and as a patient, at first. Then as my employee. I did not ever want to cross the line into impropriety. Which I have now done spectacularly."

She laughed, relieved that his grin negated regret. "I suppose I ought to begin searching for a new doctor, if not a new employer. I would hate for you to feel conflicted between your professional and personal circumstances."

"Unless something horrifying occurs that would hamper my abilities to treat you, I would be grossly insulted if you were to look elsewhere for either."

She quirked one corner of her mouth. "Perhaps the next time I must impose upon you to treat a sprain or a broken bone, I'll offer a kiss to show my appreciation."

His smile deepened. "Perhaps I'll offer a kiss to help speed the healing process."

The banter was exactly the distraction she needed. She also realized the more time she spent with him, the less she looked at him with eyes full of hero worship and the more she felt his equal. He'd never patronized her, never treated her like a child, and the solicitude she'd always defined as fraternal concern was likely an unwelcome, burgeoning interest that threatened his professional standards.

He tapped her foot once more and then settled back into his seat. He nodded to the book in her lap. "Have you learned all there is to know about spells?"

She looked down at the book. "Probably not *all* there is to know, but I'm reviewing passages that seemed pertinent."

"Can the spells be removed from the objects?"

She glanced around the car, wondering if they truly were being recorded, and crossed to sit next to him. She lowered her voice. "They can, but not easily. Binding a spell to something solid makes it stronger." She yawned.

He nudged her back against the seat. "Put your head on my shoulder. When we arrive at the inn, I'll awaken you."

She was tired. "Just for a moment," she murmured and leaned against his side.

He pulled the ottoman toward them and propped her feet on it, resting his foot next to hers. He took her book and began reading. "Close your eyes," he said. "As your doctor, I order it."

She chuckled. "Suppose someone enters? We really should bring Eugene back to act as chaperone."

"Mercy, no. I need a reprieve, and staying in the 'ton car keeps him humble. Besides, I shall simply tell anyone nosy enough to insinuate themselves into our affairs that we are courting."

Her heart skipped a beat. "Are we?"

She felt him turn his head and look at her. "Are we not?"

She looked up at him through her lashes. "Having never been courted, I wouldn't know."

"Having never courted anyone, I don't presume to know either. But your mother is not here, which means I should probably ask your uncle for permission, but I'll sleep on a bed of nails before giving him the right to anything concerning you. So, I shall ask you directly—you are a grown woman, after all. Hazel Hughes, may I court you?"

She lifted her head and met those blue eyes she loved. "Yes, Dr. Samuel MacInnes, I would be delighted." She smiled. "What a scandalous pair we are, flouting convention. What would traditionally be the next step in this courting business?"

He tipped his head, pretending to think. "I would call on you at home, bring you flowers, perhaps take you for a ride through the park in an open curricle, accompany you to balls and soirees, stare daggers at other men penciling their names on your dance card, that sort of thing."

She laughed, and he continued.

"But as you so perceptively observed, we are nowhere near conventional circumstances." He lowered his voice and leaned close. "We are on a train bound for an isolated castle high in the Transylvanian countryside where we will, presumably, set up a temporary home while we search for answers that may help your sister, whom we have never met. Your nobleman uncle may be hiding terrible secrets and definitely possesses strange, magical artifacts, and his assistant is—was—an awful brute. Have I forgotten anything?"

"Only that my nobleman uncle seems to find joy in lulling all around him into a false sense of complacency. Did you take your dose of palistocin this morning?"

He tapped his temple. "As soon as I awakened. Eugene suggested I take another dose at lunch because he believes my brain needs more help than most to fight the effects of hypno-control."

Her lips twitched. "To which you responded?"

"That he should take his advice to the underworld and remain there with it."

She laughed again.

He gently tipped her head back down onto his shoulder and lifted the book from his lap. "You rest. I have some reading to do. With any luck, I shall absorb the basics, and you can explain the rest to me later."

"I do not like falling asleep these days."

"I will be here with you the entire time."

She yawned again and nodded. The thrill of being near

him, of being courted by him, no matter how unconventionally, would surely prevent her from getting any rest at all. She was caught by surprise, then, when her mind began to wander and then drifted pleasantly into oblivion. She blinked once, sighed, and allowed the sway of the train and the security of the shoulder beneath her head to lull her to sleep.

Chapter 29

When the train pulled into the station, the world outside was completely dark. Further travel to Vania, their destination for the evening, was impossible by train due to repairs down the line. They were obliged to take a carriage to the inn, which added nearly two additional hours to their journey. Eugene begrudgingly rode outside with the 'ton driver at Sam's request that he gather as much information about the locale as the driver could provide.

Sam and Hazel sat on one side of the vehicle, with Petrescu sitting across from them. The silence was a pronounced, tangible thing.

The dark countryside was thick with trees, punctuated periodically with small towns and villages, a few buildings cozily lit from inside. The carriage climbed steadily, and the terrain became more difficult to navigate. The wind picked up as the night wore on, and Sam noted the first fluttering of snow in the air. "Is it early in the season for snow?" he asked, his voice sounding loud in the silence.

Petrescu glanced out the window. "A bit. The station master's predictions were correct." He chuckled. "The old peasants always seem to have a sense for the elemental parts of life. Not so much the sophisticated parts, but that's just as well."

Hazel arched a brow. "Why 'just as well'?"

"Can you imagine how society would flounder if the lesser among us were allowed access to anything of value?" His nostrils flared. "When I was a young man, my father hired a woman and her son, also my age, as domestic help. I had begun collecting antiquities, and upon my return from a holiday in Persia, this son, Hector, acted as my valet. I came upon him as he was sorting through my laundry and belongings, tidying things, you see." He waved a hand. "He was about to toss aside a figurine I had purchased at great cost because he assumed it was a cheap trinket."

Hazel's eyes narrowed. "How could you expect him to recognize the item's value when he'd never been taught it?"

Petrescu laughed. "I would have known that item's value as a child in the schoolroom. Again, to my point," he said and crossed his legs, "there are those among us who are simply ill-equipped to live beyond the most basic. And thank goodness for that, for who would tend to life's menial tasks otherwise?"

"I believe anyone can be taught, can learn," Hazel said.

"You find me elitist, perhaps?"

"That would be one word for it."

He chuckled. "Ah, my dear. You remind me of my mother. A large brain, and an even larger heart." He sobered. "I fear it leaves you vulnerable."

"Vulnerable to what?" Sam said.

Petrescu turned his attention to Sam, his posture suggesting Sam was interrupting a conversation to which he had not been invited. "To those who would take advantage of a generous nature."

"Tell me more about your mother," Hazel said to Petrescu before Sam could say the testy words he wanted to. "You've told me she was a Light Magick practitioner. What were her strengths?"

Petrescu nodded. "You have every right to know about your bloodline. My mother was an accomplished Healer, but her skills lay more with herbal concoctions and spells—things she could make. You possess internally the strengths she manufactured externally."

"Did she work among the people?"

A ghost of a smile crossed his face. "She did. Helped the weak and the ill, the wealthy and the poor. My father tolerated it."

"He did not approve of her service?"

Petrescu shook his head. "He did not."

"I would also assume you did not approve."

"I loved my mother. I overlooked softness in her that I might have criticized in another."

The carriage was quiet, and Hazel watched her uncle patiently. Sam sensed she was waiting to see if he would continue on his own. Finally, she asked, "Why did he kill her?"

Hazel had told Sam that Petrescu's father had killed his mother, but she'd not learned any details beyond that bare fact. Sam now watched the count carefully, hoping the man would forget there was anybody else in the carriage beside

Hazel. The fact he was reluctant to share details indicated his response was probably significant.

"He was not actually my true father. My mother's first husband died when I was an infant. The only father I knew was her second husband, my stepfather. He was a military man, conducted campaigns to both defend the homeland and take new territory. My mother was protective of me, and one day when he was in a particularly foul mood and angry with me, she stepped in his way. He sent her flying, she hit her head on a stone wall, and she was gone."

Hazel winced. "I am sorry for your loss. Were you raised by nannies, then? Other family?"

He shook his head. "My father took me into his life, taught me the things he knew, things he considered valuable. He felt I had been coddled too long."

"My curiosity is piqued; please forgive my prying."

He smiled. "My mother was curious as well, insatiably so."

"And your sister, also?"

He blinked.

"*My* mother?"

"Mmm. Not nearly so much. From her, I suspect, you gained your compassionate heart. It is from my mother, however, you received that inquisitive brain."

"What was my mother's name?"

Petrescu paused, then finally answered. "Johanna."

Sam eyed the count with new insight. The man had adored his mother above all others. Hazel was the mirror image of the woman, and Sam wondered if Petrescu saw in Hazel a reincarnation of the mother he'd lost—perhaps not literally, but certainly figuratively. It went a long way toward explaining the man's fascination with Hazel.

"Did you also develop your mother's love of Light Magick?" Hazel asked.

Petrescu looked out the window at the snow flurries that danced on the air. "She taught me small things. The rest, I learned from my father. He didn't possess much natural magick skill, but he was resourceful, inventive."

"What did he invent?"

"All manner of things. Spells, enhanced artifacts to aid in battle."

She smiled. "And you inherited that proclivity for artifact collection."

"One of several useful skills he taught me."

Hazel looked out the window at the snow, and Sam studied her profile. Then he glanced at Petrescu, who also watched Hazel with speculation. Sam needed to understand what the man was about, understand his motives. He advised himself to be patient. The opportunity would present itself soon, and he would take it.

In the meantime, he wanted nothing more than to nuzzle the spot on Hazel's neck just below her ear, to hear her sigh, to anticipate the moment when she would turn her face and meet his lips with her own.

Despite the uncertainty swirling around their circumstances, his heart thudded. He smiled at his own sense of infatuation, the blush of affection that had deepened from something enjoyable and light to something much more profound. He was *courting* her, and the notion made him happy. He would propose, of course, but he didn't know when. They were immersed in a journey that had no definite end in sight, but the timing didn't matter. She was his perfect match as he was hers, and he would wait an eternity if necessary.

They finally reached their destination. The carriage slowed as they drove into a village complete with homes, pubs, and an inn. When the carriage halted, Sam followed Petrescu out and turned back to give Hazel his hand. As they gathered their belongings, Eugene, who had been sitting atop the uncovered driver's perch with the 'ton driver, shook his hat and dusted snow from his shoulders and lapels. He leaned close to Hazel, and Sam heard him say, "I've learned some things. Perhaps you shall find me once you're settled."

She looked at him carefully and nodded, and Sam noted a book detailing the region's history in his coat pocket. She opened her mouth to say something but stopped when Petrescu came around the side of the carriage.

He took Hazel's hands with his. "I must see to some business, but I've reserved rooms for our group. I'll join you presently, and in the morning, we shall continue on to the castle. Only one more hour in the carriage." He smiled.

Her brows drew together in a pretty frown. "But it is so late. Can your business not wait until morning?"

Sam hid a smile. She should have been an actress with how effortlessly she dug for information.

"Regrettably, my business cannot wait. I'll not be long, however." He kissed her gloved hands.

She returned his smile and nodded. "Very well. I trust you will be safe. I confess, the nearer we draw to home, the more I worry about how Marit will accept me."

"All will be well," Petrescu said. "Trust me."

He spoke briefly with the driver, then climbed back inside, and the carriage headed away into the night.

Hazel's eyes followed the conveyance and hardened.

Sam knew Hazel didn't trust Petrescu. And she wasn't worried anymore about Marit liking her. She was Marit's champion, and heaven help the person who stood between her and her twin.

Chapter 30

The town of Vania was aglow with lighted homes and alive with strains of music sounding from pubs. Vania was much larger than Hazel had expected, and after long hours of travel, anxiety, anger at the count, and rage at Renton, the feel of a normal town was soothing.

Hazel entered the inn's small reception area and stomped her feet on the rug. Her clothing was warm, but she was glad for the inn's cheery, warm interior. The establishment was old, but cozy. She felt more at home in it than she had during the luxurious travel in the *Magellan* or on the train.

Hazel approached the front table where an older woman was bent over, reaching for something on the floor. Hazel stooped, picked up the thimble, and handed it to the old woman. She met the woman's eyes as she straightened.

The woman, old enough to be Hazel's grandmother, dropped her mouth open in surprise and fell back into a chair, bumping her hip and settling hard.

Hazel gasped and reached forward for the woman's hands. "Oh! I apologize. I did not mean to startle you."

The woman put her hand to her chest. "Johanna," she murmured.

Hazel stilled, her smile fading. "I . . . who?" Her heart beat harder. Dravor had only just told her that her mother's name had been Johanna.

A young woman Hazel's age appeared from the stairway and approached. After a quick check on the old woman at the desk, she looked at Hazel and Sam with a bright smile. "I am glad to help you," she said in accented but clear English. "I am Elana, and this is Auntie Ursula. How many rooms will you require?"

Sam stepped forward and relayed the information that the count had already reserved rooms for them. He and Elana discussed the details while Hazel and Ursula stared at each other. After completing the transaction, Elana pointed to the stairs that led to their rooms and told them that, although the supper hour had passed, she would have the kitchen warm a light meal for them immediately.

Hazel, who still hadn't found her voice, looked at Elana and her aunt. Elana was a pretty woman, with dark hair that hung in a simple braid over her shoulder and light-brown eyes. She looked as though she could climb a mountain with only a walking stick and a knapsack.

The girl smiled at Sam. "May I show you and your friends to the dining room, or would you prefer to freshen in your rooms first?"

Hazel shook herself, and reached out, taking Sam's arm. "Courting," she said. "Not friends. We are courting."

Elana's smile deepened, and her brows lifted in delight.

"How wonderful! Many congratulations to you. You are English, yes?"

Sam's lips twitched as he glanced at Hazel. "We are," he answered. "And on holiday, visiting family."

"Splendid," Elana said. "I was a governess for the English ambassador living in Budapest. They returned home, but I am here for the season to help Auntie Ursula."

Elana reached behind the desk for their room keys. "Follow me, and we will have you settled in no time."

Elana was lovely and friendly, and Hazel couldn't dislike her. Not really. But she kept a firm hand on Sam's elbow, anyway. Eugene followed them, carrying their bags, as they climbed the stairs behind Elana, who was chattering about supper, the accommodations in each room, and the time for breakfast in the morning.

Hazel's nerves were frayed from the strange and tense journey in the confines of the carriage with Dravor, who always seemed to leave her with more questions than answers. Now he was attending to some "business" in the middle of the night, Auntie Ursula had called her by her dead mother's name, and pretty Elana had beamed at Sam as though she wanted to serve him dinner herself. Hazel's old insecurities rose with a vengeance, and she was so irritated by it she wanted to cry angry tears.

Elana indicated their rooms, handed them each an enormous, black iron key, smiled brightly, and bounced back down the stairs.

Eugene unlocked Sam's door, entered, and closed it.

She and Sam were alone in the hallway; the quiet hum of voices downstairs was barely audible.

Sam took her hand. "Hazel," he said. "My darling." He folded her in his arms and placed a kiss on her forehead. Then he pulled back and cradled her cheek in his hand, and she couldn't help but smile.

The world had upended itself and dumped her in Romania with one man who had filled her dreams for more than a year and another man who was quickly beginning to haunt her nightmares. She had a sister going mad in a locked room, mysteries and secrets swirling around her at every turn, and a mother at home in England, whom she was beginning to miss quite keenly.

Sam traced her cheek with his thumb, and she closed her eyes, turning her lips into his palm, kissing him gently.

He exhaled slowly, and when she opened her eyes, he leaned down and captured her lips with his. He kissed her with such deliberate slowness that she quite forgot she was in the middle of a hallway of a very public inn. When he finally lifted his head, she couldn't remember her own name.

"Freshen up," he whispered and took her key, opening her door for her and handing her the portmanteau. "I'll knock in ten minutes."

She nodded, dazed, and stepped inside her small room with its tidy bed and washbasin. Sam smiled and closed her door, and she stood still for a moment, wondering when she had become Alice who had fallen down the rabbit hole.

Later that night, Hazel was still awake, braiding her long curls and watching the snow swirling outside her window. It hadn't stopped for even a moment, and she hoped the carriage would be powerful enough to climb up the mountain the next day. Every time she had closed her eyes, she saw an image of herself with platinum hair, growing progressively, terrifyingly more mad. Unable to sleep, and almost glad she couldn't, she donned a robe over her nightdress and cracked open her door.

She winced at the creak, which sounded like an explosion in the quiet of the inn, and made her way down the stairs. She eased her way down the dark hall, following moonlit shadows that indicated windows, until she reached the inn's small kitchen. She hoped no one would mind if she fixed herself a cup of hot tea.

When she entered the room, she stopped in surprise. Elana was there, teapot already in hand and a cup on the table.

"My lady?" Elana asked. "Is something amiss?"

Hazel blinked. "Oh. No, nothing is wrong. I just couldn't sleep and—" She tightened the sash of her robe and glanced at the table.

Elana followed her gaze and smiled. "Would you care to join me?" She set down the teapot and placed another cup next to her own.

Hazel smiled. "Yes, thank you." She leaned against a counter and hesitated for a moment. "I also wanted to ask you some questions, but I was unsure . . ."

Elana filled the two cups and handed one to Hazel. She turned on a small lamp and indicated for Hazel to take a chair next to a table set along the wall. Elana sat opposite her and blew gently across her cup. "Might I assume you have questions about Auntie Ursula and your mother?"

Hazel nodded. "How did you know?"

"Auntie was afraid when she saw you, and was rather shaken for some time after you arrived. She recognized you because she knew your mother, years ago, and you look exactly like her. Her name was Johanna, and she was married to a blacksmith from the north. She grew an herb garden and provided remedies for minor illnesses. Auntie often suffered when the weather turned, and she said Johanna always helped her."

She paused, and Hazel was grateful for the moment to absorb the details. "I never knew her," she said quietly.

Elana nodded. "I know." She took a sip of tea. "Auntie said she remembers a rumor about two babies."

Hazel's heart stuttered and then beat hard. "I wish I knew more. The count—my uncle—has told me a little, but—"

Elana's mouth hung slack. "Count Petrescu is your uncle? He was Johanna's *brother*?"

"Yes." Hazel swallowed, wondering if another mystery was about to be uncovered. "You seem surprised."

"I suppose 'intrigued' is a better description. How much do you know about the history of the Petrescu family?"

"Apparently not enough," Hazel muttered.

Elana refilled her teacup as though settling in for a story. "Centuries ago, after the Crusades, a Hungarian prince established his home here and took the name 'Petrescu.' He built a massive home for himself and for his new wife and her child—his stepson. The castle was called Coppergate because he had a preference for the metal."

Hazel nodded. That was nearly the same information Dravor had told her.

"After the prince's wife died in a terrible accident, he began spending all of his time in the tower, which was situated above the family crypt. These days, the doors at the bottom of the tower are locked tight and sealed with magick, and thorny bushes surround the base and have crawled up the tower itself." Elana smiled. "As children, we imagined it was haunted. There is a window at the top, and we imagined Lady Petrescu's ghost wandering in there at night."

The words hung in the air, suspended, and Hazel felt as though her breath had been sucked from her lungs. In her memory, she recalled looking through Marit's eyes over the landscape from high above, as though from a tower window. Hazel swallowed. "Strange to put a tower atop a crypt."

Elana shrugged. "His reasons must have made sense to him. People said he grieved her loss greatly. There were other rumors, though; he was quite cruel."

"How so?" Hazel asked.

"When the prince was young, he cut a wide swath across Eastern Europe and beyond. His enemies often referred to him as 'the Impaler.'"

"Vlad the Impaler?"

"Yes, exactly," Elana confirmed. "But he seemed to have reserved that brutality for his enemies. Once he moved to Vania, he seemed more determined to focus on his magick."

Hazel chewed on her lip. "What happened to the stepson?"

"Prince Petrescu raised the child. He grew to adulthood, married, and sired a child, but during a dark period when the region experienced a wave of attacks from Dark Magick practitioners, the wife was killed, and he vanished. The stepson's child survived and was raised by his mother's family."

"What was the name of the prince's stepson?"

"Dravor. In fact, the current count is named for him."

A knot formed in Hazel's stomach. "What became of the cruel prince?"

"He was brutally murdered shortly after the Dark Magick attacks. Other than the young child, the Petrescu line had died."

Hazel's breath quickened. "You said the stepson, Dravor, disappeared when his wife was killed?"

Elana nodded. "He was never seen again. So when this Count Petrescu appeared twenty-five years ago to claim the family seat, most people assumed he was descended from Dravor's son—the young boy who was raised by his mother's family. Coppergate was in ruins, even the tower, and he restored the whole of it, even the grounds."

Hazel rubbed her forehead, piecing together the information and following the history of her family.

Elana continued. "We had no idea Johanna and the count were related. Though it makes sense, then, why he took in Johanna's child when she died in childbirth."

Only one child, Hazel thought. *The other one was sold to a stranger.*

Elana finished drinking her tea. "Auntie Ursula does not care for the count. She says there is a darkness to him. In fact, she claims that your mother was descended from the son of the original Dravor. Her proof is that Johanna looked exactly like Prince Petrescu's wife. People believe Auntie is daft, though. Johanna, herself, never claimed relation to the Petrescu name."

Hazel's heart thudded again. "How did your aunt come by that opinion?"

"From a medieval painting of the princess and her son, Dravor."

Hazel grew light-headed. Legends, princes, paintings, her mother—all swirled in her mind until she was able to narrow her focus to one fact. If Hazel looked just like Johanna, and Johanna looked like the original princess, whose painting depicted her and her young son, she didn't need to see the painting to know the truth of her uncle Dravor's true identity.

He was the boy in the painting she'd seen on the *Magellan*, as he had claimed, and he was more than five hundred years old.

Chapter 31

S am awoke with a start. Dawn shone clearly through the window, but he'd not heard a word from across the hall. It was possible Hazel had slept through the night without incident, which would be ideal. He'd had to leave Eugene in the 'ton charging room at the end of the hall, which had not been his first choice, but a 'ton without a charge was a 'ton who couldn't function.

He rose and quickly made himself presentable, and then crossed the hallway. When knocking on the door produced no response, his concern grew. Rather than wait, he withdrew a small packet of tools from his pocket and maneuvered them in the stubborn lock.

The mechanism finally clicked, and he opened the door. Hazel's room was in chaos. Clothes were strewn over her travel trunks, and her portmanteau was gone. The blankets had been rumpled, as if she had risen but not returned to bed.

The doors to the wardrobe on the far wall were cracked

open an inch. Blood suddenly running cold, he crossed the room and yanked it open.

Eugene had been crammed inside, legs drawn up, and slumped to the side.

"Eugene!" Sam grasped the 'ton around the middle and pulled him out of the wardrobe. Eugene weighed more than Sam did, and as unresponsive as the 'ton was, Sam struggled to maintain his grip. They both tumbled to the floor.

He looked around the room, heart beating rapidly as his adrenaline shot skyward. Where was Hazel?

He gently rolled Eugene onto the floor, face down, and noted the crack in his cranial covering under his hair. His back panel was intact, but a quick examination showed severed mechanisms connecting the head to the torso had been broken.

Sam stood and ran his hand across his forehead and down to his mouth. Petrescu must have her; it was the only possibility. Sam ran from the room and down the hallway, banging on the door of the room he knew had been reserved for the count.

"Petrescu!" He pounded the door repeatedly, hard enough to rattle it on its hinges. He tried the knob, surprised to find it open, and peered inside.

The room was empty, as if nobody had set foot in it.

Cursing, his fear like a black veil hovering at the corners of his eyes, he ran down the stairs to the main room. Ursula and Elana were there, and looked up at him with wide eyes.

"Hazel . . ." Sam gasped. "Miss Hughes . . . have you seen her? Where is the count?"

Elana shook her head. "I spoke with Miss Hughes last

night, I would say near midnight, but otherwise I've not seen her."

Ursula said something, and Elana translated. "Neither of us saw the count at all."

Sam ran his hand through his hair and paced away, his mind racing, frantic. "Wait, you saw Hazel at midnight? Where? Why?"

"She said she couldn't sleep and had come down for a cup of tea," Elana said, looking truly nervous. "She asked questions about her mother and about her uncle, the count."

"And then she left? Did she say she was returning to her room?"

"She was with me for thirty minutes or so, and then she left." Elana lifted a shoulder helplessly. "This is all I know."

He looked around the room, hands on his hips, naturally falling back to the quick decision-making process that had served him so well in the military. "Miss Elana," he said, "I need tools, anything your maintenance workers use to repair your 'tons. And then you need to tell me *exactly* what you told Miss Hughes last night." He paused. "How far are we from the castle? From Coppergate?"

Elana pointed outside. "An hour by carriage, nearly to the top of that peak."

Chapter 32

azel's head hurt. She felt as though she were floating underwater and couldn't reach the surface. A
voice, softly singing, pulled her upward. She didn't
understand the language of the song, didn't recognize the
voice.

She felt a cool hand on her forehead, but when she
gasped, the hand was gone as if suddenly yanked back. The
song turned to chanting, a litany of fear, worry, and surprise.

She blinked her eyes open, and the light in the room
pierced through to the back of her skull. She groaned and
rolled slowly to her side, cautiously peering at her surroundings.

She saw faded, painted walls that had once been a vibrant
forest scene, a multitude of books stacked and scattered, an
old toy box, painted stars on the ceiling, and one window
with shutters open to the snowy sky outside. She had seen
this room in her dreams a thousand times.

"Marit," she whispered, and shoved herself upright in the
bed she found herself in.

Standing against the wall was her sister, who seemed equal parts hopeful and terrified.

"The tower at Coppergate," she murmured. She looked at her sister—familiar because it was like looking in a mirror, and because she'd seen her in her dreams—and felt her eyes burn with tears. "He has had you locked in the tower for your entire life."

What was her uncle's ultimate purpose? Perhaps he wanted both of his nieces locked away, just like the artifacts he collected. Or possibly he had a task requiring the two of them, and he truly did need Hazel's help reaching Marit.

She pressed her hand to her forehead, forcing herself to recall the events of the previous night.

Tea with Elana. The shock of discovery. Returning to her room. Opening the door. A shadow looming over her.

Then a flash of light, a screech of twisting metal, and then darkness.

Petrescu must have lain in wait for her, rendered her unconscious, and brought her here.

She looked again at Marit, who regarded her with wide eyes, still murmuring under her breath. Hazel's heart sank. How would they communicate? And even if they could, would Marit be lucid?

"I don't suppose you speak anything other than Romanian?" she tried.

"Speak, speak," Marit responded, her eyes lighting up.

"You speak English?" Hazel shifted on the bed, putting her hand to her head at the dull ache that lingered.

Yet, beyond the word "speak," Marit's English seemed limited.

Hazel tried the only other two languages she knew—French and German—and Marit seemed conversant in both, although she continued her singsong litany of nonsense words, regardless of the language.

"German, it is," Hazel said. "Slightly better than my French."

Marit nodded. "German and French . . . German and French . . ."

Hazel stood from the bed, her eyes filling with tears. She was afraid, she had no idea when Petrescu would return or what he had planned, and she feared Sam would be out of his mind with worry, but before her was her sister, a stranger, yet someone she'd known her whole life.

"Marit," she said and approached her slowly. "Do you know me? I am Hazel. I am your sister."

"Sister, sister, Hazel sister," Marit murmured.

"Oh, what has he done to you?" Hazel's heart ached. It had been just over a year ago when Dream Hazel had begun looking . . . different. Her eyes had taken on a wild glow, and she had ceased smiling. "You have not always been . . ."

She stopped a few feet away and swiped at a tear that fell despite her efforts to keep her emotions in check.

Marit's eyes slowly hardened, and her expression tightened. "Where have you been?" she asked Hazel in German. "You left me here to rot."

Hazel shook her head. "I did not. I didn't know you were here. Our uncle"—she paused—"well, our *ancestor*, Dravor, only just found me and told me you were here."

From her periphery, Hazel saw a book levitate. She

turned her head, stunned, and then looked back at Marit, who regarded her evenly.

"Marit, are you doing that?"

The book flew forward, hitting Hazel's head.

"Stop!"

Book after book launched at Hazel, beating her from all sides.

"No, stop!"

Another book smashed into her face, and Hazel's temper snapped.

"Marit, stop!" Her shout echoed through the room, and the books immediately dropped to the ground. "I did not know you were here! Do you understand me? I only knew you from my dreams, which made no sense!" She paused, her chest heaving, and wiped a trickle of blood from the side of her mouth. "Did you know of me?"

Marit's eyes clouded, and she put a hand to her heart. She shook her head and winced. "Dreams, dreams, many many dreams, dreams . . ." The singing returned, and Hazel was unsure which she preferred—lucid anger or benign madness.

She looked around at the books strewn over the floor. She picked up one near her feet. *Mathematical Theory*, she read in French on the cover. She picked up another. *Latin Primer*. She slowly crossed the floor, looking at more titles. The languages were varied, but it seemed Marit had books on every subject under the sun.

"Do you have a perfect recollection of everything you read?" she asked Marit quietly in German.

"I remember I remember I remember."

Hazel turned back to Marit and tapped her lip thoughtfully with her fingertip. "What do you call him? Petrescu? Does he visit you? He brought you these books, yes? How do you eat?"

Marit's eyes widened at Petrescu's name. Her eyes clouded then cleared, and she shook her head again. "Uncle . . ."

"Do you know who he really is?" Hazel spotted a journal on the floor. She picked it up and flipped through the pages. The entries were written in a feminine hand and mostly in Romanian, but a smattering of other languages were decipherable to Hazel. Anything with a Latin or Germanic base gave her a basic understanding of the thoughts expressed.

The journal was dated two years earlier, and the name in the journal's front flyleaf was Marit Lehn. Yet the content was not the ravings of a madwoman. They were things Hazel might have written herself, only these contained yearnings to experience the world, to see all the things she'd learned of only in books.

"Is this yours, Marit?" Hazel glanced at her sister, who had retreated back against the wall.

"Marit's books, Marit's books . . ."

There were magick spells in the margins, and as the pages progressed, the spells seemed to grow more complex. She walked to the window and looked out over the snowy outside world. The tower was nearly encased with a tangle of vines and wicked-looking thorns. It was also slowly turning, she realized. The movement was so gradual she hadn't noticed it, but with the trees as reference, she suddenly also felt it.

She reached out to the window, confused by the fact that

there wasn't a glass pane in place. But no cold air was blowing in. The room was warm, and had been since she awoke.

"No!" Marit shouted as Hazel's fingers brushed the edge.

Pain shot through Hazel's hand as soon as her fingertips broke the plane of where the glass should have been. She cried out and pulled her hand to her chest as Marit crossed the room and grabbed her.

She pulled Hazel's hand into her own and looked at it. Welts were already rising on her fingers.

"So that is how he has kept you here." Hazel looked at her sister, sick inside. "I am so sorry I didn't know. I would have come for you. My mother would have come for you." She realized she'd spoken in English, and though Marit seemed to understand, Hazel repeated it in German.

Marit's eyes filmed with tears, and the corner of her mouth lifted in a smile, but no sooner had she seemed to regain her lucidity, than she winced in pain and grabbed her head. When she looked at Hazel again, the hardened expression had returned.

"No, no, no," Hazel murmured, and began speaking to her rapidly, reaching for her hands and telling her about the world outside and all the things they would do together when they were free.

Marit became distracted, then docile, and Hazel walked with her back to the bed and sat down. She kept up the chatter, wondering how long she could maintain the pace before going mad, herself.

They settled back against the white-painted iron headboard, and Hazel held tight to her sister's hand. Her gold bracelet touched Marit's wrist, which Hazel might not have noticed except for the sudden warmth she felt along her skin. Her bracelet connected with Marit's platinum chain, and instead of the burn Hazel had felt from the touch of platinum the first night she'd met Dravor Petrescu, this time it was comfortable.

Marit also looked at the joined chains, and her expression turned to delight. Her deep lavender eyes sparkled, and for a fraction of a moment, she seemed to recognize Hazel. Almost immediately, though, she winced and again raised her free hand to her head.

Hazel anticipated the change in her demeanor, so she began chattering again about her adventures and her life. After a time, she settled on singing nursery rhymes and songs Rowena had sung to her. The memorized lyrics came freely, and as she felt her sister relax against her, their fingers still clasped, she tried to piece together what Dravor had done.

Clearly Marit had not gone mad of her own accord. Seeing the behavior firsthand, Hazel was confident that Dravor had manipulated Marit's thoughts—possibly with a spell, or something he'd fed her or infused her with. Hazel's best guess was that Marit had grown more proficient, both in intellect and capacity for magick, as time passed than Dravor had anticipated. Now, whenever her head seemed to clear, the madness abated, she was afflicted with a bout of pain.

As the day wore on, Hazel's stomach rumbled, and she wondered how Petrescu provided for Marit. The tower maintained a mellow hum. Now that she knew they were turning, she figured the machinery operating the movement was the source of the noise.

Suddenly a loud churning and clanking of gears rang

through the room, and Marit shot from the bed. She ran to an open wardrobe and beckoned for Hazel to join her.

A section of the wardrobe rolled back, and a tray appeared with a large basket. Marit grabbed the basket, and when Hazel put her hand into the wardrobe to see if she could somehow keep the panel from closing, Marit yelled and pulled back Hazel's hand.

"He thought of everything, didn't he?" she muttered to herself in disgust.

Marit opened the basket and pulled out food that, Hazel admitted, smelled delicious. They ate together on a blanket spread on the floor, and Hazel wondered how long she could maintain her calm control before going mad, herself.

Chapter 33

S am clamped the last two wires together. He reattached the covering on Eugene's spinal simulation and opened the back panel, securing the tins in place. He held his breath and hoped for the best.

He pushed the "live" switch and watched until Eugene finally moved. His eyes blinked open, and the sound of his whirring cogs grew. Sam had never been so happy to hear the familiar sound.

He gripped Eugene's shoulder and forced the 'ton to look at him. "What happened here? Where is Hazel?"

Eugene put his hand to the back of his neck. "I had finished charging and was returning to your room when I stopped to check on Hazel. I saw Petrescu—he must have been waiting for her—and when he saw me, he pointed his hand at me. I flew through the air, and just before I hit the wall, I saw Hazel crumple at his feet. I tried to stop him, sir, but my circuits . . ." He gestured to his chest, where an odd dent remained from the attack.

Sam nodded, sober. "He has her, Eugene. I need your help."

"Of course. I shall compute our odds of success via several different scenarios."

"I would rather not know our odds, as I suspect they will be depressingly low. Elana has told me what she knows of the count's castle and tower—which is where I suspect he has taken Hazel—and we can evaluate our options when we get there."

"Very good. I must add, however, that Miss Hazel herself says 'Knowledge is power,' and knowing the odds may help you—"

Sam held up his hand. "Knowing the odds will not change my mind. I will get her out of that tower or die trying."

Eugene raised one brow, but nodded as he stood. "If that seems reasonable to you, I'll not argue."

"Good."

"It is not a sound position to take, but the choice is yours."

"Yes. Excellent." Sam gathered the tools and put them in the trunk Elana had secured for him.

"I suppose a human brain may not appreciate the sound logic that rules a 'ton's behavior, but I'll do my best to understand why waiting until later to know your odds is the best course of action. After all, the odds will change depending on if you mount a rescue attempt from inside the tower versus the outside of the tower."

Sam looked at Eugene, his nostrils flaring. "An urchin off

the streets would reason that odds are better for rescue from the inside than the outside."

Eugene shrugged and lifted the trunk from the floor as if it were as light as a feather. "Depends on the interior construction, I should think."

Sam retrieved his coat from a chair where he'd draped it earlier. "How can you possibly measure odds, then, not knowing what the interior looks like?" He shook the coat and slipped it on.

"That is why the calculation is based on averages. One would assume the tower interior is not empty, like a grain silo, and assuming Miss Hazel is at the top, there must be a mechanism in place to have transported her up there. Utilizing the mechanism should be much simpler than attempting to scale the outer wall."

Sam sighed and opened the door to the hallway. "Throw a grappling hook into the equation, now where are the odds?"

"One moment . . ."

Sam rolled his eyes and followed Eugene from the room. Perhaps, he reasoned, the best benefit of having a 'ton with superior programming was that in times of trouble, he was a wonderful distraction.

Chapter 34

The hours seemed to turn as slowly as the tower itself. Hazel wondered how long it would be until Petrescu appeared—if ever. Marit was relatively calm. She occasionally paced in circles, muttering in Romanian and sometimes in German.

Hazel examined every inch of the room, paying close attention to the wardrobe, which seemed the most likely means of escape. But whatever barrier the count had placed on the moving panel and the window was powerful enough that jumping through it wasn't an option.

Light outside the window dimmed by degrees, and still the snow continued to fall. The tower had made a full rotation, showing the land for miles. Villages could be seen in the distance, looking like toy houses, and Vania, closer to the castle, lay in the valley below like a page from a picture book.

Sam was down there, if Petrescu hadn't already done something to him. Was he worried? Even now trying to find her? The thought of losing him was worse than the notion that she might be stuck in the tower with Marit forever.

"Now I understand why you walk in circles," Hazel said in English as she made her own slow pass around the room. "The most amazing thing, really, is that you weren't driven mad long before now."

"I came close," Marit said, picking up books and putting them back on their shelves.

Hazel's attention whipped to Marit, who seemed to have responded without realizing it. And she'd answered in perfect English.

Marit suddenly cried out and tunneled her fingers in her hair.

Hazel's heart thudded "Oh, no, no, no!" She rushed to Marit and grabbed her hand, touching their bracelets together, and began singing the nursery rhyme Rowena had used to sing to her as a child. It was the one Marit seemed to like the most, and to Hazel's relief, she was quick enough to ward off a violent attack.

She was still singing, Marit humming along, when the gears inside the tower turned. Marit looked up, delighted, and ran to the wardrobe.

But instead of the small panel that had opened earlier to deliver a basket of food, a larger side door opened.

Marit stopped, then took a tentative step back.

Hazel moved toward Marit as the door slid open, revealing first a pair of men's shoes, then trousers, a coat, and then a face.

Marit screamed and scrambled back, and Hazel's breath caught in her throat.

It was Renton.

Hours had passed by the time Sam successfully repaired Eugene, gathered supplies, and found a driver willing to brave the elements and rough terrain between Vania and the count's castle. Hazel had been in her uncle's clutches the entire day, and the thought that he might be too late to find her—to save her—had Sam sick with worry.

He now brushed the snow from his eyes as he stood at the base of Coppergate's tower. It was a massive structure, originally made of solid blocks of stone and brick but now showing signs of age. Missing chunks revealed enormous cogs and gears churning and clanking inside. The copper-covered roof had taken on a green tinge but had probably shone brilliantly when newly constructed.

A knot of brambles and thorns provided a barrier around the base and climbed midway up the structure. The tower itself turned so slowly, he thought he might be imagining it, but the thicket of thorns remained stationary. He blinked quickly, feeling dizzy.

Some of the vines were nearly as thick as his arm, with thorns as big as his fist, and the thicket itself was a meter deep.

"It appears Miss Elana was correct about the thorns," Eugene said.

Turning to Eugene, he said, "And I was correct that we'd be better off going inside."

"We won't be needing this, then." Eugene tossed a heavy grappling hook to the ground.

A scream echoed from inside the tower, faint behind the thick, stone wall, but loud enough that Sam heard it and felt his blood run cold.

"Find the entrance," he said to Eugene. "Now."

The grin on Renton's face was smug, and Hazel nearly went blind with fury. She clenched her fists and debated her odds of doing enough harm to him to render him useless long enough to get herself and Marit to the wardrobe.

"Marit, shh," she said to her frantic sister, who grabbed her arm and pulled her back, nearly tumbling them both to the floor.

Marit cried, speaking in Romanian, and Hazel was forced to struggle against her to remain upright.

"I see she remembers me," Renton said.

Marit let go of Hazel and scrambled to the wall, where she crouched down and pulled her knees to her chest.

Hazel planted herself in front of Renton. "Why are you not in jail?" She matched him step for step, always keeping herself between Renton and Marit.

"Did you honestly think the count had me arrested? He has friends in every police force between here and London."

"I saw them take you into custody." She shook her head as realization dawned. "It was all a show for me."

"And a good one. I was actually on the same train you took, you know. And riding on an animatronic horse is much faster than traveling overland by carriage."

"I assume you were the 'business' my uncle needed to see

to last night." Hazel was pleased to see he still bore the marks of the scratches she had inflicted on his face.

His eyes narrowed, and she braced herself for a blow. He leaned toward her, and the effort it took to restrain himself was clear.

"Renton, why are you here?"

"To deliver you both to the count. It's time you proved you're worth all the trouble you've caused."

She realized the door to the wardrobe remained open, and since Renton had been unaffected as he entered, that passageway down should be shock-free.

If she could get her sister and get past Renton, perhaps there was a chance . . .

"Marit," Hazel said in German. "Get up, and come to me. We are leaving."

Renton reached behind his back and pulled a long knife from a sheath. He twirled it in his hand as he advanced on her. "What did you say?"

Hazel imagined Sally's fear while running from the man, and despite her own rising anxiety, her anger built. "Killing Sally was unnecessary. My uncle would have quietly returned her home."

He shook his head. "You're as stupid as he is. She would have eventually talked. I couldn't let her go back to England."

Hazel took a step toward him. "Who would care for one poor servant girl? She could swear you attacked her, and nobody would lift a finger to look for you!"

Renton's eyes suddenly left her face, and his gaze darted over her shoulder. She realized Marit must be moving, and to her surprise, she felt her sister lock hands with her.

"Bad, bad, bad, bad . . ." Marit chanted under her breath.

Hazel stepped back with her and angled toward the wardrobe. She had no idea how to protect the both of them, but to her surprise, she realized her Marit-inspired urges for bravery over the past year now strengthened her resolve. They would not die at the hands of that odious man.

He was huge, and he had a weapon. But this was their only chance. One step, two steps, three steps. She and Marit moved together as he advanced, and Hazel locked her eyes with his, trying to anticipate his moves.

They were steps away from the open door in the wardrobe when Marit yelled "Run!" and pulled Hazel with her.

Renton shouted and then snarled, his face red with rage. He grabbed Hazel's shoulder and nearly took her to the floor. Marit held tight to her other hand and pulled, and, as Renton advanced, Hazel kicked as hard as she could between his legs.

He bellowed and fell forward, and the tip of his blade caught her cheek, slicing across her skin. His grip on the weapon loosened, though, and she blindly grabbed at it, her hand landing on the edge where the blade met the handle.

She yanked the knife from his hand, gritting her teeth as the blade cut into her palm. Marit pulled her arm so roughly that Hazel feared it would pop from its socket.

Renton, still bent double and swearing, caught the edge of her dress just as Marit hauled her into the small space. Hazel quickly scanned the walls, hoping to see a handle that would lower the lift.

"There!" She shouted and pointed to Marit's side. Her cheek was on fire, and her hand burned from where she had grasped the knife. Using her good hand, she managed to rip her skirt from Renton's grasping fingers.

The door began to slide closed, and Hazel gasped for breath when her head was yanked back. Renton had grabbed her braid and was pulling her back through the closing door.

She cried out and lifted the blade, and, desperate with fear, sliced through her braid, cutting it completely off.

Renton stumbled back, and the door closed.

Sam and Eugene circled the base, until they found a spot where a segment of the thorns appeared to have been disturbed. He looked closer, pulling a Tesla torch from his bag and shining it inside the mass of vegetation.

"There it is." He glanced up at the tower, praying that Hazel was safe, but knowing she was not.

"A trap, perhaps?" Eugene shook his head. "That was a simple search."

Sam frowned. "Trap or no, I don't see another way to do this." He glanced at Eugene and tried for levity. "And those odds, remember?"

Eugene lowered the heavy pack he carried and pulled out a long, sheathed knife. He gave Sam a look, and Sam took a large step back. Eugene whacked at the opening in the thorns three times, enough to give Sam room to wriggle through.

"Thank you," Sam said, checking his ray gun. "You'll wait here, and—" He broke off as the thorns rustled and magically filled in again.

"Bother," Eugene said dryly. "It appears you will need to

be quicker." Eugene motioned him back and whacked again at the branches.

'This time when they opened, Sam shoved through with an arm over his eyes, wincing as the thorns tore through his coat and caught his neck and chin. He reached the tower and ran his hands along the side. The door was a mechanism that slid open along an interior track. That it was now open a scant five inches was testament to someone's earlier haste in entering.

"Not that I'll complain," he muttered and grasped the edge, shoving with his might to open it past the gap currently available.

The thorns filled in behind him, tearing into his back and legs, catching his arms and hands until he was nearly immobile.

"You must be quick, I said." Eugene's voice sounded muffled as he again chopped and hacked with the machete.

"I *was* quick," Sam muttered and winced as a thorn scratched along his arm.

Eugene shoved his way through and stood next to Sam, who tried to shrug out of his coat, which was caught tight. Eugene pulled on the tower door, trying to slide it open wide enough for Sam to fit through. He finally managed it just as Sam muscled out of his coat.

The thorns closed behind Eugene, and Sam winced as the sharp needles tore through the 'ton's clothing down to his exterior covering. The tower was slowly inching away from them, and Sam's opportunity to dive into the opening was going with it.

Sam cursed and reached out to Eugene, but the 'ton was quickly trapped by the unnatural thorns and vines.

Eugene still had use of one arm, which he used to roughly shove Sam into the tower. "Go," he said as the door began to slide closed. "You are supposedly a surgeon; fix me later."

Sam dove into the blackness of the tower as it rotated, and the door slid shut behind him with a loud clang.

In the resulting darkness, he wondered if he had indeed walked into a trap.

Chapter 35

Marit's eyes were wide and terrified as the lift descended. Hazel's legs trembled and threatened to give way, but Marit threw her arms around her and held tight. She said something over and over in Romanian, a constant litany in Hazel's ear as her breath came in ragged, crying gasps.

Renton's roar sounded from high above, even over the sound of the clanging and connecting of the tower's internal cogs and wheels. Hazel turned to face the door as the car reached the ground and shuddered to a stop.

She sucked in a deep breath and rubbed her eyes with her sleeves. She clasped Marit's hand, and holding Renton's bloodied knife out in front her, she steeled herself to face whatever awaited them on the other side.

The lift door opened, and Hazel struck swift and hard with the knife.

"None of that now, Hazel," Dravor said, wiping the blood from his face with a snow-white handkerchief. The red smear was a stark contrast, and Hazel's thoughts flitted to Sally, to Renton, to Marit, who still clutched her hand and chanted like a frightened child.

He pointed at her hand, and she dropped the knife against her will. When she bent to grab it, he pointed again and sent it flying into the tower machinery, which ground it into bent, mangled pieces.

He ushered Hazel and Marit out of the lift, through an ancient door, which slammed behind them, and then, because they refused to descend the stairs, levitated them down and dropped them roughly to the stone floor of an underground crypt.

"You ruin lives," she gritted through her teeth. "I *demand* to know what you are about this instant!" Her ragged shout echoed throughout the cold room and circled back.

"You want to know what I am about." He folded the handkerchief and placed it back in his pocket and looked down at his coat, where a single, dark stain dribbled down the lapel. Tsking, he removed the coat and set it on a stone lid, under which lay a box that probably contained one of her ancestors.

"Have you not reasoned it through, yet?" He looked at her in mock sympathy. "Hazel. Do not disappoint me. Not after all of this."

Marit gripped tightly to Hazel's hand. "Healing, healing, healing . . ." she murmured quietly, and Dravor's brows shot high.

"Now, that—*that* is impressive. She should not be able to recognize the time of day. Tell me, did my safeguards against her possible lucidity hold true?"

Hazel's eyes blazed. "You mean was she comprehending one moment and attacking me the next?"

He smiled broadly. "Oh, excellent."

"You have us both, now. Release her from . . . whatever this is you've done."

"I cannot possibly do that. Those two brains working together? Against me? I dare not risk it. All I need is the two of you physically together, and one able to think through the process." He paused as if only then noticing something. "Where is your hair?"

"Renton," she said through clenched teeth.

"Ah. He has always been a bit . . . unpredictable."

Hazel wondered if she should stall for time or simply press forward through to whatever end he had planned. She didn't know where Sam was, and he stood no chance of finding them down here anyway.

There's no one coming. It's just us. The thought ran through her head, and she glanced at Marit, who remained still, glassy-eyed. Hazel amended her thought. *It's just* me.

"Now, do not be glum." Dravor raised his hand. "What do you know thus far?"

"You are five hundred years old."

He tipped his head. "True, but gauche of you to mention age. What else?"

"Your stepfather was Vlad the Impaler."

"Yes! You've done some research."

He's a mage, mage, mage . . . Marit's singsong voice sounded through Hazel's head, and a cold realization washed over her. Marit's voice was in her head, and Petrescu might eventually realize it. She steeled her thoughts, determined to keep the mind-reading gift to herself.

"You're a mage," she said.

"I am—because of my mother, but also because of the study I did with my father."

"Vlad?"

"He was the only father I ever knew. By the time he married my mother, his impaling days were over."

"That did not stop his cruelty, however."

His face tightened. "No, it did not."

"Why did you study magick with him?"

"What choice had I? I was a child!"

"But then you were an adult, with a wife and child. You could have taken them away, left him behind."

His eyes flashed. "Why would I leave? With my natural ability and his resources—you have no idea of the power we wielded, the spells we worked together."

She looked at him silently, fitting the pieces together. "You were looking for eternal life and used a spell that blended elements of a fossilized creature and a rare plant from central Africa."

"Oh, you are excellent."

"So why are we here, in the family crypt, and one of us mad?"

"Because, Vlad tampered with the elixir we created." His jaw tightened. "The elixir required two different incantations—one from each of us. He did not trust me."

"Should he have?"

"Of course not. I drank it as soon as I could and then ran him through with my sword."

Hazel smiled slowly, enjoying the irony in spite of herself. "But he had not spoken his half of the incantation. Not all of it, anyway."

Petrescu eyed her, and his fingers twitched. Her throat began to close, and she fought for air. He released her as suddenly as he'd captured her, and she gasped.

"No, he had not. And although it took him some time to die, he waited until he breathed his very last, gurgling breath before telling me."

Her temper flared despite her fear. "I confess, I do find humor in it. And I might remind you that if you choke me to death, I'll not be able to do whatever it is you require of me."

"My time is coming to an end," he said. "The incomplete elixir granted me five hundred years, but no more. I have searched the world for talismans to prolong my life, but have gained only temporary time."

She looked around at the stately, ancient, and eerie stone coffins, visible in flickering torchlight, and her heart began to pound. She reflected on the fundamental elements of spell casting and magicks she'd recently studied. "You need an incantation spoken by one from Vlad's lineage. But since he died without a direct heir . . ." She swallowed. "You need him alive again." Images of Eugene's notes in her journal flashed through her head, and she felt faint. "You believe we are more than Healers. You believe we are Resurrectionists."

He chuckled. "You *are* Resurrectionists. I created you myself."

She clenched her fist until the wound from Renton's knife throbbed. The surge of her rage that had carried her thus far ebbed, and she feared she would fail after all. After everything. After dragging Sam away from London and straight into this nightmare.

"What do you mean, you 'created' us?"

"The same elixir that granted eternal life, when altered the slightest bit, and given to a woman carrying an unborn child, will produce a Healer of exceptional powers. That child will be a Resurrectionist."

"You gave our mother the elixir." Hazel narrowed her eyes. "Did you stalk the women of the village until you found one expecting a child?"

"Don't be daft. I couldn't use just anyone. As it happened, Johanna worked in my gardens and thus was in close proximity. She was ill, and I caught her husband attempting to steal medication from my personal laboratory in the castle. I granted him leniency." He placed a hand on his chest. "I, instead, provided medication that would be much more effective for his pregnant wife. The timing couldn't have been better, as I had just procured the last of the African plant."

"You gave him the elixir."

"Indeed. And he gave it to Johanna. Tragically, he died in a hunting accident within a week."

"Convenient."

"It meant Johanna became my responsibility, of course, much like vassals of old who depended upon the lord of the castle. I told Johanna that I would help her and raise the child as my own. The baby would have a place in the castle to live, my undivided attention—everything a mother could want for her child and more."

Hazel finally understood. "But you frightened her."

His eyes snapped up to her face. "She had no reason to be frightened. I promised her I would give the child the world."

"Except there were two of us."

"Except there were two of you. At Johanna's urging, the midwife spirited you away before I was aware you even existed. She would have given away Marit, as well, but I'd heard Johanna was in delivery and arrived just after your birth but before Marit's." He circled around to a stone box on the far end of the room. The lid bore the stone-carved image of a man in peaceful repose, hands clasped in prayer on his chest. Dravor looked at it and rolled his eyes. With a flick of his wrist, the lid flew off and crashed to the ground.

"In the years that followed, I could not understand why my darling Marit was unable, despite years of training, reading, studying, and exposure to the world's best learning, to raise even the simplest thing from the dead. Nothing!" He huffed out his irritation. "It was because I required *both* of you." He scowled impatiently. "Come closer!"

Hazel moved forward reluctantly, and after a step, Marit joined her.

We are holding the wrong hands, she thought, and wondered if Marit heard her. *Our chains must touch.*

Dravor's head came up sharply. "Are you talking?" he barked.

Hazel wrinkled her brow, glanced at Marit, and then returned her attention to him as if in confusion.

He watched them for a moment and then returned his attention to the body in the coffin.

Hazel and Marit stepped closer, and dread grew in her

stomach. She wished desperately for more time to think. "Did you kill Johanna?"

He frowned, the flickering torchlight casting shadows on his face. Dravor's eyes narrowed. "It was my herb garden, and descendant or no, she had no right to steal from me."

Hazel swallowed. "You knew she was your flesh and blood—and still you killed her?"

"She looked like my mother. As do both of you." He sighed. "Besides, a mother's love is a powerful thing. I couldn't have her interfering."

Hazel thought of the young, frightened woman—her *mother*. "She was familiar with Light Magick so she may have known you, recognized you."

He scoffed. "She couldn't have known me."

"I knew you."

He looked at Hazel with narrowed eyes. "You did not."

"I did. I knew I had a sister, recognized the pieces of truth you told me. I even felt a . . . kinship . . . with you." She shook her head and looked away from him. "I wanted . . ."

"You wanted a father." The mockery in his tone chased away any remaining traces of sadness.

She straightened her shoulders and moved forward, pulling Marit with her. "This thing you are doing is dangerous, Dravor. We are Healers, not Resurrectionists, and there are no instructions for this procedure."

He smiled. "You forget I have access to your betrothed."

"He does not know where we are." She swallowed.

"He does. In fact, he is already upstairs as we speak. I heard the lift."

Oh, Sam. Hazel's heart hurt. She'd led him to his doom.

"The sooner we finish, the sooner you can go to him. Come closer, both of you." His expression was hard, and when they hesitated, he lifted a hand and brought both of them to the side of the stone coffin, where they looked down on the remains of Vlad the Impaler.

Chapter 36

S am took stock of his surroundings. A corridor circled the perimeter of the tower, and he spied an opening. He stepped inside and looked up into what seemed an eternity of gears and cogs. He felt as though he'd stepped into a giant clock. The mechanisms turned in perfect precision, enormous and loud, and he quickly realized that to scale the pieces themselves would lead to a bloody mess if he slipped.

How had Petrescu gotten Hazel to the top? Elana and her Aunt Ursula had confirmed there was a room at the top of the tower, which meant there must be a way to deliver food and basic supplies to whoever was in that room. He skirted around the base of the machinery, eventually spying a long shaft on the wall that shot upward. Just before him, at the base, was a door, and he realized it must be a lift that led to the room at the top. To the left of the lift was another door, but it was larger, ornate, and aged.

He assumed Hazel was in the top of the tower, but Ursula had said the original family crypt was underneath. The larger of the two doors was clearly the one leading to the crypt. He moved closer, undecided, when something glinted in the light of his torch. Several strands of golden hair were trapped in the lift door.

He swallowed, his mouth dry, and opened the lift door. He grasped the strands and shone the light into the interior of the box. Blood had been smeared along the frame and wall. His heart beat faster as he stepped inside the lift.

He found a lever and pulled it. The door closed as the lift began to rise. Uncertain of what he would find at the top, he braced himself and pulled his ray gun from the holster. The lift climbed higher, before eventually grinding to a stop. One heartbeat, two, and the door finally slid open.

There on the floor was Hazel's braid. He dropped the torch, lunged forward, and grabbed the hair, and a violent shove from the side sent him sprawling. The gun went flying, and Sam cursed his stupidity. He ought to have been steadier, ready for an attack, but the sight of Hazel's braid had stunned him.

He scrambled to his feet, and when he finally caught a glimpse of his attacker, he stumbled back in surprise.

"What are you doing out of jail?" he grunted, and then coughed as Renton caught him in the ribs.

"Your little pretty asked the same thing," Renton snarled. "Just before I sliced off her hair."

Sam muscled his way free of the man's grasp and felt a cold violence in him that he hadn't experienced since returning from the battlefield in India. "What did you do to her?" He grasped Renton's lapels and shoved, forcing his back against the wall near the window. "Where is she?" he shouted, shoving his forearm against the man's neck.

Renton's face turned red, but then he smiled. "Took them both, I did, pretty little mirror images." He thrust his knee up, but Sam twisted away in time that the blow hit his thigh. He still flinched backward, and it was enough that Renton could shove Sam's arms away.

"'Course, they're a little different now—one with hair, and one without . . ." He grinned, and blood showed in his teeth where Sam had hit him. "Though neither one will be pretty at all when Petrescu finishes with 'em."

"Where are they?" Sam shouted again as Renton grabbed him and swung him around and shoved him hard into the window's shutter.

He strained against Renton's grip, trying to twist and spin into a better position, looking for the gun. He finally shoved Renton back again, reversing their positions so Renton's back was to the window. He tried to tear free and dash across the room for his gun, but Renton held tight. Sam smashed his forehead into the bridge of Renton's nose, and as the man howled in rage, Sam angled to lift Renton's body in an attempt to shove him out the window.

Renton's head and shoulders were finally out of the window, and as the other man screamed, Sam realized his own arms burned in pain. He tried to loosen his hands and pull his arms back, but Renton held tight. In his own attempt to escape the burning barrier, Renton lunged back, grabbing Sam's arms and pulling him out with him.

Sam went through the window with Renton, the sensations slowing to searing, hellish pain. His head was on fire, his eyes burned, and the inferno scorched and burned his body from head to foot as he plunged through the window and out into the night. They tumbled and fell, locked together, the wind trapping Sam's scream in his throat.

The side of the tower sped past him, and then he landed atop Renton's body on the spiked thorns below. The searing pain of the thorns tearing into his skin began to fade as he lost all feeling, all rational thought.

The last sensation he registered was the soft braid of long, curling hair—hair that glinted in the sunlight and felt like spun silk in his hands—that fell from the window above and landed on the back of his neck like a caress.

His breath left his body in a long, ragged sigh.

Chapter 37

Hazel looked over the bones in the crypt. Clothing that had once been rich now lay in tatters over a skeleton that wore a talisman and several rings.

"I find it oddly satisfying to see him in such a state." Dravor looked at the remains dispassionately. "It will be far more satisfying to subject him to my will, however. I have uses for him elsewhere."

Hazel swallowed and looked up at Dravor. "You mean to remove him from the crypt? For what purpose?"

"To serve me."

Silence followed his pronouncement.

"He will be nothing more than a zombie," Hazel said when she found her voice. "And should he prove . . . difficult . . ." She swallowed. "I imagine your plans would be complicated if the Impaler were again turned loose on the world."

Dravor regarded her with the look of feigned sympathy she'd come to hate. "He'll be under my control, my dear, not his own. Have you not read extensively on the zombie condition?"

"I have read enough to know there is more that we *don't* know about the condition than what we do."

"Because the world has never seen a zombie raised by a truly gifted Resurrectionist." He extended his hands. "Or two, as the case may be."

"Why not let the body be at rest once the incantation is complete?" Hazel finally said. "That is a variable that may escape your control."

"Because he killed my mother!" Dravor's roar echoed through the chamber, and both women jumped at the suddenness of it. "I thought that ending his life would bring me satisfaction, but it has not!"

Hazel tugged subtly on Marit's hand, and they moved to the foot of the coffin. It was logically a better vantage point, but she couldn't decide if she and Marit would be better served to run at the first opportunity, or if they could possibly do more good if they remained. Perhaps they could learn how to reverse the process and be certain the dead man remained where he belonged.

Hazel glanced at Marit and back at Dravor. "We have never done this." She gestured to her sister. "You've bound my sister as surely as if she were tied and gagged, and I have no reference to draw on, no idea how to proceed."

"I have seen you heal, Hazel. You meditate, and the power flows from you. It is rather a sight to behold." Dravor smiled. "We will learn as we go, the three of us."

Hazel stared. "I was exhausted after Sally's surgery. Suppose this kills us?"

"You will be all the more motivated to master the art of Resurrection quickly, then."

Hazel released a breath, a laugh, and put her hand to her temple. Madness. It was madness, and she and Marit would be held captive to it until it destroyed them.

Dravor indicated the coffin. "Enough delays, no more arguments from you. I never dreamed parenting would be so trying. Join hands." He waved his hands and crossed them. "The other hands, with the chains."

They hesitated.

"Now." His voice was cold.

Hazel thought of Sam. Was he even alive? The sooner they finished this business in the crypt, the sooner she could protect the ones she loved from Dravor's evil.

She glanced at her sister, whose eyes were glossy with unshed tears. Hazel traded her hand, their chains touched, and the warmth spread. Turning her attention to the body in the coffin, she visualized, reluctantly, a healthy form.

She held the image, and narrowed her focus. Sweat beaded on her forehead, and pain radiated from her head. Her own ignorance of the process both frightened and frustrated her, and she concentrated on her mental image more firmly, shutting out everything around her.

Nothing happened. Nothing!

If she couldn't figure something out, Dravor would either kill them or keep them locked together indefinitely. She felt her nose run and wiped it, anxious to see her hand come away smeared red with blood.

Marit, she thought, and imagined sending the message to her sister. *This isn't working. Focus with me. Imagine the body well and whole.*

Marit squeezed her fingers in reply, and Hazel felt both a sense of comfort and a surge of energy.

To her horror and fascination, the bones began to twitch and quiver. The biological matter beneath it gathered and spread, becoming sinew and muscle, tissue and organs, that knit and fused together over the skeletal structure.

Marit's grip on Hazel's hand tightened.

Hazel glanced at Dravor, whose face glowed in satisfaction as he watched his father reappear. Energy passed through her and around her, obliterating reality. She lost all sense of time and place. It might have been moments or hours, but suddenly, to her amazement and horror, a fully-formed man lay in the box. His eyes slowly blinked open.

Dravor reached down and clipped a few strands of his father's hair and placed them in his jacket pocket.

"That will insure obedience?" Hazel murmured.

"Possibly." Dravor watched, fascinated, as the zombie slowly rose to a seated position.

Hazel looked at the risen man, and her heart stuttered at the blankness in his eyes. This creature lacked a soul.

"Hazel!"

She snapped her attention back to Dravor, who glowered at her in rage.

"Focus!"

The zombie swayed in the coffin and clutched the side for balance. Hazel's distraction had weakened the process, and Marit was unable to sustain the animation alone.

Dravor barked something in Romanian. The creature blinked, and responded in a monotone that grew in inflection and speed. Conversation between father and son began to flow, and to Hazel's amazement and dismay, the zombie soon became more animated, its voice surer, its gaze sharpening.

The zombie turned its attention to Hazel and Marit, whose hands were clasped so tightly Hazel figured she'd be sore afterward. It said something to Dravor, still looking at the twins, and its mouth turned up in a smile that had Hazel feeling cold despite the warmth of the spell she and Marit cast.

Marit blew out a soft breath and retreated half a step, pulling Hazel with her. The horrid satisfaction on the zombie's face made Hazel feel ill. It seemed more fascinated by the twins' abilities than anything Dravor had to say.

Dravor must have realized it, because he shouted at the zombie, but the creature's attention remained focused on the women. It said something to Dravor, the awful smile spreading, and braced its hands on the side of the stone coffin. It shoved itself upward and slowly began climbing out.

Hazel and Marit retreated until their backs made contact with the wall.

"We must release," Hazel said and lifted their clasped hands. "We must stop this!"

"No!" Dravor moved toward them, watching the zombie.

"You are not controlling it!" she shouted.

The zombie's feet touched the ground, and it rose to its full height, watching Dravor and the twins with dark, soulless eyes.

"One such as the Impaler will be impossible to manage," Hazel said, her voice shaking.

"I have a lock of his hair!" Dravor protested.

Not adequate. For one who was docile in life, perhaps, but not this one. Marit's voice sounded in Hazel's head, and despite her fear, Hazel felt a surge of hope. *We must reverse it, sister. Before it is too late.*

Hazel slowly began to release her hold on the mental image of a strong, whole man. The zombie stumbled against the coffin and caught itself with its arm.

Dravor yelled, his calm and rational behavior vanishing. He rushed to the twins and grasped their joined hands. A spark flew from where he touched the metal chains the twins wore, and he withdrew quickly with a curse, examining his palm. With quiet fury, he said, "He has not yet spoken the full incantation! Do not release him until I instruct it."

Hazel eyed the zombie, who had again stood straight. Something was different, progressing. It seemed to be gathering strength as it slowly approached them.

"The longer we hold him, the stronger he grows on his own," Hazel said to Dravor. "He will destroy us all, including you."

The zombie was nearly upon them.

Hazel made a decision and wrenched herself apart from Marit. The glow that had grown between them immediately faded, like a torch switched off, and the crackling sound in the air subsided. Echoing howls of rage from both zombie and mage bounced off the stone walls, and Hazel clamped her hands over her ears.

The zombie fell to the floor, and the reanimation process reversed itself as quickly as it had happened. Skin, muscles, and organs dissolved away and disintegrated into bones and dust. The last of the echoes faded, and the room fell quiet.

Dread built in Hazel's stomach as she felt Dravor's eyes on her.

"Bring him back," he bit out on a low growl. He grabbed their hands and forced them together, but even when their bracelets connected, nothing happened. "Bring him back!"

"It won't work." Hazel's voice trembled, but was firm. "You can't force us to do something we haven't studied."

Dravor dug his fingernails into their combined hands, and Hazel sensed the rage coursing through him. His goal may have been thwarted, but he was still lethal. He could kill either one of them in an instant.

"You've killed me." His voice was a quiet whip of fury.

He is already dead, Marit's voice rang in Hazel's mind. Her eyes were clear, the calm before the storm. *He is living on borrowed time—time that is not his own.*

Marit's clarity added to Hazel's anxiety. *Please, do not attack me, Marit. Please. I cannot fight both you and the count.*

Dravor looked over his shoulder at the remains of his father, now far beyond reanimation. "Five centuries I have waited for this." His tone was so low Hazel almost didn't hear him. Still looking at his father's skeleton, he grabbed Hazel by the throat with one hand and Marit with the other and slammed them up against the wall at their backs.

She and Marit kicked and struggled, but he did not budge an inch. He tightened his hands, cutting off all air.

Hazel clutched at Dravor's hand with her free hand, clawing and tearing, to no avail. Spots gathered before her eyes, and from the corner of her eye, she saw Marit begin to slump.

Hazel's vision tunneled, the edges of her periphery

dimming to a black circle that grew smaller as Marit's voice echoed again in her head.

He is already dead . . .

Hazel grabbed for Marit's hand, twisting with her last remaining strength to touch their chains together. She closed her eyes, feeling her consciousness fluttering, but envisioned Dravor as a living, breathing, five-hundred-year-old man.

They could not kill, but they could heal. They could give life.

Hazel felt warmth on her wrist, her chain connected to her sister's, and her thoughts were peaceful.

As suddenly as he had struck, Dravor dropped his hands, and the women collapsed to the ground.

Hazel choked and gasped but clung to Marit. She looked at Dravor, who examined his hands in horror and then looked at her.

"What have you done?" His voice was gravelly, dry.

"Brought you back to life," Hazel choked.

"You have ended me! Reverse it!" His form thinned, his cheeks growing gaunt. His coloring turned an awful shade of gray as his lips pulled back, revealing discolored teeth that began to fall out. He lunged at Hazel and Marit, his eyes large and furious even as his face decayed around him. His bony hand clutched at her clothing.

He uttered one final shriek that echoed horribly around the cold chamber as his form completely dissolved into the dust he would have been had he died centuries earlier.

Hazel collapsed against the wall, still wheezing for air, and Marit, coughing and choking, managed a laugh. It was different, though, not the crazed, confused laughter Hazel had heard so often over the last several hours.

Marit's laugh was bright and strong, though mixed with tears and coughs.

Hazel glanced up at her to see clear eyes, free of the spells that had caused her thoughts to tumble and her reasoning to disappear.

Hazel managed a laugh of her own and laid her head on Marit's shoulder. They sat together for a long moment, simply breathing.

Eventually, Marit rose slowly and extended her hand to Hazel. When they stood facing each other, Marit closed her eyes and gathered Hazel into a hug. "I knew you would come for me."

Hazel returned the embrace, finally feeling the missing piece of her life slip into place. She couldn't wait to introduce her to Sam.

She pulled back with a gasp. "Sam! Oh, no, no . . ." She turned and ran across the crypt, hearing Marit following, and tore up the stairs to the ground level and base of the tower.

"Dravor said he was here—" Hazel said, her thoughts filled with panic.

She had taken a step toward the lift when a shout sounded from outside. She tipped her head and listened. "Eugene?"

"The machinery has stopped!" Marit pointed.

The gears had ground to a halt, and the outer door was visible through the corridor. Night had fallen, but the snow was bright on the ground, and the sky was a lighter version of its nighttime self, displaying shades of dark purple and gray.

She heard Eugene's shout again, and she ran around the base of the tower. The thorns and vines she'd seen from her brief glance out the window earlier had disintegrated, turned to dust that had fallen to the snow. It was as though the count's toxic hold on the building had dissolved.

Eugene came into view, and Hazel stopped short. He was carrying an inert form, and her knees buckled. Marit grabbed her before she collapsed to the ground, holding her close as Eugene stumbled forward and dropped to his knees, his exterior casing scratched. He was missing pieces on his arms and shoulders.

Sam was a mass of cuts and burns, and Hazel put her hand to her throat.

"He is alive, Miss Hazel," Eugene said haltingly, "but I fear his wounds are serious." The 'ton looked down at his employer. "And his eyes are horribly burned. If he lives, he will be blind."

Chapter 38

I f he lives? If he lives . . ." Hazel slipped from Marit's arms and sank into the snow. "Sam . . ." She reached for his still form and held his shoulders and head. "No, no, please—Please! You cannot leave me here, not now! Sam, we've done it!" Her voice was raspy from Dravor's assault, and her words broke on a sob as she rocked him back and forth in her arms.

"Sam!" She lowered her head and kissed his hair as choking, gasping sobs wrenched from her heart. "Please, please, please . . ." She turned her tear-filled eyes to the heavens, the snow falling gently on her face.

Marit dropped next to her in the snow, her face stricken, her eyes filled with tears. She reached a hand to Hazel's shoulder and squeezed hard.

"He must live, he must!" She looked down at him again, at the welts and burns striping across his skin and especially his eyes. "He's a surgeon. He's a brilliant surgeon and inventor," she cried to Marit. "He needs his eyes . . ." She choked again, coughing and crying and feeling as though she'd inflicted the injuries herself.

"He offered to come, and I should have told him no. I should have refused!" She looked at Marit, whose face blurred through her tears. "I should have told him I didn't want him with me, because then he'd still be well and in London, working and saving people and—"

Her voice cracked, and she looked down at his head, cradled in her arms. She touched her hand to his chest, which rose and fell with shallow breaths. The time between breaths lengthened and then shuddered out with horrifying finality.

"No!" Hazel's scream sounded through the night, and she shook Sam's still body. "Sam!"

"Give me your hand." Marit grabbed for Hazel's bracelet. She clutched Hazel's fingers tight and touched their bracelets together as they rested their hands on Sam's still chest.

As Marit murmured something in Romanian, Hazel threw an anguished plea for help heavenward, and as she squeezed her eyes tightly shut, she imagined Sam's heart beating, his lungs filling with air, his organs working in concert and continuing his life. Hazel opened her eyes when she felt blood trickling from her nose. A glance at Marit showed her wiping blood from her own nose, but her focus remained on their clasped hands.

Hazel looked at Sam's still face, and a sob broke free. "Do not leave me, Sam! You must come back!"

He coughed, then, and she gasped. She stared at Marit, who looked at Sam with huge eyes, and then Eugene, who returned her astonished expression.

Marit slowly released her hand, and Hazel rubbed Sam's

chest, as Eugene sat flat in the snow and hefted Sam into his lap. Hazel cradled Sam's face in her hands and shifted closer, heedless of the snow seeping through her clothes.

His eyes fluttered, and in the dim moonlight, she saw the redness, the lack of focus. He coughed again and turned his head, sucking in a deep breath of air and releasing it again.

"Sam?"

He raised fumbling hands to her shoulders and then cupped her head. "I found your hair," he mumbled, and coughed again.

"Oh, sweet man, did Renton do this to you? I hate him! I will kill him with my bare hands."

Sam shook his head weakly. "Already done." He lifted his hand to his forehead and touched his eyes. "Dark out here, is it?"

Hazel bit her lip, then leaned forward to place a kiss on his forehead. She rested her head on his as tears flowed from her eyes and down his face. The tears were warm, and a soft glow lit the space around their heads. "Sam, I am so sorry. I love you. This is all my fault." Her shoulders shook with sobs. She would never forgive herself, ever.

"Hazel?" Marit touched her back. "Hazel, look."

Hazel sniffed and raised her head. Sam was rubbing his eyes and blinking. He finally squinted against the muted night sky.

"What . . . what happened?" She looked first at Marit, then Eugene.

"I keep telling you that you're an amazing Healer," Sam mumbled and wiped his other eye. "Not so dark out here anymore."

Hazel sat back on her heels. She looked at his eyes, at the abating redness. They looked sore, but his pupils were dilating, and when he blinked, he was focused on her face.

"Can you see me?" she asked in a whisper.

He smiled. "You'll be glad to know your hair is lovely, even short."

She put a hand to her mouth and stared. "You can truly see me?"

"I can see you. Many thanks for crying into my eyes."

Eugene shifted and helped Sam sit up straight, which he did with a groan.

"You would be Marit, then?" Sam winced in pain and tried to smile at Marit.

"I am." Her eyes were huge, and she looked overwhelmed. "Thank you for bringing Hazel to me."

"My pleasure." He shifted and winced again.

"You must visit a doctor," Eugene told him.

"I *am* a doctor," he murmured. "And my soon-to-be-betrothed is a Healer. Get me back to the inn, and I'll be fine." He gave Hazel a crooked smile. "I wasn't teasing." He held up a long rope of golden hair. "I found your braid."

Hazel laughed a little. "You loved my hair." She ran a hand through her sloppily cut mop of hair, now wet with melted snow.

He reached up and grasped her hand, pulling it first to his mouth to kiss and then holding it to his chest. He closed his eyes and smiled. "Long, short—I do not care. Hazel, let's go home."

Epilogue

H azel, the groom still has scratches on his face that haven't fully healed. Are you certain he won't wait?" Rowena fussed with Hazel's wedding veil in a guest room at Blackwell Manor.

The house was beautifully decorated. The holidays were approaching, and the guest rooms were completely filled with loved ones and friends. Hazel looked at her mother in the mirrored vanity and smiled. "He does not want to wait any longer, nor do I. We've been home for a month."

"Exactly! You've been home for one month! You and your sister are Romanian countesses and nobility; I ought to have much more time to plan!"

Lucy Blake, Countess Blackwell, gently put her hands on Rowena's shoulders. "Mrs. Hughes, I have a quandary with the bouquet, and I wonder if you would offer your opinion. I've placed a white rose at the center, but now I'm undecided . . ." Lucy guided Rowena to the foot of the enormous bed, where flower arrangements were laid for final inspection.

Marit smiled at Hazel from her seat near the hearth,

where she chatted with Isla about possible training in Shapeshifter Relations and Therapy.

Marit was slowly finding her way in London, and while Hazel sometimes found her sitting quietly in the library, her expression sad, she was hopeful that, as time passed, the sad moments would be replaced with happy ones.

Emme flounced next to Hazel on a stuffed ottoman. "You are beautiful, you know. I believe you've created a new fashion trend. Half the debutantes have cut off their hair, and their mamas have lost their wits over it." She grinned, and Hazel laughed.

"I like it." Hazel looked at herself in the mirror—her thick, golden curls had been artfully cut by an experienced French stylist. "And so does Sam."

"I should say so." Emme's eyes glistened. "Now, you know how I hate excessive dramatics, so I will say this only once: I am so very glad you arrived home safe and whole, and I am happier still that you and your charming doctor will now live happily ever after." Emme squeezed Hazel's hands. "I love you dearly."

Emme stood, kissed her cheek, and then clapped her hands at the room of laughing, happy women.

"It is time! If we are one minute late, we will have an anxious groom wandering the halls."

The chatter increased as people bustled, passed around flowers, and then headed from the room toward the beautiful, curved staircase in the front of the house. They all descended, though Isla hung back with Hazel and Rowena.

"Hazel, as your matron of honor, I must tell you that

I've seen the groom, and he is stunning." She kissed Hazel's cheek.

Hazel smiled, her stomach full of butterflies.

Marit made her way through the crowd of people outside the library and to Hazel's side.

Hazel hugged her sister quickly and looked at her pretty, deep lavender eyes. "You are well?"

Marit bit her lip and nodded. Hazel recognized the nervous habit as one of her own, and smiled. "Are you certain?"

"I am. You go, now, and marry your handsome love."

Isla took Marit's arm, and they found their places in line, along with Oliver Reed, Daniel Pickett, and Miles Blake, who were Sam's groomsmen.

The music began from inside the library, and Hazel turned to her mother, who was still fussing with the veil. "Mother, everything is beautiful."

Rowena flushed, but smiled. "I am so proud of you, my Hazel." Her eyes filled, and she waved a hand. "Silly mother, I am."

"A wonderful mother, you are."

The procession moved forward, and as she and Rowena walked down the aisle, she locked eyes with Sam, and her heart swelled. The butterflies—good butterflies—took flight again in her stomach, and as much as she loved being with the people gathered in the room, she couldn't wait to have Sam all to herself.

Eugene stood at the end of the line of groomsmen, and while many considered it odd, Sam insisted the 'ton be part of the proceedings. Eugene pretended he hadn't cared one way or the other, but when Sam had insisted, Eugene had smiled.

Sam watched her approach as if there was nobody else in the room, and Rowena tearfully kissed her cheek and handed her to Sam.

"Happiest day of my life," he murmured and clasped Hazel's hand. He still bore some of the scratches and scars from their traumatic day at the tower, but Hazel thought they only increased his handsomeness.

They exchanged their vows, and Sam gathered her close before the priest had even finished pronouncing them married. He kissed her soundly to the laughter and happy cheers of their friends.

"I hope you realize this means you must include me in all of your mad schemes from now on," he whispered in her ear.

She laughed. "Now that Marit is free to explore life on her own, I doubt I will be compelled to undertake any more mad schemes. I am content to be the reserved one."

"Reserved, perhaps. But you, Hazel Hughes MacInnes, are the bravest person I know."

Acknowledgments

So many, many thanks go to my patient family, who got really used to dinners without me, outings without me, house-cleaning chores without me, just about everything else without me as I wrote and revised this book. I am so grateful. I am also grateful for my extended family (Allens and Faulsticks!) who forgave my spotty attendance at the family reunion so I could write.

Thanks, also, to Bob Diforio and Pam Victorio, of D4EO agency, for their work on my behalf, and also to Heidi Taylor Gordon, Lisa Mangum, Heather Ward, Richard Erickson, Malina Grigg, and the rest of my publishing team at Shadow Mountain for helping this book be its best. Additionally, I couldn't do my job half as well if not for my writing friends, The Bear Lake Monsters, and especially to Josi S. Kilpack (*Daisies and Devotion*) and Jennifer Moore (*Charlotte's Promise*).

To my sweet readers who have embraced my steampunk world, thank you so much for sharing in the fun. There's a genre for everybody, and that there are readers who enjoy steampunk fairytales (who knew?) makes me so happy.

Discussion Questions

1. *The Lady in the Coppergate Tower* is a steampunk retelling of "Rapunzel." What elements of the fairy tale are present in both stories? Where do the two stories diverge?

2. Hazel has a quieter personality than Lucy, Isla, or Emme, but that doesn't mean she is any less heroic than her friends. In what ways does Hazel demonstrate her heroic qualities?

3. Hazel's particular gift is in healing other people, but she doesn't believe that talent is remarkable. What talents do you have that you could value more than you do?

4. There are several mother figures in the story—Johanna, Rowena, Dravor's mother, and Sam's mother. How do the relationships between mother and child help drive the story line? In what ways were Dravor, Sam, Hazel, and Marit shaped by their respective mothers?

5. Sam suffers from claustrophobia due to his wartime experiences in India. In what ways does he overcome his fear during his journey aboard the *Magellan*? What are some of the ways you confront and conquer your own fears?

6. The steampunk 'tons play a large role in the story, especially Eugene, who has more of a personality than other automatons. If you could have a 'ton of your own, would you want one with a personality and a measure of independence? What might be some of the difficulties that could arise from that?

7. Hazel and Marit are able to defeat Dravor by joining their powers together. Is there someone in your life who brings out the best in you, and with whom you are stronger than you are on your own?

8. In the story, Sam sees himself as Hazel's protector, but in the end, she saves him. How did you feel about that?

About the Author

NANCY CAMPBELL ALLEN is the author of fifteen published novels and numerous novellas, which span genres from contemporary romantic suspense to historical fiction. In 2005, her work won the Utah Best of State award, and she received a Whitney Award for *My Fair Gentleman*. She has presented at numerous writing conferences and events since her first book was released in 1999. Nancy received a BS in Elementary Education from Weber State University. She loves to read, write, travel, and research, and enjoys spending time laughing with family and friends. She is married and the mother of three children. Visit her at nancycampbellallen.com.

FALL IN LOVE WITH A

PROPER ROMANCE

BY

NANCY CAMPBELL ALLEN

Available wherever books are sold